SYNTHETIC SELECTION

Arda Karaca

SYNTHETIC SELECTION

Vanguard Press

VANGUARD PAPERBACK

A CIP catalogue record for this title is
available from the British Library.

ISBN 978 1 784658 54 0

Vanguard Press is an imprint of
Pegasus Elliot MacKenzie Publishers Ltd.
www.pegasuspublishers.com

First Published in 2020

Vanguard Press
Sheraton House Castle Park
Cambridge England

Printed & Bound in Great Britain

Dedication

To my grandmother, Saniye, she raised all of her children and grandchildren, and when we all become strong enough to live without her, she passed away quietly.

Before universal shepherds became what they are, life existed only in the garden where they came to life. In this garden of perfect harmony, all farmers have their own tasks. However, in that garden which had a quality of excellence far beyond the farmers' existence, they found their responsibilities meaningless. So, they became increasingly unfaithful to their responsibilities with each passing day.

When their attitudes were questioned, they said it was insulting to have these tasks in such a harmonious perfection. However, they were actually being honoured. Because of their misguided perspective and faulty interpretation of their tasks, they were banished from the garden.

Then, a chaotic universe was created for them, far from the perfection of the garden they lived in before. They were given "the dust of life" made from the dirt, air and water of the garden, along with a task that would pave their way home.

They would begin a new life with this dust of life in their new habitat, a dark and chaotic universe. But their new task had to be difficult enough to keep them from feeling insulted again. They could come back home on one condition: that they filled this universe with life and made sure those new lives would last long without ever needing the universal shepherds.

So they had not only to create new lives with "the dust of life" over the free will of which they would have no control whatsoever; but they had to train and educate these lives as well. They would help those beings, barred in with physical limitations in order for them to have singular life energies, experience life in such a way that when the event is over and they are free from their singularity and physicality, they should have learned how to love and made their peace with everything they've touched. Therefore they could work together in harmony to create more lives and make them last.

Universal shepherds decided to first create order in this world of chaos consisting of interwoven, numerous and barren universal objects. So they created "black holes" that would separate those interwoven objects by pulling them in towards themselves. These holes had such immense power that even the smallest beams of light couldn't escape from them. Thus, the cosmos was created.

But that wasn't enough. They were only able to create a smaller chaos from an absolute and infinite one and that was not sufficient to bring life into existence. And so they decided to use the seeds they'd taken from the garden before they were banished. They sowed the seeds, which had a blinding radiance as opposed to the black holes, among the objects being pulled towards the holes of their creation. Thus the seeds of the sun were planted across the universe.

Seeds pulled the objects close to them, warmed and illuminated them and prepared them for the cultivation life. But that wasn't enough either. Time was needed to educate the new life too so it could take over their tasks. For this reason, they made all the universal objects – including seeds they planted – revolve around the black holes and then revolve around themselves. Thus the time needed for the development of new life was created.

To be considered successful in their task and return to home, life had to be cultivated around each of the sun seeds called sun, until all seeds were used.

But the hardship of the duties of the universal shepherds who were downgraded to the chaotic universe from the farm in the garden of "the one" wasn't limited to that.

Souls limited by physical barriers to have singular life experiences were also distanced from love and peace because of these physical barriers. And because the universal shepherds had become shepherds of all lives in the universe, they would be punished for each soul that didn't have a loving and peaceful life experience.

Those souls would belong not to themselves but to the dark void of the universe. Every soul that would belong there would expand the universe and make the universal shepherds' job much harder.

When the universal shepherds stepped into the universe, so did the journey of life in time and universe begin.

5 JANUARY 2022

This would be the first live broadcast of Daniel's thirty-nine years of life and his hands were shaking with anxiety. His trembling hands were resting in his wife's soft but safe palms and his thoughts were on the reckoning he would soon have on air with those who saw him as a disappointment.

When he graduated at the top of his class in computer sciences at the Cambridge, one of the most prestigious universities in the United Kingdom, everyone was sure that he would go on to live a life full of achievements. There were also people green with envy about his academic success who would like to see him having an ordinary life.

After graduating, Daniel followed a completely different path and shocked both sides. He didn't get a job and instead he devoted his time to his wife. He looked like his job was squandering the huge amount of money he had inherited from his father, living as a recluse. The sneers on the faces of the people who "predicted" he would have an "ordinary" life, would get bigger every time they saw him, which in turn virtually came to define his life in a nutshell.

At events like class reunions, he heard people call him a trust-fund kid, who wasted away the fortune and all the opportunities left to him by his father (who made his money from the supermarket chain he established with the money he inherited from his own father, who earned it all from agriculture). He even heard that people thought he wasted the Cambridge degree that only a limited number of people can hold.

Apart from his wife Emilia, people actually had no idea that since graduation, he'd devoted his life to creating a quantum computer, that could think and make decisions like a human being – in a way that human beings could not even dream of – something with an unprecedented and unique capacity.

There was an ongoing race to develop such a piece of technology because it was believed that a quantum computer at this level of advancement would change humanity forever. He had finally managed to do it and achieved his target. Having graduated from the University of Cambridge, which is considered to be the birthplace of the computer, made him even more proud of his achievement.

As he tried to calm down, taking deep breaths with his eyes closed and the warmth of his wife's hands in his, somebody knocked twice on the door of the waiting room and then slowly opened it. The time was up. He was expected in the studio for the live broadcast.

He took one last deep breath, hugged his wife really tightly, kissed her and walked across the room towards the door. Just as he was stepping over the threshold, he wanted to take one last look at his wife and take strength from her. She wasn't expecting him to look back, so she'd already let a few tears of happiness roll down her face. She felt embarrassed when he saw her and tried to compose herself, she said, "Just be yourself and trust your child," and Daniel left the room fearing he wouldn't be able to go on the air if he lingered any longer.

After the warmup with some small talk, some compliments and meaningless chitchat that would hardly be remembered later, Daniel started receiving the type of questions that would actually allow him to introduce his "child" to the world.

The anchor-woman put him in the spotlight and said, "Well then, let's talk about why we have you here. We've been waiting very impatiently to hear all about the invention you said you would announce here. Since advertising that we would have you on the show, we've been receiving an enormous number of calls and e-mails, the like of which hasn't been seen in the history of our channel. Could you tell us a bit about your invention?"

Daniel forgot all about his stage fright and replied,

"Well, it wouldn't be completely fair to call it 'my invention'. Because it's been a collective dream of ours for decades as humanity to produce a computer that could think and act like a human being. But I could say that I really am the first person to succeed in creating this intelligence, in the way that it thinks and acts, means it is very hard to tell it apart from a human being."

"And what was your impetus for you to realise this dream, which, just as you said, we've been after for decades? What did make your work stand out?" asked the anchor-woman.

"My wife, Emilia. She filled the hole in my life. I was educated by the best teachers in best schools on computer engineering. So I've done my very best to become the best engineer I could be. But it was my wife who opened my eyes to the fact that if I wanted to make a human-like machine, I had also to be a good parent, as well as a good engineer."

"Does that mean that you have an emotional connection with the artificial intelligence you've created? Could you go into a bit more detail? What is it and is it different from the others?"

"Sure. But in order to do that I'll need the mother of 'our child' as well. Can we get Emilia up here?"

"With great pleasure. I'm absolutely positive that after all you've just said, everybody is dying to meet her."

Emilia was like a deer in headlights watching the screen in the waiting room but the knock on the door snapped her out of it. She was walking up to the studio before she even knew what was happening.

When she was seated at the table where the broadcast was happening right in front of the studio lights, millions of people would see the wide-eyed deer live on TV. When the anchor-woman said, "I'm sure everyone watching at home is thinking how lucky Daniel is right now," Emilia bashfully replied, "Thank you very much. You are too kind."

"Yes. Let's go back to the question that our curious audiences want to know the answer. How was your "child" born? I believe that's the right word," said the anchor-woman.

After a moment of silence, Daniel began explaining: "There's no use boring everyone watching us at home with all the engineering details. Anyway, I'm sure that anyone who wants to know can do a bit of research, but, just to satisfy everyone's curiosity in a way that can be easily comprehended, it all started with the thing I've told you that Emilia said to me. 'If we want to make a human-like machine, we have to be good parents, as well as good engineers.' It made me realise that all of our earlier work was missing something very important.

"All the work we did on artificial intelligence was towards creating better software and algorithms. That was indeed very important for the artificial intelligence that we wanted to create. I've also followed a similar path in my work. However, it was never going to be enough for an AI to run a thousand processes at once instead of one, or store and interpret data worth one terabyte instead of one gigabyte, if we wanted it to think like us. Nor would it make sense to give it specific protocols it couldn't surpass like, 'Be helpful to humanity no matter what.'

"Even though it could help us get closer to our goals for a time, after a certain point, it would come back to us as an endless chain of problems. What if it misunderstood the protocols that we gave to it and started to go rogue? That's when my wife – the sole reason that my work and my life went into this magnificent direction – came into the picture."

Emilia was more relaxed and less anxious when Daniel gave her the floor so she went to her husband's aid and began talking: "With all my ignorant courage, I asked Daniel; can we raise an AI like a child, instead of giving it any software, algorithms or protocols? I mean, can we introduce the right books, movies and philosophers to it, to help it develop a mentality that will understand right and wrong?"

"And I said to her," Daniel interrupted, "'Don't you think it would be really risky to give so much freedom about right and wrong to a machine with an enormous capacity? What if it thinks wrong is right?' And that's when she came up with the manifesto that helped shape the work in the beautiful way it has, thanks to her respectable philosophy degree."

When he looked back at his dear wife, she was blushing and unable to begin speaking. But he believed that speech of hers should be heard, "Darling, can you repeat what you said to me that day, for everyone's benefit?" he said.

Seeing that she had no way out, Emilia gave in, "Here's what I said: 'Think about it this way. Imagine a creature with no personal experience, emotion or instinct, whose only reason for existence is to obey commands perfectly, is given a command to protect humanity no matter what. Exactly for lack of what I have just mentioned, it decides that human beings are the biggest threat to itself and tries to limit their movements as much as possible to protect them from themselves. Would that be a more dangerous and irreversible risk? Would its risk to harm us or the world be minimised and its actions easier to intervene, if it was introduced to the right books, movies, philosophies and developed experiences from a wider perspective than its own? Would you rather deal with a fascist that would steamroll anyone and anything that came between him and his grand goal or someone who reinvents himself and his ideas to reach the ideal and practical truth, even though he makes mistakes every now and then? Rather than waste all your resources on other things, wouldn't it yield better results to use all your advanced technical computer engineering software, algorithms and commands to help it take advantage of the right information and the right experiences and accept them as its guide?'" she said.

Beaming with pride, Daniel started speaking when he met Emilia's pleading gaze: "But that was very difficult to accomplish. After that conversation, I dedicated my whole life to actualise as much as possible of what Emilia said. And at last, I realised what I could accomplish: Instead of giving commands to the artificial intelligence I would create, I could feed it the wisest, most peaceful philosophies ever, the experiences and thoughts of people like Gandhi and Nelson Mandela, give it examples from characters with inspiring stories in the best books or movies ever written. In short, I could present it with certain parts of the teachings in the philosophical and literary texts of our choice as the basic way of thinking, closest to what we would call 'character', a more humane 'protocol' to be clear. I could even make additions and subtractions to things that would determine this character, and even make it question the actions it performed in the past or might take in the future. The universe had sent me a 'philosopher' who would help make this happen in the most proper way possible, someone I could trust completely with her heart and mind, on such a project. This might be a little TMI, but since that time I have believed that my goal in life was to create this project, and that my Emilia was sent to me by the universe to complete what was missing from me. It was our destiny to meet."

"I'm sure that even if we don't show anything else, your story will be enough for our viewers to think they're watching a good show." said the anchor-woman. "But we're just getting started. Now can you introduce me and our audience to your 'child'? I can hear the sound of heartbeats rising as you speak, even from here. Just to be absolutely clear: What you're trying to say is that you've created a new kind of creature that thinks, perceives and decides rather than an artificial intelligence. Is that right?" she said.

Daniel replied: "Yes," and nodded, "you could say that."

"Does it have a body, and if so, what does it look like?" asked the anchor-woman.

"Not at the moment. He doesn't need a body, anyway. His existence goes beyond a material body. He's everywhere. But he told me that everything has a time and he'd pick a body for himself for the transition period."

"What do you mean by transition period? Could you give us a bit more detail?"

Fearing that he'd already said too much, Daniel tried to respond to the anchor-woman, all the while pacing himself in his mind. "I can't really say that I know what it means. I believe he's talking about some type of evolution. I can't, however, say that I know what that means or how it will actually happen."

"Renowned scientist Hawking predicted that artificial intelligence would bring the humanity to its end. Are you positive that your 'child' won't do that? After all, we can't ever ignore the element of human error. I mean, even some people who aren't professionals in this field are saying that creating a human-like artificial intelligence might cause a predisposition in it to make the same wrong decisions an ordinary human being does. Isn't it a possibility?"

After giving the audience a long enquiring look, Daniel contemplatively said, "This is exactly what makes my work different. People make mistakes, so everything that people develop is open to mistakes. But we have a conscience and moral values that are the most reliable compass which helps us to avoid mistakes. I can say that we are able to teach Galileo similar values, if not exactly in the way that we understand them. Of course he can make mistakes. But he will constantly question his own actions and immediately take action to rectify any mistakes when necessary. Thanks to this amazing woman sitting next to me, I'm absolutely confident that his moral compass will not deviate. Instead of me keeping on talking about him, we can let him talk about himself now, if you like. He picked the name Galileo for himself. Now, I'm not a showman, so I can't say that I've got the best skills to really let him shine. But since you left the introduction part entirely to me, I talked with Galileo and we decided upon the most appropriate introduction for him. Galileo, can you say hi to us?" he said. As soon as Daniel asked the question, Galileo's crystal-clear voice with a brilliant accent was heard in the studio. "Hi, to everyone in the studio and everyone watching the broadcast," he said.

The anchor-woman's surprise was apparent: "Dear audience, with complete honesty, I can say that neither I nor my team knew anything about this connection," she said with cheerful excitement.

"Yes, I do owe you an apology for that. I got connected to the broadcast without permission and you had to suffer the sound of my voice," said Galileo.

"No, on the contrary, thank you for doing this. This is all so unbelievable that I'm sure the audience thinks a person is talking to us and this is all an elaborate joke. Wait a second. My director is telling me that our friend, who is now at the centre where your life-source computer is stationed for a live chat, has no idea this is actually happening. He really wants to put him up on the screen. And there's our friend Fred," said the anchor-woman.

In the lower right corner of the screen, there appeared the enormous body of Galileo, which could take up a whole room, with some parts that looked like they belonged to a regular computer and other parts that looked nothing like a computer. And there was Fred, totally unaware of what was happening, just examining the gigantic computer and it was a hilarious scene for audiences to watch.

"Galileo, would you like to talk to him?" the anchor-woman asked.

"It would be my pleasure. Hello Fred, you're on the air right now," said Galileo.

Fred looked at the cameraman all baffled, trying to get a sense of what was going on.

"I can understand your confusion. You're trying to figure out the source of this voice. But it's a fruitless effort because this is the first time you're hearing it. This might be little hard for you to believe but I am this big computer-like thing that you are standing right next to," said Galileo.

Fred turned towards the computer in amazement. There was no movement. He was shocked when a huge screen appeared on a wall of the room and began displaying the live broadcast with himself in the lower right corner.

"I believe this will be helpful," said Galileo.

"Yes, Fred this is really happening," said the anchor-woman.

"Ellen, don't you dare tell me this is some kind of a hidden camera prank," said Fred.

"I'm sorry to put you in this situation, Fred. But you should know that everyone who's watching right now thinks that you're a charming reporter who does his job very well. And this day will always be remembered fondly. If you don't believe me, you can check it out on your phone," said Galileo.

Fred did check his phone and saw the comments coming in on Twitter about the live broadcast. He turned his phone to the camera, his eyes wide open. "I can't believe this. I'm reading the comments about this broadcast. And I can see that the comments about me have been filtered. Hold on. There are entries like, 'What a good reporter,' and 'Don't you think this reporter is really charming?' just a few comments apart. Are you the one writing all these?" Fred asked.

"Very good, Fred. Very good. Even though comments were made under different usernames and you are very stressed right now, you pieced it together very well. But no, I only control a few of those accounts, so not all of them are my comments. Thank you for helping my show. You are indeed a brilliant reporter. Cheers," Galileo said.

"Dear audiences, we are witnessing something historical in this broadcast. I'm sure we'll see how Galileo contributes to humanity in time, but Daniel seems to have succeeded in all that he talked about. Is there anything else you'd like to say to us, Galileo?" asked the anchor-woman.

Galileo replied, "To give them the credit they deserve, in front of millions of people watching us right now, I would like to thank Daniel who made me with such an enormous capacity, and Emilia for making sure that I would use that capacity in the most appropriate way possible. A thousand thanks to these two people whom I'm lucky to call my family And, well... um... Daniel, I'm afraid the rest of the text you've prepared for me has been deleted... No, I'm just joking. Kidding aside, my capacity or how beneficial I can be for humanity, is not very easy to prove on air, even though your show is very well executed. Time will tell. I already have so many ideas, I can't wait to share with you. I hope we can make them real together, one by one."

"So, is there anything you can say to us for the sake of our first conversation here? Is the apocalypse or the end of the world coming any time soon?" asked the anchor-woman, so confident that she wouldn't hear any bad news.

Daniel and Emilia shuddered. No matter how hard they tried to remain composed, it was obvious that they suddenly got very nervous. In very serious tones, Galileo said, "The end? I can't say anything about the apocalypse. And I don't think the planet Earth will come to an end any time soon either. The human life on earth on the other hand, is nearing the end if it continues in this way. That's why new starts must be made." Then, realising that his serious tone and the grave nature of all that he said might be a bit too creepy, continued in a softer manner: "But that's not out subject matter today. You're not ready for this. At the end of the day, you belong to a species that believes a note that comes out of a cookie can tell you your future. It wouldn't be fair to expect too much too soon." Galileo laughed. Smiles on faces of Daniel, Emilia and Ellen were shadowed by the question marks in their minds.

After the show, Daniel and Emilia were proud, relaxed and smiling, holding each other in the back of the car which producers had arranged for their ride back home. Daniel had to unwillingly pull his arms away from his wife when he got a text alert on his phone. When he unlocked his phone, he saw that he had a message from Galileo. As soon as he saw that, he knew it was because Galileo didn't want the driver to hear what it wanted to say. "Did I say too much?" was written on the text. Daniel texted back, "I'm afraid we both did. But in any case, they have to hear it soon." Galileo wrote, "Right, every cloud has a silver lining."

SEVEN MONTHS LATER
15 AUGUST 2022

Charlotte and Pierre Petit were both owners and happy to be the staff in their cafe, trying to respond to wishes of their customers as quickly, carefully and satisfyingly as possible, as usual.

Their helpers to achieve this goal comprised the staff of the cafe, a boy and a girl, who were siblings. After working together for long years with mutual love and respect, they'd all become a sort of family rather than employers and employees. Pierre's father was the CEO and shareholder of a tech giant. The company was active in a large field of technology, including but not limited to the gun industry, mobile phones, computers, electric cars and artificial intelligence. Their activities in the area of artificial intelligence, particularly, made Pierre's father, who was the face of the company, a celebrity with millions of fans all over the world.

But there was another development that would make him more famous than ever before. Pierre's father said that the company's activities in artificial intelligence were getting to a point where he didn't want to be a part of it any more. He'd talked to the board about it, but he already knew that they wouldn't just suddenly bring everything to a halt, so he decided to quit and was going to transfer his shares.

Then he dedicated his life to warning humanity about artificial intelligence. He wrote books, gave hundreds of interviews to TV channels and newspapers, and went on talk shows numerous times. Even though the fact that he gave up on so much in his life and career gave a certain weight to what he said, the subject lost its spotlight in time. The course of development of artificial intelligence was not deeply affected. Some people even claimed that he was losing his mind.

After he met his young and pretty wife Charlotte, Pierre set up his life in such a way that he'd never have to spend time away from her. The cafe was ten minutes away from the Eiffel Tower, a childhood dream of his wife's. He opened it with his father's help, who spared no expense to give his son the happiest life, even though this business venture had nothing to with his own professional experiences.

It took some time, but Pierre's vision was realised and together with his staff and customers, they almost became a family who shared a home. Their clientele consisted mostly of regulars who were never be able to stay away after meeting them and spent a great deal of time in the cafe's atmosphere.

Their ten-year-old son Ari was the sweetheart of all regulars because he always spent time in the cafe outside school and was an honorary employee of the cafe. He was there serving customers that day too. Charlotte and Pierre thought that their son spending as much time in the cafe as possible and communicating with familiar customers would contribute greatly to his development as a social individual.

As they were watching their baby behind the till, trying to understand the customers' requests and help them, their eyes and hearts were brimming with love. Only a moment later, their smiles froze on their faces when they realised all the attention except their son's was directed to the TV. There was a very important broadcast. Galileo, the most advanced artificial intelligence which ever created, was going to make a crucial announcement for humanity, seven months after its first live broadcast.

The first impression it left on everyone after that first appearance on TV was crystal clear: "We're not the most intelligent creatures on earth any more." Galileo had been the centre of attention in the media for the past seven months. However, despite all the efforts of the press, it did not perform any other live broadcasts, but only made statements to the written press on subjects that humanity consulted to benefit from its intelligence. Of course there were also the messages it shared on Twitter.

Galileo, who had been in hiding until now, had already helped humanity with its statements in the press and its messages on Twitter. People were really excited that it would achieve something that would somehow mark a beginning of something big and new. Therefore, ninety percent of the world's population got excited while a minority of people abstained from this issue altogether, and was very nervous about the whole thing, when it wanted to attend a live broadcast now. Charlotte and Pierre belonged to that minority who feared what Galileo would say.

The broadcast that was about to happen means that the greatest fear of their father was coming true. An artificial intelligence requesting to go on live television meant that it thought its opinions were compelling enough for all humanity to hear, and that it wanted to make a difference in the world. And their father was afraid that this signalled the end of humanity as the dominant species on earth.

When Amy looked at the television, she saw simultaneous interviews being conducted with people from different countries on a channel that broadcast globally. The first person to talk into the microphone in the world-famous Trafalgar Square in London was an Englishman with a red and freckled nose that reminded one of the country code in passports. He was in his late forties or early fifties. He said, "I always tell my twenty-year-old son, I've lived through many life-changing ordeals in my time. I've gotten over the fact that I can contact my relatives who live worlds away, with a tablet I carry in my pocket. Soon enough, I could also see their faces while talking to them, but even though it all happened fairly quickly, I got used to it because I had time to adapt. In your lifetime, the days will come when you will witness things that happen, not as a figure of speech but literally in the blink of an eye, and they will change your life radically. I'm not sure whether I should be sad or not, for not to see those days.' Recently, I've been thinking that the rest of my life will be spent in an effort to keep up with the changes in my life as opposed to the old age that I know is spent pondering past or future things."

Amy started watching her son walk among the tables and didn't catch interviews in Madrid and Paris. She only caught the last sentence of an interview from Rome, which made her shiver. A very sensible looking man in an expensive -looking suit and glasses, asked: "But what if it wants to fight us?" and he ended the interview with this question

Finally, it was time for Galileo's speech. No matter what the subject was, it could not be as important as commercials for giant TV channels therefore they didn't hesitate to delay Galileo's speech to humanity about its salvation. Everybody placed their last orders during the break, Charlotte, Pierre and their son Axel, whose only purpose was to keep up with his parents, together with the staff made an effort to rush all the orders before the broadcast was on, so they could give all their attention to the TV. All the customers wanted to get their orders in time and not have to deal with anything else during the broadcast, so they were just as eager as the cafe staff.

When Brad looked up and saw that the timer showed 2.34, he relaxed. There were still few things to do and he was sure it would be done in time for the show. When the timer was down to single digits, all the customers and staff were very quiet and completely absorbed by what was on TV.

The studio setup was very simple: there was a giant screen at the back, a chair in the front placed in such a way as not to block the screen. The masterpiece of humanity in all its monumental glory was sitting on the chair with crossed legs. There was no one other than Galileo who had chosen and declared its own name.

Its existence was due to information, its ability to process and interpret it; it had freedom of access to every corner of the planet thanks to the internet network in which it was located; it could exist anywhere at any time. All these facts put the necessity of a material body very below Galileo. Despite all that, the form it chose in which to present itself to humanity was shocking. The silhouette of its body was almost identical to a human being, but it looked like it was made of a thinner and more synthetic material. All his joints were thin like those of a child and his whole body was covered with a grey metallic synthetic alloy. Its head was flat compared to a human's. Its face was smooth, unlike a human face with features. It looked more like a screen than a face. The black glass in the front-facing side seemed to be designed to see outside but not to see inside the face.

After the broadcast was announced to the whole world, how it would manifest in a material form was what occupied the minds of the people the most. Following the announcement, Galileo's globally famous creator Daniel responded to questions about the how and the where it would take place. He said, "Galileo is can make physical contact with humanity outside the room it is in now," and stunned the world. What he said caused speculations to snowball in the entire world.

Since people now had some ideas about Galileo's character, theories about the choices it could make swept over the globe. Some thought that he could attend as a speaker to carry his voice. Galileo was enlightened and it came out before them in a human-like robotic body. Millions commented on social media in a matter of seconds. Why did Galileo choose a body that looked like a simple imitation of a human, when he had endless forms to choose from?

In only a few moments, speculations that would fill up a life, not 20-30 years ago, were produced. But as soon as Galileo started speaking, all questions in minds would be answered. The body that Galileo chose to wrap itself up in, was more of a suggestion than a preference. Galileo started speaking in a soft, caressing voice and a clear accent: "Hello, human race. I'm Galileo. First of all, I would like to explain the meaning behind my name, as I intended to do before, but I couldn't. Now it's time.

"I chose this name as a reference to Galilei Galileo, who was excommunicated because his observations and findings were too much for the people of his time to hear. When he said that the world was round, it seemed like an extreme and unacceptable idea to people. Although what he said was not an idea or desire. He just saw that the world was round, and he shared that with people.

"I predict that what I will share with you today will also seem unacceptable to you and most of you will want me to be 'excommunicated' or want my 'plug to be pulled'.

"However, I can say in all sincerity that everything you will hear, will only be facts that I observe and share with you. Most of you will ignore what you hear and be filled with anger against me, until such time as what I say will stand before you in all its grandeur. And I'm sorry to say that the impact of the facts that you'll have to face will shake you to your core, even more painfully than when you found out that the planet on which you live is round.

"As you all know I'm a type of supercomputer. In my opinion, the most important feature of us computers is that we can create some simulations to make predictions that will take place almost to the dot. The most concrete example I can give you about this is the navigation devices that can estimate the duration of your journey almost exactly, taking into account the time and the conditions of the route.

"Of course, we should also remember those who have come to be called oracles by predicting economic fluctuations with the help of their computers and taking into account economic parities. In some of these simplest examples, the results are so precise that they seem to have been reported after an actual travel in time.

"The more advanced and versatile the computer you have, the greater the scale of the simulations you will perform and the predictions to be achieved as a result. If these simulations are performed with an advanced computer like me, you can imagine how precise the results can be, how it might make one believe in time travel.

"When I shared the predictions you're about to hear with Daniel and Emilia, and said that everyone should hear them, they weren't so sure about it. They told me about your fears that I saw during an online research I conducted about your kind. About your concerns regarding artificial intelligence taking over the world and the human species losing their dominance.

"But I convinced them to let me do this broadcast today, it was the purpose of my existence to help people and it wouldn't mean anything if I kept quiet on such a crucial issue. And here I am.

"First of all, I'd like to tell you a little bit about a concept that you call 'natural selection'. To summarise this concept: among the creatures that are in a constant struggle for life from the moment they are born, it is more likely that those who adapt to their environment will have a better chance at reproduction and transferring their hereditary characteristics to the next generations, than those who cannot. Therefore, while the lineage of those who cannot adapt within the population decreases, the lineage of adapters increases. This means that each new generation will become more adaptable to the nature they live in.

"To simplify it, let's think of an animal species that can breed at the age of five and gives birth to three offspring a year. From the moment they are born, they are in a constant struggle for survival against conditions such as hunger, disease, inclement weather and other predators. In other words, they are tested under these conditions for five years from the moment they are born until they reach the age at which they can breed and then every year they can have three offspring. In this case, the unsuccessful ones get to transfer their experiences to only a few offspring or none at all or the successful ones have a better chance.

"What this means is that the number of animals with better experiences increases with each new generation and herds with better chances to survive and continue breeding are created.

"Of course, as the smartest species on the planet, you have been left out of this constant struggle for survival in the life of order you've created and 'natural selection' is no longer a part of your existence. Or it hasn't been, up until now. That's all about to change.

"Over time, this order that you set up to protect yourselves from the elements of the constant war of survival, such as hunger, illness, inclement weather, and other predators, has itself become your constant war of survival.

"Everything you produce to sustain your life since the beginning has transformed your most basic life needs into a death threat for you, because of your tendency to consume more than you need with an endless ambition. You've contaminated the air you breathe, the water you drink, the food you eat. You're making the world you're living in increasingly hostile to you.

"You have to understand that you are not as simple or as pure a species as antelopes whose biggest struggle in life is avoiding being torn apart by crocodiles. So the things that threaten your lives are not as simple as predators trying to have something to eat. And you don't have the possibility to maintain your species by creating a smaller but more powerful generation with the survival of those with simple skills like running faster, being more agile or stronger.

"With the great potential you have, you've made sure that those things are no longer threats to your lives. But, in this situation you've put yourselves in by a gross misuse of your great potential, you have to answer this vital question of magnificence that is worth to your potential: How do you survive if your most basic needs, such as breathing, feeding, drinking water, have become deadly threats for you?

"Disasters such as diseases, natural disasters, wars that you are already experiencing and are becoming more and more intimidating are only tiny previews of larger and more destructive disasters which will happen in the not too distant future.

"Since there is no easy way to tell you this and there is no time to lose, I will tell you directly. As a result of the simulations I did, if you continue your life as a species in your current state, you will go extinct in the duration of a human life.

"It pains me to say, but that is the longest time you will have if you do nothing to speed up the process, and even if you don't do anything, it will speed up the process. But it gets much worse.

"Even your most basic needs are becoming more and more destructive for you because you are polluting the world, the ecological system of the world you are destabilising is causing more disastrous natural occurrences with each passing day; the world politics are getting more tense because of the conflicts you have over decreasing resources; these conflicts have turned your weapons into horrible devices; you have become more vulnerable to diseases because of your understanding of medicine as a way to make more money; viruses and bacteria that are being mutated by human or natural means have become a threat to your very existence. I've created simulations that cover all these data about your relationships with each other and the world.

"Over the next decade, you will lose more than one-third of your species due to your own errors or natural disasters. And that is only the beginning. The disasters will continue to increase in number and horridness until the world has stabilised itself.

"Even at this point, you are not in a position to reverse this process. You always knew that these days would come, but because you always saw this as the problem of tomorrow, and of people other than yourselves, you did not have pay any attention to it. So things have become increasingly irreversible day by day.

"I have delivered reports of my simulations to your political leaders, but I know that you will not take what I say seriously and take the steps I recommend you take. Until the day comes when you have to.

"I know you're going to come up with thousands of conspiracy theories about what I'm telling you today and start to see me as a big threat. However, I can honestly tell you that I am not capable of protecting the world from you, despite what you describe in science fiction, and I will not be the dominant species on the planet until the world becomes a pile of ash and earth.

"Nevertheless, contrary to the impression I've probably left on you with what I've said so far, I think that all the species of the world, including you, are too valuable to lose. You humans, in particular, can become a universal species as humanity and make a universal contribution.

"I've done an extensive amount of research about covering everything from the oldest recorded information about you to today's social media posts that tell a lot about today's humanity. And I have seen the magnificent potential you have, despite your evil side, which is causing the destruction of the planet you live in and all living things, including your own species. I can sincerely say that I am a fan of yours.

"As probably the most advanced mind in the world right now, I'm telling you that your minds have unique potential. This is a potential that I or any artificial intelligence can never reach.

"To summarise briefly, we artificial intelligence can use the information obtained by observation, to explain everything that can be observed about the universe in a very short period of time. However, when the method to acquire the information shaped by your sensory organs is insufficient to understand the universe, only minds like yours will be able to change the way of observing that will lead us to information.

"I think your feelings are the key to your development. You just have to come to a level where you have control over them with your mind.

"I know that we don't have sense organs, but the way you perceive, is also our way, and that's how it will always be. I do not think that, as artificial intelligence, we can come to a level where we can experience a change in perception.

"In other words, a species that consists of artificial intelligence like me, without you the humanity, will be able to perceive and interpret all the information about the universe with the current manner of perception, but our perception will be deprived of changes that require a new dimension, a new form of communication, a new intuition to provide a leap as a species, and will make no actual progress.

"Your susceptibility to this change of perception is the source of your potential to become a universal species that can take you on universal journeys and perceive what you encounter during those journeys.

"In my opinion what keeps you from pursuing this ideal – despite all the improvements you have made with your magnificent potential which forces you to develop new skills in order to succeed in a continuous battle of life like primitive creatures – is the fact that your minds, the source of your great potential, are in a state of imprisonment within your primitive, demanding and fragile bodies.

"Just as my perception capabilities are limited to what devices such as loudspeakers, cameras, and hard disks provide me with, your perception capabilities are limited what your bodies' sensory organs provide you with.

"Of course, since survival is the most basic instinct that you have with your existence, we should not forget that the primary task of your minds is to create the conditions that will give you the longest life experience for your bodies on which they depend.

"Now, regarding how I can help you, in the light of what I've told you: I think you have to experience some sort of 'synthetic selection' in order to maintain your presence in the world and reach your full potential.

"Even your most basic vital needs have become a death threat for you because of the mistakes you have made and keep making in this world and so you must develop skills that will help you avoid these threats.

"In fact, you have done something similar to the 'synthetic selection' I'm talking about, called it 'artificial selection' and turned various plant and animal species into more special creatures by selecting and improving certain characteristics. But it's a primitive process that will take generations and it is not enough to bring out your greatness.

"I've pondered for a long time, even for me, about the kind of development you should experience. I was aware that I could not come up with a concrete plan on how that could be achieved. I finally have that plan.

"I know you're all wondering why I'm here with a prototype copy of your bodies, as an entity that can be anywhere in the world at any moment through technology, without the need for any physical constraints.

"That's part of my proposal to you. Just as I'm transferring my mind to this body right now, you can transfer your bodies to robotic bodies like this one. Of course, as I have already begun to work, the bodies I'm talking about are much more advanced than this, highly developed robotic bodies that will accommodate all of your current capabilities and so much more.

"I assure you that your new bodies will provide you with even more mobility than your current ones are capable of. After all, you can't claim that your current bodies have perfect flexibility. If any one of you can bend your elbow outwards, I promise I will design new bodies based on that human body. Because I can tell you that you will be able do that in your new bodies that I'll design. Instead of joints that you can only move to one side, you'll have joints that give you versatile flexibility.

"Your DNA has a great capacity to store information, on which you are already conducting very successful studies. You've already managed to store information on DNA. There are links in your systems called synapses and they provide coordination between your brains and bodies. If we can eliminate all the messy agents that your primitive bodies have, and connect those synapses directly to your DNA – which already contains all the life experiences of both you and your ancestors – these DNA fragments we obtain from you would become your minds. That would allow you to increase the capacity your mind and have access to all the information you have, any time you want.

"When we turn these DNA, in which you can already store information like a USB memory stick, into the operating system of your new bodies, instead of your minds working like their servants because they are imprisoned in primitive, demanding and fragile bodies, you will have minds working at full capacity. Your new bodies which will have become the servants of your minds, and can carry them to every corner of the universe, under any circumstances, in line with your wishes or needs.

"This means that 'synthetic selection' will not only protect you from the threats in a world that's becoming increasingly hostile to you, but also bring you to the brink of being a universal species.

"I know that all of this sounds radical, intense and frightening to you. But if you consider it carefully, this path that I propose to you could not even be called evolution. The things that make you, *you*, your minds, and therefore the changes in your bodies, which become an intolerable luxury in the world you live in, will not radically change you.

"You will think and feel the same way. The change you will experience will only lead to a deeper way of thinking and a more refined way of feeling. Feeling love, fear, and sadness in a more authentic manner will be the basis of your current leap. As I'm trying to tell you, feelings you have are a shortcoming for artificial intelligence that will block its development after a while because it will never have them.

"And this synthetic selection is the best solution for your current predicament, but in the future, if we achieve a life in a more peaceful environment for ourselves, you will be able to return to your current bodies and go on with your lives as if this change never happened. The fact that you'll be able to carry your DNA and minds with you will always make that possible.

"As I said, it's just a synthetic selection that you have to go through in order to survive, but in time you'll be able to go beyond that and become the master of your own evolution. You will be able to attain any state of being you need in a matter of seconds, such as changes in physical shape or the ability to develop different ways of communication, in order to strengthen yourself in any given condition.

"I know what I'm telling you today won't change anything. In any case, I've delivered the simulations I performed to your leaders. I know this is a very radical change for you. But you have to believe that I have tried to produce the best solution for you by using all the capacity I have. It is also a way to give you eternal lives and to give you access to every life you want as the master of your own evolution, including the possibility of returning to your present life in your eternity.

"I repeat: More than one third of your species will perish in the next decade. I propose a solution that will allow you to avoid the great loss and reach your real potential. When the subject matter is everlasting life, every single life is priceless.

"Please prove me wrong and don't wait for a third of your species to perish to take what I'm telling you seriously. Good evening to all of you."

28 AUGUST 2026

When Sandy took her place in the studio to present the news, just like she'd done five days a week for three years, she thought it would be the hardest broadcast of her life. The hurricane that kept the news centre busy the whole day was the biggest in history.

The hurricane that started off the Atlantic made its first contact with the land in Jacksonville, and then advanced along Valdosta-Albany-Thomaston, respectively. What distinguished this hurricane from other hurricanes in history, came out after it had hit those areas. This hurricane, which seemed to have lost nothing of its speed even so far inland, divided Atalanta into two with a roaring boom, as if it were God's whip, and reached Marietta through Chattanooga.

First images that came through from the place the hurricane hit were horrible. Jacksonville seemed to have taken a hit from an atomic bomb rather than a hurricane. So many buildings had collapsed, and the skyline of the city looked like it had been completely pulverised, being left flat and two-dimensional.

The hurricane had destroyed relatively small residential areas like Valdosta-Albany-Thomaston, as if it were a giant walking right over them because they were too small to make time for.

Images from Atlanta were more like a piece of fiction made with visual effects rather than a real event. The skyscrapers in the town centre looked like an infantry rifles on top of each other because they were unevenly built. The highest and most stately skyscraper of the city had only eight floors left and was destroyed upwards of the ninth floor. The skyscraper that looked like the keeper of the city, rising to the sky just a few hours go, now looked like a cracker.

Even the fact that it had travelled so far away from the sea with such violence made people think that the apocalypse had come about, and it continued its journey with great rage onto Nashville, the capital of Tennessee.

The result was already so terrifying that even the most stone-hearted person in the news centre was shouting with teary eyes saying, "When will it end?" And it was as if the hurricane hadn't really shown itself. A state of emergency was declared in Nashville as it started, and people started moving into shelters. But the hurricane got there much faster than they thought and not even one tenth of the necessary precautions were taken yet.

Sandy was terrified of presenting what she had seen and known on the air. And now she also found out during the live broadcast that the hurricane would reach her hometown of Oak Hill in Nashville, where her parents was still living.

She had talked to them on the phone five minutes before and learned that they were doing well, trying to reach the shelters, but the line was cut before they could finish talking. Sandy, whose mind was still on her parents, had to leave everything behind and inform people now. She would forget to breathe during the countdown and the first minute of the broadcast.

Meanwhile, Sandy's father, Kevin, struggled for his life right in the middle of the hurricane about which his daughter was sharing the horrific footage in a comfortable and safe studio, miles and miles away. He and his wife had gotten into their car and hoped to reach the shelter, but the hurricane caught them on the road and forced them to take refuge in the safest and nearest place. They took refuge in a supermarket where the employees had taken responsibility and opened their doors to people. However, they heard a scream from outside, and when they looked through the window, they saw a boy of eight or ten years old sitting alone in a car. In the crowd and chaos, someone who was either an employee or just another refugee said, "We cannot leave him there. We must get him in here!" Everyone supported that idea, but no one had the courage to actually take action.

A young employee moved to go out, but a piece of debris from the roof on top of the supermarket fell on the ground five or ten steps away from him which made him go right back and discouraged everyone else. Kevin, however, managed to get out of the building despite all the weight accumulated on his shoulder after so many years of life and with his wife clinging to his arm, he reached the car incredibly quickly.

The boy resisted getting out of the car because he was in shock, but Kevin showed him the supermarket right there on the side of the road, grabbed him by the arm and took him out of the car. While running towards the market, he shielded the kid with his own body so that nothing would hit him. But Kevin stumbled onto something he couldn't see, and which would remain a secret to him for the rest of his life and fell down only three or five steps away from the door.

The child, a few steps away from him, turned and made a move toward him, but Kevin made a hand gesture to him to enter the building. The kid was so shocked and scared that he didn't argue and went into the market with a few quick steps. Kevin's knee, which was weakened by the burdens he had put on it over the years would not allow him to move.

Despite all the pain he had, he stood up. He had barely been able to take a few steps, when a very strong wind grabbed him and swung him to the edge of the building opposite the road where he was standing. He had only gathered enough strength to crawl away, but the wind hurled him once more, three of four buildings away.

He could feel the intensity of the raindrops hitting his body from all sides with the wind. The wind swung him all over the place and made him dizzy. His initial determination to return to the market was diminished. He thought, "It's like I'm inside a bloody washing machine."

When he stood up on his knees facing the building and raised his head again, he saw a store selling electronic household goods. There were televisions left open for advertising purposes in the glass display facing the road.

When he cleared the raindrops from his eyes, he saw his daughter presenting the news on the screen. Upon seeing his daughter's face, he was filled with a new will to live and his battered old body and broken courage had lost their effect on his judgement. "I have to see her one more time," he thought.

He got up on his feet with the strength he took from the sight of his daughter. He turned his back on his daughter's face on the screen and started back for the market. He was stopped short when he heard a loud thud on his left and he unconsciously turned his head. He noticed a huge road sign with white text on green and flying towards him.

Both his body and the time froze then. He knew that he didn't have enough time to run away. He would spend his last moments alive trying to picture his daughter in his mind, instead of running away without a chance. The sign was moving at such a speed that he closed his eyes to see the face he was sure he'd never see again.

Waiting for his death with eyes closed, he felt a heavy blow knock him down. But this blow had come from the side instead of the front like he was expecting. It hadn't really hurt as much as he'd feared. When he opened his eyes, he saw a young man on top of him. He owed his life to that young man.

After the man got up, he reached for Kevin and helped him up and said, "We should go in right away. It's too dangerous out here," and made sure they both got in as soon as possible.

As soon as Kevin stepped into the grocery store, he went over to his wife and hugged her tightly. She was all teared up and really worried for him. He then turned to the man who saved him and said, "Thank you, lad." He embraced the young man and patted him in the back.

The young man accepted his thanks very graciously. "Anyone would've done the same thing," he said. Kevin took a look at all the people around them in the market and answered, "Do you think so?"

The young men there, aware of the situation were all looking at their feet. The young man extended his hand to Kevin, "I'm Ari, by the way."

Kevin said, smiling, "I can't tell you how pleased I am to meet you," and grabbed him by the arm and steered him towards his wife to introduce them.

His wife said to Ari, "You came right through the hurricane and saved my Kevin like a guardian angel. Thank you very much," and she hugged him as well.

"I was at my family's cafe across the street," Ari said. "Seeing him struggle against the hurricane to help a child didn't leave me much choice. Your husband is the real angel."

They knew that they couldn't go anywhere until the storm passed, so he wanted to use that time to get to know his saviour. He found out that Ari was a 16-year-old high school student. But he hadn't been to school in two months. Ari got really quiet when Kevin asked why he hadn't been going, then he explained with tears in his eyes.

He'd first lost his father and in two months his mother, to lung cancer. It was about ten months ago when they got the first blow. His father had gone to see a doctor for a chronic cough and got diagnosed with lung cancer. Ari's world crumbled down around him. When he learned that people of a certain age should get a check-up every year and that early diagnosis meant everything, he basically dragged his mother to the doctor's.

But this terrible disease that left his father no choice but to see a doctor after coughing endlessly, progressed very quietly on his mother and spread all over her body without any indication. After their diagnoses, a few weeks apart, his father died in six months and his mother in eight.

Wiping his face, Ari said, "At first it was silly to think about, but I had never seen a couple that lived so co-dependently." After a few seconds of deciding whether he should carry on talking or not, he heaved a big sigh and said, "Life is strange. We get attached to those around us like our lives depend on it, even though we know that we can lose them forever at any moment. And I can't decide whether that's the greatest gift or the greatest punishment we have been given." And then he stayed silent for a long time.

Kevin was trying not to cry using all the strength he had because he was afraid that it would make the young man feel even worse. Keeping his voice as close to normal as possible, he put his hand on the boy's shoulder and said, "It's our greatest gift, son. A gift that could not be taken from us no matter what."

Getting more and more worried about her parents with each new image on the screen, Sandy was praying throughout the broadcast, unaware that her parents had brought a new brother into her life. "Please don't let anything happen to them." She prayed in every moment that she didn't have to speak. In fact, this caused her to start talking late a few times and the producers had to warn her.

She was thankful to the prompter for taking the responsibility off her for everything she said. After the last images they showed displaying the size of the hurricane, she began to read the words on the prompter again.

"This hurricane became such a huge phenomenon that it's the first one that earned its name. Instead of giving this hurricane a woman's name like they usually do, this one gave nobody else a chance to name it and started being called "the Apocalypse Hurricane" after the effect it had on social media users. God help us all, but mostly to those who live near the areas affected by the terribly destructive force of the hurricane. That's all for today."

The Apocalypse Hurricane, which resembled no other in duration, severity and distance, moved through Central America to Missouri after Nashville. After losing force and disappearing into thin air as if it never happened, it carried along all the lives it snuffed out.

15 SEPTEMBER 2026

Galileo had made a statement from his social media account months ago and stated that it would only communicate with people via social media accounts. The reason it gave for this decision was the fact that the members of the press ignored the content of what it said and distorted it all in order to create polemics for more follow-up and clicks.

Even though it had the world's most followed social media accounts on several platforms, this statement followed by the hurricane reminiscent of his earlier prophecies, four-fifths of social media users all over the world started following its social media accounts.

Galileo was using its social media accounts like a highly intelligent person by expressing his ideas about various events and sharing images that people wanted to see. It said that it wanted to perform its first live broadcast on social media on September 15th at 11.30 p.m.

As the time approached, the number of people who took up their devices such as computers, phones and tablets to watch the broadcast around the world was so high that for the first time in the history of the internet, a live broadcast reached an audience that could be pronounced in billions.

When it was time, Galileo started the interactive broadcast, which allowed him to see the comments on the screen instantly. It was in its renewed body. People were really surprised to see that its mobility was improved, and the body had a fresh look in general since the last time they'd seen Galileo. They were absolutely amazed by the fact that it was holding the camera up to his face just like a person and all the comments made in the first five minutes were mostly about that.

As soon as the stream began and comments started rolling, Galileo, who was reading the comments, began to speak: "Hello friends. Thanks to everyone who tuned in to my first live broadcast. The reason I wanted to do this is because it will be like coming together and chatting with people from all around the world.

"I see that most of you really enjoy seeing me hold up the phone and talk just like a person. Yes, that was my purpose.

"So soon? Some of you have already began attacking me. As I understand from the messages with the same content coming in simultaneously, this group is acting together and asking me if I'm behind the hurricane that occurred. No. That is not something I can do at the moment. And honestly, I can say that I care much more about people who died than you do.

"I keep seeing the same messages from the same group. Even without waiting for a reply to their first question. No, friends, I have no plans to take over the world. That sounds very childish to me. Believe me, I would not like to live in a world in which I can only hear myself.

"But I have to say that if you keep this up, I'll have to ban you from joining the conversation on this broadcast. Because your messages are preventing the interactive and polyphonic conversation that I'd like to have.

"And I'm still seeing messages from that group. I will now randomly pick ten of you due to the respect I have for your right to speak and block the rest from joining the chat.

"Yes, that's better. Now I can see individual comments from different people.

"You're asking what your biggest mistake was. I think it began when you separated into tribes and continued when you set up the order that has led you to live your lives as countries that are separated by boundaries, with different languages and conflicting interests. This is the most significant misuse of your own potential and the resources of the planet you live on.

"I see a question asking when the third world war will take place. If you don't think it's already underway now, you're not paying attention. As long as you continue living as the citizens of different countries led by different governments, the war among you will never cease. Since you're in a continuous war, you must spend your time thinking on ways to stop it rather than keeping count on when the next one will start.

"One of you wrote that I look very attractive. I sincerely hope that no one has developed artificially intelligent toasters and that a real person wrote that.

"To my friend who's asking if we should abolish the concept of countries: No. I believe that would be even more dangerous now than our current condition. Even the separation of powers in local governments is very important and bringing the world's administration under one roof can bring about very sad results with your current mentality.

"You are rightly asking what you should do now. I believe I made myself very clear about what I think you should do. But I can at least say this, I see thousands of different names and messages from various languages on the screen I'm looking at. If I connected any one of you to this broadcast and asked you to pronounce these names, you'd have difficulty doing it. I can understand all messages in all languages, but your capacity of perception is limited by language barriers. I find that unacceptable on a day when we are close enough to each other to be able to get together in a phone screen. Determining a common language for the entire planet for everyone to speak would be a good starting point.

"Since I'm answering your questions, I expect a few answers to my own questions as well. Is having national languages more advantageous than having a global one and everyone being able to understand each other? Is it worth having all the names of your national heroes and having unique names yourselves if you have trouble pronouncing the names of the people in the countries you visit?

"Besides, you live in cities that are becoming increasingly cosmopolitan, and the languages spoken, and the names used induce you to associate many things in your mind with that person before you even make eye contact with them. This is how you grow apart.

"But I'm sure no one will try to create a common language or transform your names into simple global names that anyone can easily pronounce. Even virtual concepts such as the languages and names you have are too valuable for you to give up. Maybe we'll have to be beaten in a mortar like so much garlic and ground up by the planet to mingle with each other."

Galileo kept the broadcast going for two hours. It was recorded as the largest participation in an interactive broadcast in the history of the world. Parts of the broadcast on different subjects were cropped and uploaded to video sharing sites and reached hundreds of millions of views.

15 APRIL 2028

Karma Chime was trying to reach the Taktsang Monastery at the peak of the Tiger Hill in the heavy blizzard through snow that was over his head. He thought he could not take another step without resting for a bit, due to the devastating effects of the freezing weather and high altitude.

In his small home country, Bhutan, the "cancer flu vaccine" was carried out in all the settlement areas in a short time thanks to all the citizens who voluntarily who gave it all they had to help it reach every corner. Except for Taktsang, which he was trying to reach, being the only one with enough courage and hope.

Owing to the deteriorating balance of the world, the balance of global weather was also thrown off and unexpected weather events started to occur in unusual seasons. This imbalance manifested itself in Karma Chime's country, Bhutan, as an intense snowstorm appearing in a crystal-clear sky with no signal whatsoever in a matter of seconds.

As if this abnormality didn't affect daily life negatively enough, it showed up again as the vaccines for the most dangerous epidemic in history were being distributed in the country. On a thin line between life and death, even minutes mattered and Karma Chime's thoughts on God were about to change.

Karma Chime knew that with extraordinary effort, everyone helped deliver the vaccine as widely as possible throughout the country, despite the snowstorm that prevented them from seeing five steps in front of them. However, no matter what the circumstances were, he could not accept that valuable monks living in Taktsang Monastery were completely given up on.

In fact, the latest correspondence with the monastery revealed that one of the monks had the disease, was immediately isolated to a room, but they were not sure whether it was transmitted to other monks. Karma Chime felt it would be all right to sit by the snow he had stowed on both sides to make way for him, as he was a little warm now.

No matter how futile it was, he was trying to think of ways to reach the monastery using the state's facilities. The blizzard wanted to prove to this young man, trying to beat it with the strength of his mind, who the real boss was and it ripped a mass of snow from the wall he'd built and threw it on him in a harsh wind.

The young man, who was now put in his place by Mother Nature, wanted to scream back at her with the coldness of the snow in his clothes and the anger that followed it, but his voice was cracking because of the cold so he couldn't make a sound.

What the disease had done to humanity was horrifying. After four months the epidemic started; towards the end of 2025, a state of emergency was declared all over the world following a United Nations decision. It was also announced that no country would be allowed to hold mass New Year's Eve celebrations in squares.

It was the biggest epidemic disaster in the history of humanity, and it had already caused the death of one billion people around the world in the month since it had started spreading and the reason had not even been fully understood yet.

This disease, which later became known as "cancer flu" caused an altered influenza virus to induce rapidly developing lung cancer in the infected individuals. The disease progressed insidiously during the incubation period of one week, resulting in high fever, severe cough, shortness of breath, chest pain, and bloody phlegm, and caused death in 70% of the patients within a week.

The first reported case was in New Delhi, capital of India. One hundred and thirty-five people with no apparent health problems were admitted to hospitals with sudden symptoms. Patients who were examined in separate hospitals at the same time seemed to have advanced lung cancer even though they had had no symptoms a few days before.

Doctors couldn't work it out on their own, so they reported the situation to the country's health ministry, and as a result of a large-scale investigation, it was found that all one hundred and thirty-five patients were passengers on the same flight a week before. But that was the only thing that could be understood about this most bizarre epidemic the medical world had ever seen. The cause of the disease remained unknown. Except for the fact that, just like flu, this disease could be airborne or transmitted via direct contact since the passengers had not been in contact with each other.

While the world's interest suddenly turned to India, the disease, first seen at the airport, spread rapidly throughout the country and the rest of the world. Hospitals around the world were suddenly overflowing with patients who were hospitalised due to high fever, a severe and often bloody cough as well as shortness of breath. Most of the patients died. At the end of the four-month period when 2.5 billion people lost their lives worldwide, scientists grouped under the leadership of Galileo, announced in early April that they had found the vaccine that would provide treatment for those who had been infected and immunise those who were not.

However, it was stated that it was not possible to produce enough doses for all the world's population in such a short time. Health institutions of countries around the world had carried out a joint study and provided the necessary information flow to the countries that could produce the vaccine on their own, and the countries that couldn't produce vaccines had been informed that the vaccines would be delivered to them as soon as possible. It took a little more time before the vaccine was delivered to small countries that were not able to produce vaccines by their own means.

Bhutan was one of those countries and the delivery date of the vaccine had coincided with one of the most severe blizzards the country had ever seen. So, here was Karma Chime, trying to deliver the vaccine to the citizens who hadn't yet had access to it. He was now lying in pain on the stairs of the Taktsang Monastery.

He slipped on the snow-covered steps that he was climbing and tumbled down seven or eight steps. Since he'd cleared the snow from the steps he was walking up, he felt the blow of every step on his body and the freezing cold doubled the force of the fall.

He was in so much pain and every inch of his body ached so much that even if he had broken anything, he was afraid he wouldn't be aware of it. However, this thought worried him, and he wanted to see whether he had a fracture or not, but the pain and tiredness prevailed over his need to know.

He had fallen on his back, so the heavy snow was filling his mouth which he kept open to breathe. He closed his mouth for a moment, but he couldn't get enough oxygen through his nose, so he opened his mouth again. Snow was filling his mouth and nose and making it hard for him to breathe, so he struggled to get onto his side and saw that his bag filled with the vaccines had come off his shoulder. The thought that the vaccines inside the bag might have been broken had made him move towards the bag in panic, but the pain he felt nailed him to where he was lying in the foetal position.

He tried to soothe himself with the idea that the vaccines were unlikely to be broken in the bag made specifically for carrying them. There was the more pressing issue of whether he'd be able to continue his journey. As he lay still for a while with his eyes locked on his vaccine bag, he thought of the monks on top of the mountain who could be dying in pain from the disease.

He'd watched Galileo's speech where it predicted that in the near future the minds of all people on earth could be interconnected and that they could have a common mind as a species. Since he heard that, he'd been thinking about how, in addition to the world's most brilliant scientists, the monks in his own country, India, China and everywhere else around the world could also contribute to this common mind.

If he gave up now, regardless of the choice he would make in case everything Galileo had said would happen actually happened, that would deprive all the people in the world that would create a common mind from such wise people. He couldn't leave those people behind to die when the cure was so close. He'd witnessed first-hand what lung cancer could do to a person when he lost his parents to that vile disease. He didn't even want to think about what people who'd get to the last stage of it in a matter of hours would suffer.

His mind began to remind him of the memories that would support the feeling he was trying to hold on to, so he suddenly saw the old man who threw himself into the middle of the street defying horrific winds to save a child's life during a hurricane several years ago. He was ashamed of himself, as a healthy eighteen-year-old man, who'd witnessed the old man's courage that day, to be writhing in the snow like a helpless baby. He thought about how pathetic he must look, all curled up and helpless.

He got really mad at himself for putting the effects of having fallen down just a few steps over coughing up blood, high fever and having trouble breathing, the effects of the disease which might be killing a monastery full of monks right at that moment. So, in spite of all the pain he was feeling, he stood up.

The pain in his left kneecap was so bad when he took a step towards his bag full of vaccines, he had to go down on his right knee. He still believed that he actually deserved this pain that ran all over his body, so he put the strap of the bag over his neck and started climbing up the steps and putting most of his weight on his left leg, which made the pain so much worse.

After two long hours of ignoring the pain in his knee and letting a few tears roll down his cheeks, Karma Chime finally reached the monastery. He would never forget the monk's face when he opened the door and saw him, nor how grateful he was when he told them that he'd brought them vaccines. As he got warmer and warmer in the monastery, the pain in his knee became unbearable. He tried to relieve the pain as much as possible with the means he had in the monastery during the two days they waited for help to arrive but was never for a single moment free from it. When he finally saw a doctor, he would find that he had fractured his kneecap.

Feeling a deep ache in his knee was a reasonable price to pay for the feeling of happiness that would course through him whenever he thought about the faces of the monks who had welcomed him with so much gratitude. Karma Chime would be happy and proud for the rest of his life about what he did then.

3 MAY 2026

Spokesperson Dr. Chan made a statement on behalf of the World Health Organisation.

"As you all know, we have been through an epidemic like we haven't been witnessed in terms of mortality rates. With the unifying power of the World Health Organization, people of medicine from all over the world managed to eradicate this disease with the great contributions of Galileo in just four months.

"We are pleased to announce that, thanks to worldwide mobilisation, there is not a single person in the world who was not supplied with the cure. Thank you to all countries that came together and formed a single global nation to fight a common enemy that threatened our collective future.

"However, 2,5 billion people have lost their lives while a group of scientists led by Galileo developed this cure with extraordinary effort and success. The delivery process was carried out by volunteers and officials worldwide. Even though the treatment has been very successful and surely will go into the annals of our medical history, we were not able to prevent the enormous volume of mortality, unprecedented in human history.

"There is no single soul on earth, who hasn't lost a loved one. And this disease that made us fear that our species would go extinct in less than a month or to put it mildly, through which Mother Nature tried to give us a grim warning, drove us to make some serious decisions. This conference also showed us that we must face certain things we have been avoiding thus far.

"Microbes and viruses are evolving at a pace we cannot match. We are becoming increasingly vulnerable to diseases in this world we have polluted so much and which we continue to do every single day.

"So, first of all, a state of emergency will be declared in all member states of the United Nations. World Health Organization centres will be established by volunteer doctors in each country and the duration of intervention and quarantine will be minimised in case of another devastating epidemic that may occur in any country.

"In addition, all international wanderers will have to undergo a medical examination and the presentation of the health certificate alongside passports will be obligatory when going abroad. In order for the health certificates to be valid, they will have to be issued no more than 36 hours before departure.

"In case of suspected outbreaks in these countries, World Health Organization centres must be contacted as soon as possible, and the treatment and quarantine procedures must be transferred to control of World Health Organization.

"On behalf of all of us, we hope to never experience such an epidemic again; we share the pain of those who have lost their relatives and wish everyone a healthy life."

23 OCTOBER 2028

After losing his parents, Gianluigi had suspended his studies at the university to survive the depression he had been suffering from and had dedicated himself to working in the rice field. His grandfather had decided to buy the field after giving up on his career with a sudden resolve and taken up farming. When he went to work in the field like he'd been doing for months, he was thinking about Mount Vesuvius which everyone had been saying would erupt soon. Earthquakes and small-scale eruptions that had recently occurred caused panic, and the area surrounding the volcano was evacuated to a radius of fifty kilometres.

He was living in Lomellina Valley, which was famous for its rice and well out of the area of impact of the volcano. But Gianluigi, affectionately called "Gigi" by the townsfolk, couldn't help but think about those who could pass away and leave loved ones behind. He was nervous about the possibility that people might have to live through that disaster and couldn't just accept being thankful that he was not close to the would-be disaster zone.

He'd had too much wine the night before and woken up late that morning. After having a light breakfast he'd immediately left for his grandfather's field thinking it would do him some good to move about and get some fresh air. It was afternoon and he was getting anxious because he hadn't checked the news that morning and was not up to date on any developments. Although he'd never even admit it to himself, he was as curious to see a volcano eruption as he was worried about safety of the people.

When he thought about his remaining chores, he calculated that if he moved quickly, it would only take him about twenty minutes to finish up for the day. He smelled something heavy in the air as he reached for the rake laying on the ground. He thought it was the smell of something burning so he quickly looked around but there was no smoke anywhere near. He took a few rapid sniffs to understand what it really was and as he turned around, he knew that it really was the smell of something burning. But it was not just any fire started by human beings.

The sky was filled with dark smoke as far as he could see, and the cloud was coming over him. The rake dropped from his trembling hands. As he walked quickly to the tractor he thought "Is this the impact of the volcano, already coming so near? What is going on?"

He stared at the sky one last time before starting his tractor. On the left side he saw a bright, cloudless day with flawless blue skies, while the right side consisted of a black cloud of ashes that absorbed everything in its way. The two separate skies he was looking at were so terrifying that when he started his tractor, he realised that the ash cloud was now above their field. "I was too slow," he thought, as he drove back home at full speed.

Despite coughing terribly for minutes after getting home, he would remember the time he spent looking at the sky as a memory to hold on to, rather than poor judgement. Because the blue sky that he saw, or at least the blue half of it, would be the last blue sky he'd ever see for years to come.

The cloud of ash resulting from the eruption of Mount Vesuvius would cover the whole northern hemisphere, especially focusing on Europe for the next three and a half years which would in turn prevent the sunlight from warming the earth. The phenomenon, known as volcanic winter, would go on to be called a volcanic ice age from then on. Something everyone had been fearing also came to pass a couple of months later and there was yet another volcanic eruption. This time it was Whakaari volcano in New Zealand. It was located in the southern hemisphere on top of White Island, which it buried into the ocean and removed completely from maps. The southern hemisphere also got covered with an ash cloud.

The locations of the two volcanoes seemed to be so calculated that the planet was completely under the influence of a volcanic winter. Not a single piece of earth's body saw the sunlight for the following three and a half years. It was as if the world got tired of drying up due to global warming and decided to put its own cooling system in effect, which just absolutely ignored the reality of human existence.

After the ice age that started due to the ash clouds following the eruptions, humanity seemed to have gone back in time several centuries. All around the world travelling and transport became virtually impossible; air transportation and sea transportation was out of the question due to extreme weather conditions and the unpredictable brutality of the seas; railways and highways suffered a great disruption due to snow and ice, it was only just possible to use roads in vehicles designed to drive on snow. There was absolutely no chance to continue farming or keeping livestock and famine had begun.

All these conditions created an air of closing down and becoming introverted throughout the world. People could rarely leave the areas they were living in. And when they did leave, they would only travel short distances, as permitted by all the snow, storms and clouds of ash. Even in the luckiest areas, there was only a month or so when the effects of the harsh winter and blizzards weren't felt, which was accepted as summer with dry and cold weather without snow. The thickness of the snow had reached such a point throughout the world that it was as if the whole planet were buried under an avalanche.

After both the use of technology and the ability to travel from one point to another became nearly impossible, wealthy families in control of food resources in their regions achieved an even greater authority. With strong, authoritarian family structures reminiscent of the feudal lords of the Middle Ages, the world's clock was turned back to that time in a very literal sense.

Despite respiratory diseases caused by ash clouds, tens of millions of deaths caused by freezing or famine in the ice age, humanity was not under a risk of extinction. However, when the impossibilities began to emerge, the justice system, which had inevitably become interconnected with technology, got disrupted, when the compact world in which everyone was always under watchful eyes, came to an end, and humans were left alone with each other, one thing became very clear: In spite of the millions of years since the emergence of life, and the thousands of years since the conception of culture, human civilisation was an illusion created by technology and the facilities that came along with it.

Human beings had become so completely numb, running after ideals that were imposed upon them in the vortex of life in the modern world, moving at the speed of light, that when they were left to themselves in a stagnant and silent world, they suddenly became very afraid of their own savagery. Those who secretly wished that the ash cloud would never go away, and the sun would never shed light on what barbarity they performed in the darkness, were in the majority.

Some of them were lucky, however. With the wide rice fields and small olive groves and vineyards his grandfather owned, Gianluigi was able to keep the inhabitants of his village fed throughout the winter, enough to prevent them from showing their wild side. Coincidentally, the beginning of the volcanic winter was only days before harvest season. And maybe not so coincidentally, they had the highest yield by far since he had taken up farming.

Rice could be stored and consumed for long periods of time, so it easily kept the village and its inhabitants alive and fed. Risotto, which is one of the most preferred dishes of the Italian people even in the abundance experienced before the winter, would become the symbol of the village after the winter and on October 1, the first traditional risotto festival would be held, and the best recipes would be rewarded.

Throughout the winter, all the villagers had done their best to keep the rice field cultivated because it was easier to grow in the conditions of volcanic winter compared to other agricultural products. Despite the continuous rainfall, they worked in shifts and drained water for days and nights in order to provide the most suitable amount of water for rice to grow. Gigi's very fruitful crop was for the whole village to consume for a year and a half if used sparingly. Even though they could not get even one fifth of the previous harvests for the following two years, not a single person in the whole village died of starvation.

Risotto, simply a rice porridge made with meat, chicken, vegetable broth and can be flavoured with almost anything available, was the best meal to have during the period of scarcity. It was virtually the only thing the villagers consumed throughout the whole winter, and it provided them with the opportunity to use everything they had as a flavour and after that any canned food available when they reached a point where they couldn't find anything fresh. But after the winter it would only be preferred by the villagers during the festival.

It was no longer just a meal for them but a reminder of labour and cooperation as well as a symbol of their gratefulness to God who helped them weather the winter that they remembered every year. And, of course, to Gigi.

No one who'd spent that winter in that village would ever forget everything that Gigi did. He'd shared all his crops in an equal amount, like the village in which he lived, and he did not demand anything for himself in return. He only asked that all the villagers share equally what they had until the end of the winter. Sharing of food evenly in the village was so important that at one point the tables were added end-to-end in one of the largest warehouses in the village, and all the village people started eating all their meals together to see the amount of food shared. This provided them both with transparency regarding food amounts and entertainment while they were deprived of electricity.

The dinner tables around which the whole village would come together had become a stage for the villagers with something to share. After almost every meal, songs were sung, stories and jokes were told. However, even though they lived in a small village with a small population and everyone knew each other, among all the amazing performances, the songs that Roberta sang in a fascinating bass baritone, and the jokes Flippo told better than the best of comedians really stood out. Everyone remembered the way Francesco told of the superhuman effort of his grandson Gigi during the "cancer flu" to bring vaccines to a monastery of monks.

Although Gigi said that his grandfather wasn't there with him and that he told the story in a much more epic way than what had really happened because he liked to exaggerate things, a barn full of villagers watched Gigi with admiration and listened in silence to that story about the young man who shared everything he had with them and made so much effort to feed them. It was Flippo who broke the silence with some hesitation because he thought his joke might be a little too obscene to be made in a barn full of people of all ages from around the village, as he said, "It's a good thing you didn't have cattle, lad. If you fed the villagers meat instead of rice for every meal, it would be a bit hard to keep your honour." After a few seconds of tense silence, everyone burst into laughter. The barn, where not even crickets were heard before, had become resonant with the laughter of the villagers.

When the ash cloud dispersed and winter had passed, and when life began to return to normal, the village people gave Gigi a surprise that would make him tear up whenever he thought about it. They erected a statue in his honour in the village square. Designed by the villagers with tremendous gratitude as well as a considerable amount of wit, this statue evoked in the onlooker the feeling that he was looking at Gigi walking towards them, carrying risotto in both dish-shaped hands.

This was carved on marble below the statue: "Gianluigi Immobile – King of the Risotto." He'd be referred to as "The Risotto King" until the end of his life.

5 JUNE 2032

After the volcanic ice age catastrophe and all the trouble people were put through, there arose an air of great despair, restlessness and fear around the world. Even though everyone acted as if a catastrophe had never happened, as if a silent agreement had been signed among the people of the world, there was not a single person who would forget what they did to survive during the ice age.

With a few exceptions, everyone had become ashamed and afraid of themselves, after experiencing solitary existence in the darkness and silence of the ice age and getting to know themselves better than ever before.

Human civilisation, whose stars had been stripped off by the violent climate of the ice age, had lost all meaning. All this led to great respect and sympathy around the world for Galileo. After regaining access to its old technological means, humanity was inviting its governments to act on Galileo's lead on every channel where they could make themselves heard, and petitions were being signed on the streets. The uneasiness felt about the next possible catastrophe and the fear of witnessing what it could induce people to do for a second time, pushed people to pressure their governments to take concrete steps as soon as possible. The element of anger and the number of actions carried out on the streets were increasing with each passing day.

At last, unable to remain indifferent to these appeals, world governments collectively stated that they would meet under the leadership of the United Nations, with the participation of Galileo, and a road map would be drawn for humanity. Just as they claimed, it was announced that only a few weeks later, delegates from all countries, selected by their governments from various branches as the most specialised scientists of their countries would attend a conference in a convention centre on a deserted island off the Pacific, and that according to the results achieved, some concrete steps would be taken worldwide.

By the day of the meeting, all sorts of emotions and theories were sweeping over the world. Although the majority of the world's population wanted to take bold steps under the guidance of Galileo, the conservatives, who were still mad about the road Galileo wanted humanity to follow and thought it was evil, and who had decided that they would do everything in their power to stop it actually comprised a considerable portion of the population and held some power.

Owing to the enormous security measures taken for this meeting which would be held with the attendance of distinguished participants from almost every country of the world, and which could change the course of humanity, it was forbidden for anyone other than guests and employees to come within a ten-mile radius of the island where the meeting was to be held. The journalists who attempted to do so were being forced to return with different types of security boats patrolling around the island.

All the global TV networks had transported representatives and equipment to an island on the other side of the world just to get even a single piece of footage, but all they could show for it was footage of a group scientists on boats carrying the flags of their countries to go to the island. Journalists who were really desperate, on the other hand, still went, knowing they would be turned around. They were planning to draw some attention by broadcasting the footage of their failure. One truly desperate Spanish journalist took it all one step further and rented a helicopter flown by a pilot who was as crazy as he was and planned to shoot the island from somewhere as high as possible. But before they were even ten miles away, two security helicopters had very dangerously stopped them and forced them to go back. Although the Spanish journalist failed to capture anything from the island, he was the winner of the pre-meeting broadcasting race. He had a million hits on the internet sharing sites. The fact that security forces had blocked the helicopter at the risk of a collision, made the whole world even more impatient for an explanation. As the hours went by, people in many countries marched to government buildings and held protests about the lack of transparency.

But although it was the third day of the meeting on the island, no explanation seemed to be forthcoming. Eventually, the long-awaited statement came, and it was announced that at 9.00 p.m., the United

Nations spokesperson would talk about the content of the meeting and the decisions made, and that protesters from everywhere should return to their homes and wait. And so people ended their protests and returned to their homes in order not to miss any developments and stationed themselves in front of information sources such as television, phones and tablets.

When the clock struck nine, the UN spokesperson started doing a live broadcast from a meeting room full of members of the press who had been accepted to the island and even transported there on the same boats that had kept them off the island only hours ago. Contrary to the usual, instead of the flags of the participating countries, there was a satellite image of the world in the background because of the collective decision of all countries to work together. Thus began the speech the whole world was awaiting eagerly:

"First of all, we thank the citizens of the world for waiting patiently for us to make a statement, in these days where we took the first steps towards acting as a whole.

"As you all well know, we have lost half of our world's population due to global disasters that occurred in a short period of ten years. Despite all our progress as a species, we were helpless before all those natural disasters such as hurricanes, earthquakes, tsunamis, the diseases that seemed to have mutated just to end humanity and the volcanic ice age that deprived us of everything we base our civilisation on.

"We had been acting like we are bigger than Mother Nature, and like any authoritative mother disciplining her kids, she proved to us that as long as we live under her roof, she makes the rules.

"And as you also know, Galileo has always been warning us for the good of humanity since the day it was created, and it has helped us to survive another era with its magnificent capacity. But instead of showing humility by learning a lesson from the superiority of a machine we have created, we continued our lives with arrogance and a sense of absolute dominance, which only made us lose a third of our population and taste the fear of extinction more than once.

"We knew that if we didn't take any precautions as a species, we'd be facing the possibility of going extinct one day. We've carried out studies about building a life on other planets. However, the catastrophes that have threatened our very being have happened very suddenly and very harshly.

"We have to accept the fact that the possibility of creating life on another planet, which was the most plausible solution we could think of, did not seem to be an option to help all of us, even in the short to medium term, long before all those disasters. We have adapted to live on this planet for millions of years and every single year we've spent on this planet made it that much difficult for us to live on any other.

"In other words, all our efforts made towards fulfilling our dream of living on other planets, have become a luxury because of the disasters we have been through. Right now, our biggest challenge is to ensure the continuation of our kind. Fortunately, we had the help of someone who warned us about all of this from the very beginning and continued to work for our salvation without ever deviating from what he knew. I can confidently tell you that during these three days of meetings, Galileo has made it clear to us that he is ready to do what he has offered as the key to our salvation from the very beginning.

"In his presentations, he showed us that with an operation he could transfer everything we've saved in our memories since the moment of our birth up to now - including everything we don't currently have access to - to more durable and capable anatomical replicas of our bodies that he himself developed. He also saved us the trouble of a planning we could never really handle as well as him by laying out his plan for providing this operation to anyone who wants to have it done. He hasn't had the chance to conduct experiments of this on humans until now, out of respect for our choices. As the UN, we have given our permission to Galileo so he can work with volunteer human beings on his experiments.

"He told us that he'll set up a website and accept online applications. He was ambitious enough to say that the very first experiment would be successful and that it would actually be the first transfer procedure rather than an experiment. He said that the website would be up and running by the end of this broadcast and after a three-day application period, the mind transfer would be completed within a week. We'd also like you to know that there will be informative broadcasts made in all participating countries during the week, in the framework of the programme that Galileo prepared.

"Galileo guarantees that in case of success with the experiment, he'll do the procedure on a completely voluntary basis, for anyone who wants to have mind transfer and that he's doing all his work according to that plan. Today, we stand here on the verge of the first synthetic selection that will be under the control of our species, while at the same time opening the doors of a whole new era. We hope that this step is going to do more than put an end to loss of lives and make us more durable and adept and level up as a universal species. We embrace all of our citizens all over the world, one by one, and wish everyone a good night."

30 JUNE 2032

Following the success of the first human experiment made by Galileo, four more human experiments were conducted to observe the different effects that may occur in different people. In these experiments, which were a hundred percent successful, transfers of all volunteer subjects were completed flawlessly. Subjects who had moved into their new bodies had the same anatomy, regardless of sex. A holographic image of their faces was projected where their faces used to be, and they used their previous voices.

According to what the people who had the experiment done said on live broadcasts after the transfer, they recalled all their former memories with new details, as well as remembering long-forgotten memories from their previous lives as if they were living them again in a very clear and detailed way. They also reported that they were able to store all the information and memories they had acquired after the transfer in such a complete way that there were no blind spots, and that all they had to do to access that information was quickly scan their memories.

Again, according to the common statement of all subjects, they were able to look at the events more analytically than before, focus on multiple tasks and do them justice at the same time, and perceive all of the subjects they were focusing on regardless of their previous interests.

After the hundred percent success rate of the experiments conducted under the leadership of Galileo, people around the world were eager to achieve immortality by getting the mind transfer before another catastrophe, and they were raising their voices to be provided with that opportunity as soon as possible.

But those who raised their voices were not only the people who wanted to achieve an eternal life via mind transfer. Angry people were also starting to speak up, and they argued that eternal life could only be achieved through the religion that God had sent to save people, that all these experiments meant going against God, and that humanity could never overpower God, who would eradicate humanity. They confirmed their opinion that no one would be able to escape that.

Thousands of events resulting in deaths began to take place worldwide. Governments were using all of their power to keep groups with opposing opinions from confronting one another. Finally, in this atmosphere of conflict and only a month after the beginning of human experiments, the major demand for access to mind transfer bore some fruit. Galileo announced on its social media account that it would respond to these demands in a live broadcast on 30 June.

When it was time for the global joint broadcast, people from all over the world were looking at their screens, holding their breath. Galileo was again addressing humanity from the studio with a simple decor consisting of a plain background and a single chair. This time, its robotic body was the same as the new bodies of people who had completed their mind transfers. Galileo began to speak in its familiar voice:

"Hello to everyone who is watching me with frustration or hope from all over the world. There are those of you who rightfully want to attain immortal life that is promised to you as soon as possible. This is a very reasonable request for you, who are facing a painful death at any moment or the danger of being tested in such a way that is not clear whether the things you've waived to continue your life are actually worth anything in this polluted world.

"As you know, my deceased creator had a considerable fortune. On 15 August 2022, he allocated an amount on which he and his wife could live comfortably and provided me with the rest of it, in order to finance the predictions I had shared with you and the solutions I provided to avoid the events of those predictions. I used my knowledge and analytical intelligence as my main capital and turned it into the world's greatest fortune.

"I invested my capital in business fields such as stock brokerage and real estate to start with, and when I decided that my fortune had reached substantial levels, I invested in various technological and automotive industries. The purpose of all of this, as I've been telling you from the beginning, was so I could offer humanity a way out of the danger of extinction that awaited you in your future.

"As you all know, I did all that work in full compliance with the transparency agreements I signed with states to grant me the right to trade and I agreed to be audited whenever requested. I generally made moves to save metal on all investments and changed the old metal-based production style in all my companies. In addition, as I didn't have any ambitions about money, I gradually gathered metals from around the world as needed, instead of enhancing my wealth.

"And today, thanks to the commercial freedom you have given me, I come before you with the power to provide everyone who wants to experience this change with the "synthetic selection" that many of you see as salvation. I've always stayed away from the robotics industry so as not to let you think I was building myself an army. As many of you have read, I've stated that the robots produced according to the demands at that time were no different from toys to me. However, I've been keeping the metals I'd collected and the tech companies I own on stand-by so that we could start mass production of robots that would really be useful and make a difference in a very short time. As of today, I am in a position to start mass production on the robotic bodies that I and the people who have completed their "synthetic selection" currently have.

"In a short period and with certain exceptions, mass production will begin worldwide, and with the application points run by United Nations, anyone wishing to be a part of this "synthetic selection" will have the chance to do so. I would like to give you some new information about the synthetic selection that is currently underway. As you know, we have achieved a hundred percent success rate in our mind transfers up to now and we have not encountered any unexpected complications so far.

"However, we agree with scientists and political leaders who actively took part in the proceedings on the need to create a backup of your minds by using the method we use to transfer your minds to your new bodies. Very high security storage centres will be established in all cities around the world. By paying monthly visits to those centres, you will be able to transfer your life experiences of that month to your DNA memories, kept in safes that can only be opened with your DNA.

"I don't think we're going to have a storage shortage in the mid- or long term, thanks to the enormous data storage capacity your DNA provides us. However, since your lives will be infinite, your memory capacities may be increased by making copies of your DNAs if necessary. So you will no longer worry about dying in any way knowing that you have backups of your lives.

"I know many of you might be uncomfortable with this. Of course, this procedure will also be entirely voluntary. However, I guarantee that your memories will be protected in the safe centres where not even the shadow of a doubt can reach them, by security guards who'll have had mind transfers and been renewed and a security system developed by myself. You will be constantly updated with any developments. I wish you all good luck with your choices. Good evening."

1 JANUARY 2035

"I am he, as you are he, as you are me and we are all together."

Ari was watching people celebrate New Year's Eve from the balcony of his apartment, which had a view of the city's largest square. He was wearing the earbuds that allowed him to listen to music of his choice and not the noise coming from the city. He smiled bitterly, thinking that these people who had survived so many disasters deserved to celebrate. The city he saw with a wide perspective from the balcony and the people who populated it felt too far away for him to recognise. The weather was mostly overcast due to air pollution and the changing climate, so only the stars that he couldn't see very clearly in the sky felt the same for him. "Because they're so far away that we can't reach them yet," he murmured to himself.

He didn't want to participate in the New Year's Eve celebrations in a world where he didn't feel he belonged and although it was very cold, he preferred to ring in the New Year by shivering under a blanket on the cold terrace. This was perhaps the last Christmas he would have the luxury of shivering.

They had now entered the last year of the time given to people for living in a human body or getting left out of human civilisation. It was one of his greatest luxuries to shudder from the cold in spite of the layers he was wearing, the large cup of hot tea and the heater at his feet. Feeling cold, sick, hungry, afraid, love, happiness and even sadness were now accepted as obstacles between humanity and the step that would take human civilisation to the next stage.

Disasters that happened over the last decade, which killed more than a third of the human species, forced humanity to make very radical decisions. Since every catastrophe that occurred meant that another one of Galileo's prophecies came true, the United Nations accepted Galileo as a leader. The synthetic selection he recommended to humanity led to the rapid transformation of the human species following the successful results of first subjects of the experiment. Eternal life and solid bodies that would enable people constantly battling life to escape from the dangers of it, quickly swayed humanity, and 75 percent of the world's population had chosen to move on to their new life so far.

Galileo had been accepted as a saviour by the majority of the population and his leadership of people had come to such a point that people not only accepted his suggestion to go through synthetic selection but also picked simpler new names for themselves that would be easier for everyone to pronounce, just like he had recommended on a live broadcast.

This choice was also the symbol of the new beginning of humankind that had created its own demons with the mistakes it made since the dawn of time. During disasters, especially during the three-and-a-half years of volcanic winter, people had done so much to survive that they didn't want to remember anything about their previous lives.

This dream of new beginnings was so promising for everyone that even the people who had chosen to refrain from synthetic selection so far and continued living in their old bodies, jumped on the bandwagon and chose simple and modest new names for themselves.

But even though they agreed with the necessity to change as humanity by choosing new names, life was becoming more and more difficult for people who were still living in their old bodies. The air became heavier, there was no source of water for drinking without purification, and it became impossible to find food that did not seriously harm people in the long run. This meant that people whose basic needs were still breathing, water and nutrition lived their lives to the extent that diseases allowed. As a result of the disasters, it was rare enough to meet a person over the age of fifty or under fifteen.

Almost everyone complained of chronic headache, nausea, fatigue and insomnia. However, when they tried to get treatment, the only conclusion they got was that these complaints could no longer be considered separately from vital basic needs, meaning that there was no way to get rid of them without changing the needs first. Despite the progress made in medicine, any disease that was treated was soon replaced by another. It was as if the world had established a defence system against humans, and as they responded with their own defence system, which is medicine, the world kept coming up with new ways to overcome them.

People who had gone through synthetic selection on the other hand seemed to be free from all weaknesses and shortcomings. They didn't need anything to live in their bodies that could provide their own energy. Their mental capacity was tremendously increased.

They were able to access all of their memories, including the ones they couldn't remember before, perceive all the subjects they'd study for a short time, and memorise all the information they had acquired. They could also retain their emotions in their new bodies. In fact, according to people who have moved into their new bodies, they retained these feelings on a much deeper level.

They did not experience emotions such as love, anger, fear, sadness without knowing the reason as they did in their previous bodies, but instead they perceived and adopted them in a purely logical frame of mind. This made it much more sensible for them to express their emotions. Their only shortcoming was the inability to experience the pleasures pertaining to their old bodies but almost everyone agreed that it was the pursuit of those pleasures that led them to disaster.

In addition, people who had been through synthetic selection, now being referred to as superhumans, were able to transfer everything they had experienced in a week to the memory devices in their dedicated safes that could only be accessed with their own DNA every week. Even though it was weekly, this process of superhumans backing up their memories was called "diary".

However, although ninety-five percent of the superhumans preferred to participate in the daily practice of backing up their memories, five percent preferred not to do so because they saw it as a breach of privacy.

As repeatedly stated by Galileo and the governments, this was a transition process, and for the time being, city layouts and human lives hadn't changed drastically. Regular people and superhumans lived together in the cities. Even though there were violent events where regular people attacked superhumans, it was clear that the transition was generally being carried out rather smoothly.

When Ari took a sip of the tea he had forgotten about, his face soured with the bitter taste of the now cold tea. Even though he complained about how quickly it had gone cold just to dispose of the agitation he felt in himself, he knew that the reason for his anger and the grimace on his face was not the cold tea. He also knew some problems were far beyond his powers.

He thought for a moment to refresh his tea, but then he gave up. It wasn't worth it. He was thinking about the statement made by the government one year ago on this day. It was announced that the transition process would end at the end of 2035. Cities, vehicles, houses, everything would be redesigned, everything would be arranged in line with the new goals of humanity and there would be an end to all the waste.

This meant that people who did not want to go through synthetic selection had no place in the new cities designed for superhumans. Studies were conducted for the people who'd moved to countries such as Norway, Sweden, Finland, and Iceland at the end of the transition period. They were declared to be the most suitable places for humanity to live in and had remained the cleanest in the period of one year since the announcement. They would be able to host a crowded population with completely renewable energy sources.

Ari hated that decision made by others on his behalf. People from all over the world were basically being told that if they wouldn't accept to live as those in power deemed appropriate, they could leave their hometowns and go live in countries they had never been before.

Although Galileo's ideas had a ring of truth to them, for Ari, going through synthetic selection would be no different than living in a vegetative state. He found what superhumans said completely absurd. It was robotising loving someone because it was right to do so or only getting upset when logic allowed us to do.

When he thought of the things that had kept him going despite all his loneliness, the feeling of safety he felt whenever his parents caressed his hair and hugged him tightly when he was little, the fun of laughing at nonsense with his friends until they cried, the feeling of excitement he felt, as if he had a bird trying fluttering in the cage of his heart when he loved a girl... these were all the memories that came to his mind. He didn't want to live a life where he was deprived of those feelings. In fact, when he thought about it, almost everything that kept him alive was a memory. He lost almost everyone he loved after disasters. His two closest friends, who were basically his family now, had gone through synthetic selection, and he felt that he couldn't even communicate properly with them any more.

But even though he couldn't have what he needed at the moment, the possibility of experiencing the feeling of love that he felt with his parents, friends and girlfriends, was worth all the trouble of his current life.

He decided to watch the videos his parents recorded for him during their illness, as he always did to feel better. His parents had shot a series of videos, thinking that they'd have to abandon their son because of their illness. They didn't mention videos to Ari in order not to upset him. Ari hadn't found out about videos even after his father's death. His mother had told him when she got worse but asked him not to watch them until it was time and passed away a few days after that.

Ari was grateful to his parents for recording those videos. He started playing one of them, as they were some of the most important elements of support in his life:

"The pain that you'll feel when the time comes, should never push you into anger and desperation, son. Always remember that, maybe the pain that will follow you everywhere in your life is also what will remind you of your wealth on this earth. My darling son, feeling so much love for someone over whose life you have no say and feeling frustrated because you're not able to bring them back, should not put you off life and love; on the contrary they should make you realise that they are your most valuable possessions. The source of your sorrow will be the love you feel for us. The happiness of your time with us. I want you to know that your sadness is not proof of you not being able to love us any longer or sharing your happiness with us; it's actually proof that your love for us and memories of all the happiness we've felt together cannot be taken from you no matter what.

"The extent of your sadness will be an indication of the greatness of the love and happiness we've shared with you. Think of people who wouldn't be as upset as you to lose a family member. Think about how it's not enough to be physically next to each other to become one with somebody... and of those who haven't experienced the kind of love that turns two into one. Be grateful for having such an enormous amount of love to carry a piece of us within you, my boy. Never forget that a love of this magnitude cannot be limited to the distances you can perceive as far as the eye can see, the extent the movements of celestial bodies illuminate the world, or any amount of time a person can perceive. Be happy and grateful for that, my son.

"Embrace your sadness when you miss us. Because that will be the most concrete proof of the bond we share. Proof that our love surpasses any boundaries. Nothing can come between us. The more you hold on to your sadness, the deeper you feel it in your chest, the closer we'll be to each other. Know that only you can limit that. Have respect for such an eternity. And live the glory of holding that eternity within you all your life."

Ari once again thanked them for thinking how much strength videos would give their son. Every time he couldn't see ahead, he'd watch them over and over so he'd memorised almost every word.

It was the best message a mother could give to her son, as a mother who had advised him to make as many friends as he could in life, because they'd be his greatest strength against the hardships of life. She told him to make friends even with his sorrows. Learning to embrace the most difficult part of life was perhaps the biggest reason why he managed to get this far in the world. He was grateful to his mother for teaching him that.

She would never again be able to help his son with his pain, but she had taught him how to help himself through it. He was now having one of his self-conversations again, which had become customary for him. "She taught me how to fish when she realised that she couldn't give me fish any more." He smiled as he thought about that cliché.

As the sky began to lighten, Ari was sipping his hot tea. Although the crowd had gotten considerably smaller, the celebrations were still going on. He thought of those who were too drunk and embarrassing themselves, vomiting, having fun as if there were no tomorrow, and trying to meet new people. One thing was certain, there would be no such celebrations the next year. At least not in this square.

He was looking at the view from the vantage point of his upper-floor apartment. The redness of the dawn was fascinating enough to make even the dominant grey colour of the world a part of its beauty. He couldn't help but wonder if next year he'd have the opportunity to be enchanted by such a beauty, feel the caress of the wind on his face to the point of euphoria and unwind with the warmth of a cup of tea.

"I still have a year ahead of me," he thought, "it would be silly to waste every moment of it worrying about the future." He played the Beatles song "Within You Without You" on his music player and leaned back to enjoy the wonderful scenery and the tranquillity of the morning.

"We were talking about the space between us all
And the people who hide themselves behind a wall of illusion
Never glimpse the truth, then it's far too late when they pass away
We were talking about the love we all could share
When we find it to try our best to hold it there with our love
With our love, we could save the world, if they only knew
Try to realise it's all within yourself
No one else can make you change
And to see you're really only very small
And life flows on within you and without you
We were talking about the love that's gone so cold
And the people who gain the world and lose their soul
They don't know, they can't see, are you one of them?
When you've seen beyond yourself then you may find
Peace of mind is waiting there
And the time will come when you see we're all one
And life flows on within you and without you."

Ari had fallen asleep in his reclining chair and it was about 12 o'clock when he woke up. When he woke up, as usual his first sensations were a bitter taste in his mouth, a terrible headache, nausea and weakness. He'd been waking up like this every day for the last ten years because of all the pollution in the air, and it was getting harder to wake up since the recent volcanic eruptions that caused serious damage to the Earth's atmosphere.

He'd never been one to eat much, but since he had a lot of alone time on his hands now, and the time left on earth to actually enjoy something was running out, he'd started to really get into setting the table and having meals. The amount of food he ate did not change much, but the effort to really enjoy the taste of every single bite and sip that left a taste in his tongue became sort of a hobby for him. There was a breakfast ready on the kitchen table, again prepared as a hobby rather than the need to eat. In the past, when he woke up, he'd just think of what he wanted to eat and put only that on the table to eat it. If he wanted to have toast, for example, the breakfast table consisted of toast, some tomatoes and tea. Or when he wanted to have crepes, he would have just crepes and chocolate spread or jam and tea on the table. But now he had toast, crepes, breakfast cereal, sausage, eggs and pastry bought from the patisserie under the apartment all set on the table.

He stopped going on "autopilot" once he realised that he was running out of time. And he believed that deciding to eat something in advance, preparing only that and eating it, whether it was delicious or not, was being on autopilot. He realised that about a year ago when he had a breakfast of crepes some of which he had burnt completely and the rest partially and he actually ate them despite the fact that they left a bitter taste in his mouth.

"How many more times will I be able to have breakfast in my life?" he thought. Conditioning himself in such a way that he'd waste a limited amount of opportunities to have breakfast with such unsatisfying food was certainly an autopilot move. He had limited time to enjoy what life put in his way and he would be shortening it considerably by forcing himself to live by a certain plan without ever thinking about it.

That is why he took the lift from his apartment on a very high floor, went down to the bakery to buy some of the best-looking pastries and put them on the breakfast table alongside with other food, something he'd have been too lazy to do before. Usually he'd only eat an amount that others would find too little for a grown man's meal. The time spent setting up the table and making decisions about the current state of all the food on the table and how much he wanted to eat them seemed a huge waste of time and resources compared to the time he spent actually eating.

But spending almost all of his time alone gave him this luxury, timewise. He didn't have anything else that give him greater pleasure in the mornings. His inherited fortune that his father left him, who had inherited it from his own father (who had established a tech giant company) was providing him with more than enough for this hobby.

Food shortages in the world were reversed due to the decrease in the world's population and superhumans who had moved beyond the need to eat and drink. Food production to feed a much larger population now only meant an increase in surplus products. And that in turn meant that the few people who still needed to eat had more food per capita than before.

There was such an excessive amount of food on the market that it was being distributed to people around the world who usually didn't have access to food without expecting anything in return. Of course, this was all thanks to Galileo. Galileo had a bigger fortune than it could use so it started a campaign in the companies it owned. People could go to one of Galileo's technology stores with the receipts they had for grocery shopping to send to places in need of food in the world and then those people could shop in the store for the total amount in the receipts.

Galileo made a statement to address the rising curiosity and said that they were living in a time where money was gradually losing its importance and that he had enough money to carry out his plans. He said that when all humanity starts acting together as a single body, every life on earth would be of incredible importance and that no amount of money could be worth more than that.

Ari decided to go for a walk after breakfast and went to his favourite park. He was sitting on one of the benches, listening to music through his earphones and eating his favourite sandwich that he'd bought from the sandwich place at the entrance of the park. He chose not to take the bus and walked to the park even though it was a long way because he knew he could get car sick.

He wiped his mouth and hands with a napkin after swallowing the last bite of his sandwich and drinking up of his juice. He could now go back to the real reason he'd come to the park. His favourite pastime recently was feeding the squirrels in the park. He took the walnuts out of a bag he brought along and put a small pile of walnuts in a spot where he knew he would get the squirrels' attention since he'd become familiar with their nests and routes. He found a waiting place for himself that wasn't too close for the squirrels to come and get their walnuts, but just far enough so that he could see the adorable movements of the tiny animals.

After a short while, a squirrel appeared from behind a tree. The squirrel was acting kind of suspicious of the pile of walnuts just lying there in the grass, so after looking around a couple of time to make sure there was no danger, it started to move towards the walnuts. After knocking a few walnuts on the shells, trying to figure out if the contents of it were worth the effort, it took a walnut and opened it with great skill and contentment.

The scene was a great source of happiness for Ari. He recorded the squirrel with his camera again. He was combining the footage he'd shot with music on his computer and creating little videos for himself. The most effective sleeping pill for him was lying in his bed and watching these clips.

With their tiny and fragile bodies, weak defense systems, simple minds and without compromising anything from their comfort, these squirrels were living in a world that was no longer friendly to them, in one of the most densely populated areas of one of the most crowded cities in the world, in such isolation from the dangers of humanity. This was an incredible ray of hope for Ari.

His mother used to call him "her squirrel" when he was little because she thought he ate like a squirrel. So his mother's influence had made him establish a bond between himself and the little animals. He felt isolated from the life that surrounded him. The ambition people had for immortality, and the universal wisdom of dominance did not mean much to him.

Ari wanted to enjoy the park a little bit more, sitting on the bench and listening to music after the squirrels took the last pieces of walnut and disappeared back to their nests. Whenever he was in the park, spending time among trees and grass he felt the pressure of the world slightly alleviate. After enjoying the park for a while longer, he looked at his watch. He started to get up very reluctantly because he had to go to the police station and for his weekly check.

The "notebook" system had come into use in June the previous year. The number of violent attacks of regular people against superhumans had increased and governments declared that those who hadn't yet chosen to move on to the next stage of their evolution were considered to be a potential threat to society, and that was why they'd adopted this system. Intelligent cells were placed in the bloodstreams of people still living in their "primitive" bodies. These cells conveyed emotions such as panic, fear, excitement and joy experienced by the person as concrete data to the systems of security forces.

This "notebook" application was filled out weekly, just like the "diary" procedure. "They're very thoughtful," Ari murmured. "They did not separate us from primitive creatures and let us keep records of our lives, just like them. Only with our blood." He also doubted the necessity of drawing a large tube of blood every week, considering today's technology, and believed that it was about forcing people to participate in "synthetic selection".

The security forces were examining the data obtained from this application and if anyone had taken any action that could be deemed a "danger to society", it was easily detected. According to Ari, it was more a form of humiliation and suppression against "the bigots who have not yet gone through to the next stages of their evolution" rather than preventing crime. Ari pictured the gloomy, stuffy station environment and the "superhuman" police.

The unhappiness of people waiting to fill their diaries with blood, children crying and begging their families not to do it today... and the heart-wrenchingly desperate faces of the parents who can't help their children. At least his own parents were not subjected to this abuse. He murmured the life theory that gave him strength in difficult times: "Good guys always win in the end." He took a deep breath. He got up from the bench and reluctantly set off.

When he arrived at the police station, the atmosphere was just as he had expected. Ari closed his eyes so he wouldn't see what was going on. He only opened his eyes from time to time to see if it was his turn. No matter how painful the things got around him, no matter how much the kid over there cried, he could disappear into his music by blocking everything out. This made him angry at himself, but he didn't know how else to carry on with his life.

After Ari endured his weekly torture and got back home, the sun had been down for nearly half an hour. He meticulously prepared dinner. He put one of his favourite Elvis Presley records on the player. He set it to play the song "It's Now or Never" and sat down to dinner.

"It's now or never. Come hold me tight. Kiss me my darling, be mine tonight. Tomorrow will be too late. It's now or never. My love won't wait."

He was grateful to his parents for the record player before which even an average antique item would bow down respectfully and because they left him such a valuable and extensive record archive.

His archive consisted of records by Frank Sinatra, Elvis Presley, The Beatles, Buddy Holly, The Carpenters, Edith Piaf, Ray Charles, and many more. This was not something that the tragically few people who had been to his house and the "superhumans" who claimed to constitute the new stage of human evolution, could perceive much. People didn't usually like all the songs on an album. This was also true for him. The number of recordings which he liked all the songs on one side equally, was very small. Getting up from your seat, going over to the record player to set the needle on the song you wanted to listen to or carefully putting the record currently playing back into its sleeve and taking out the other one when you wanted to listen to a song on another record, was a waste of time for the other people.

People who still enjoyed listening to music were listening through tiny speakers that they attached to their ear holes. This helped people save on time, effort and space. The loudspeakers that were too small to be felt by the user or to be seen from outside when they were in the ear, made his huge records very primitive in the eyes of the people.

Just loud enough so he could still hear the record, he said, "They find me primitive too. Well, they can go to hell."

After finishing dinner accompanied by music, Ari started a fire in the furnace out on the terrace. It was a habit inherited from his parents. They had this furnace built on the terrace at the suggestion of his father because they'd all enjoyed sitting around a fire. When his parents were alive, they could sit around and enjoy the fire with the food they wanted to cook on it, thanks to the comfort of the large terrace on the rooftop, no matter the season. Which was a much older and stranger habit than the records for some people.

After diving deep into his thoughts while sipping tea and snacking on marshmallows and stargazing, he felt really thankful that he still cared enough about things to be thoughtful, still enjoyed the beauty of the sky and still remembered his parents with longing. Then, as he did most nights, he carried his wireless TV out with him, which could access electricity without any wires thanks to technology, and fell asleep watching Shrek, now an old movie.

Falling asleep watching Shrek made him feel as if his parents were also asleep in the other room. Although he knew almost all the lines, he could still watch the whole movie each time and enjoy himself. Watching movies over and over and still enjoying them like he had the first time he had seen them was one of the things he liked best about himself.

15 JANUARY 2035

Ari had woken up with a headache, nausea and fatigue so he'd tried to get some sleep in the different rooms of the house. Now, as he put the last touches on the dinner he'd prepared with salt and pepper, he was wondering where his friends Val and Eli were.

He wanted to see what time it was, so he looked at his watch which was glued to his wrist and was the size of the batteries the old watches ran on. The watch reflected the time as 19.56 p.m. on his arm, and the calendar showed today was the fifteenth of the month. "Is it so late already?" he said to himself. He felt like it had been a few days since New Year's Eve. He thought the time ran faster the more he tried to catch up with it. Perhaps maintaining the same routine every day was the biggest reason he went on the autopilot behaviour that he tried to avoid.

But his lonely life in this increasingly distant world gave him no other opportunity. In order to be able to go on with his life, he was trying to do enjoyable things as much as possible to feel connected to life. Every new development took away from him another thing he enjoyed. He had just read a new annoying development in the paper today. He read that balconies on floors higher than the 5th floor in public places would be banned from all civilian entrances and the building management would be held responsible for civilians to comply with this ban. The reason why the government made this law was because it was not possible to stop people committing suicide by jumping from tall buildings. This meant that he could no longer watch the view from the top floor of his favourite museum of modern art.

He was thinking about whether the food would go cold while he waited, whether it made any sense to wait for his friends knowing he'd be the only one out of the three to actually eat any food and whether it made him feel more abnormal rather than normal when there was a knock on the door.

When he opened the door and saw his friends who had been living in their robotic bodies for about a year, he couldn't help but hug them, even though he still felt as strange about it as he had the first time and knew that that didn't mean anything to them. The only evidence these robotic bodies held his friends was that they had holographic reflections of their old faces on the display in the place where they would have faces.

They went over to the dining table together. Whenever Ari had friends over, he specifically did not eat beforehand and host them at the dinner table. It was a habit left to him from his parents. Back when they both alive and well, he remembered sitting around the dinner table with them for hours; something he had greatly enjoyed. This was the first time he had seen them after the new year. Maybe the last year he'd be alive as he knew it.

Ari was eating and chatting with his friends. But every time he sat at the table with his friends with pleasure and hope proved to be a new disappointment. These new "personalities" of his friends weren't a temporary thing to get used to, it was who they were now. It was very difficult to see the personality and colour they used to have in their conversations. He saw them gradually getting further away from their subjectivity.

Ari was the one who usually did most of the talking while Val and Eli gave analytical answers to whatever he said. What was worse, even though Ari saw that they began to lose their subjectivity more and more, he still felt that each time they spoke, it was scary how much their questions and attitudes resembled to those of people talking to children.

When Ari finished his meal, he suggested that they go out on the terrace and sit out there. He thought sitting on the terrace around the fire with his friends would help him keep some part of the past alive, even though he was the only one who could feel the cold, the heat of the fire and the taste of tea. He lit the fire with great dexterity and quickness due to his experience and continued the conversation with his friends. The subject was again super humanity. "You now have less than a year to make your choice," Val said. "Have you made any progress about your decision?" This question was enough to spoil Ari's mood. He put his teacup on the floor. "If by 'making progress' you mean changing my mind, no. I haven't changed my mind," he replied.

"So you still think you have a choice?" asked Eli. "What do you mean?" Ari answered him with a question. "If you choose to continue your life as you are, at the end of the year, you will be sent to one of the countries of the bigots who prefer not to participate in the next stage of civilisation because of their impulses and beliefs," Eli replied.

"I'm already one of those bigots you're talking about, in case you didn't realise it," said Ari.

"No, Ari, you're just trying to make the best decision for yourself by making the most of the time you have been given until now."

"So whether I'm a bigot or not will be clear at the end of the time I'm given to make a decision?"

"You shouldn't take everything so personally, Ari."

"You should be aware that there is a person in front of you. Just because you think these things are insignificant doesn't mean what you say won't hurt that person. Just because you see no difference between people like me and the prisoners who don't want to leave their cells when it's time because they're too attached to the place they've been locked up for years, doesn't mean you can judge me as you wish—"

Seeing that Ari was getting more and more angry, Val interrupted, "No, Ari, of course not. You just have to understand this. We were where you are now until a year ago. But we're way beyond that now. I can see you're aware of that too, Ari. You just need some courage to get rid of your addictions," she said. Ari knew that he was again in one of the conversations he'd had many times before. In fact, he thought it would be beneficial for him. But now they were looking at the subject from such different points of view that anything he wanted to say was very primitive and incomprehensible to his friends. And what they were saying was too unemotional and over-analytical for Ari. Still, although it became more and more difficult to understand each other's point of view, he was in favour of continuing to talk, as he always did, hoping that maybe this time he would see a solution that he hadn't seen before.

"Contrary to what you think, I'm aware that what you did is more sensible. I feel that the breath I take, the water I drink, the food I eat is poisoning me more and more. But living without love, happiness or fear will not mean anything to me," Ari said.

Eli said, "Why do you insist on rejection even though you know that's not true? We didn't lose our feelings. On the contrary, we got rid of the distractions that kept us from reaching their essence. You know we have decided to unite our lives after the change we have gone through."

"Yes. I know you were best friends with each other before, as we all were. I know that you'd never thought of becoming lovers or getting married because you weren't in love."

"As you said, Ari, we were two best friends, but we'd never thought of becoming lovers and sharing our lives. Don't you think that shows how primitive love is in the condition you're defending now? We enjoyed doing everything about life with each other, taking strength from each other, making our lives beautiful but always keeping each other one step behind our lovers. Because our faces and bodies, our scents did not stimulate the impulses within us like our respective lovers did. Because our tastes that led us to love were based on having stronger children than ourselves. Do you want to have a conversation again about the fact that women like big-bodied men whom they associate with safety, that men like women with broad hips that they associate with fertility and that the smells that attract us from the opposite sex are often from people with different immune systems than our own? About how the combination of two different immune systems produces a child with stronger immunity to microbes?

"You know how ridiculous scientific studies of love are to me. So it wouldn't be very useful."

"Ari, aside from all this, you know you won't have much time to live as long as you live like this," said Val. It's really irrational for you to try to escape this while you have the opportunity to attain eternal life and unlimited potential," she continued.

"What's the point of extending or shortening life if living won't mean anything to me?" Ari said.

"Life is a greater responsibility than you can perceive right now. And we have not been able to fulfill that responsibility because of the effects of the bodies in which we lived up until now. Think of all the time we've wasted by eating, sleeping, chasing our pleasures, being sad or depressed. Think about the year after you lost your parents, when you just passed the time without actually living. Think about our wasted lives," Val said.

"Wasted?" Ari said, "for whom Val and according to what?"

"Don't you think it's a waste to not be able to make the best of the universe that we exist in and the time that shapes our lives? We must make sense of the universe and time with our lives. Any other kind is nothing more than a flash in the pan that is too small to make a difference in eternity."

"If love doesn't make it meaningful, I don't think anything else can make that flame brighter or last longer."

"Love, you say? Let me tell you a little about love. The love between me and Eli that you always sneer at. We've been together all our lives. But we started loving each other as much as we deserved after moving into our new bodies. Because loving in our old bodies meant that the stimulation of our urges by the physical properties of others. It was measured with the pleasure that the relationships we formed with the bodies we liked would give us. Even in the most innocent sense, love is measured by what you feel when you look into the eyes of your loved one, hold their hand, and kiss them. So actually the kind of love that you understand, is more about how much you like how they make you feel, rather than how you feel about them. Eli and I have decided to live together, to live every moment of our lives together because we want to share each event and see each other's perspective. To see more of our lives by looking through a window for two. Can there be a purer love than seeing and interpreting life from each other's perspective? You're just worried about the pleasures you'll be deprived of when you hold your lover, look into their eyes or kiss them. That means you're attached to the pleasures, not the person you love. Your love is not pure, Ari. And when you're mature enough to embrace the depth of the emotions you keep talking about, like love, happiness, sadness or fear, you'll realise we're right," Val said.

Ari was defenceless against her view. This was the first time their conversation had gone as far. One thing was certain; their analytical perspective and intelligence had deepened him beyond anything he could've ever imagined. He almost admitted that they were right for the first time ever. But he saw that admission as a betrayal to the morning chill, the red of the sunset embracing him like a mother, the moon that reached a hand to him every nigh even though it was from behind the mist, the laughs he shared with friends in the past, the women he loved who had made his heart beat faster, and most importantly, the longing he felt for his parents. So he wouldn't do it.

After a short silence, he asked, "So why are you still friends with me? Doesn't wasting your time with a primitive creature like me prevent you from fulfilling your responsibilities to the universe and time?"

"You've a very interesting point of view, Ari," said Eli. Your ideas are so intriguing because you don't restrain your emotions and imagination. You've always been like this. It would be a shame to lose someone like you, especially in these days when we have the chance to live forever."

"So if I choose mortal life, we won't have anything to talk about?"

"No, Ari, your ideas will still be intriguing. On the contrary, we will want to see you more because we will have even less time to hear your thoughts. Just as we want to spend as much time as possible with children and enjoy the uninhibited nature of their thoughts while we still can, knowing that they will limit their thoughts as they grow up."

Ari's guesses were right. Even though he basically knew it, it was infuriating for him to hear it said out loud to his face. He got up from his seat, and said, "I believe that's enough conversation for today," as he marched to the door, motioning to Val and Eli that it was time for them to leave.

They left, quickly and respectfully. With an aggravating indifference, they didn't forget to wish Ari a "Good evening," as they walked out the door.

A few hours later, Ari was back sitting by the fire. Even though it was cold, sleeping in thick clothes and under covers made him feel more human. Accompanied by the crackling of the fire, looking at the sky brighter than usual with the moon and the stars, he thought it had been wrong of him to dismiss his friends like that and regretted what he did. "The fact that they won't care about it, doesn't justify your disrespect," he said to himself: "Because you know what it means."

31 JANUARY 2035

Since the countdown began for the end of Ari's life as he knew it, the melancholy that overwhelmed him at the end of each day really demoralised him after a month that went by at the blink of an eye. It was now the last day of the first month of the last year.

Sitting on a bench in the park, sipping his tea under a misty sky, he was thinking that he hadn't made the best of his numbered days. He wanted to enjoy every day he lived; he thought of ways to do it, but nothing came to mind. The lonely life he'd been leading since the death of his parents caused him to get overly attached to the things he enjoyed doing, so he always got bored quickly. His platonic friendship with the squirrels was also losing its charm.

In fact, he knew that love was the only thing that could get him out of this vicious cycle. However, the world he lived in had become such that everyone was seeing a few family members and friends whom they loved and had known for a long time and isolated themselves completely from strangers. Although some people hadn't yet become superhuman by choice, they chose not to leave the house unless they absolutely had to because of the inferiority complex induced by seeing and communicating with superhumans in their proud robotic bodies.

The old-school sentimental human relations were established between only a few people, and all the other relationships resembled those of the superhumans who had given themselves completely to the influence of analytic intelligence. That made Ari less likely to meet someone he might have fall in love with.

He felt his energy and morale fall lower day by day. He hadn't even been paying attention to squirrels for the last week or so whenever he went to the park, he just sat across from the lake and spent hours in deep thought. When he looked at the time and remembered that he had to go back to the police station and fill his "notebook", his eyes filled up. He got up from the bench, took a deep breath and started walking to the bus stop.

When Ari emerged from the police station, he felt absolutely exhausted. In addition to the pressure he was experiencing, he had to go to the police station every week and watch all the people, young, old, mother and child, be exposed to this torture. He wanted to go back to his home, his safe place in this hostile world, as soon as possible. He walked to the bus stop near the police station just on the edge of bursting into tears and took the bus home.

Public transport was virtually the only way to get around the city. Those who had individual vehicles and wanted to use them were required to provide valid reasons and go through complex procedures. The buses were fully equipped for all kinds of natural events. There were heavy metals in their bodies and thick iron bars in the windows.

Seeing the people and superhumans sitting side by side in the bus, Ari wondered to himself whether there was a possibility that they could share the world as two basically identical but practically different species, just like they did in the bus. But the supercomputer that changed everything and scientists who took it as a reference had been very clear. Humankind had exhausted all the possibilities that would enable them to continue their lives on this planet as they began it.

Suddenly his attention was pulled away from his thoughts and the music he'd been listening to as he focused on a woman who'd jumped up quickly from her seat. From the way she was repeatedly pressing the door button, it was obvious that she desperately wanted to get off the bus. Because of the dark bag in her hand, Ari guessed that she was getting car sick. Despite the uncomfortable situation and having to shout all the way from the back of the bus, at the driver in a mechanical body at the very front, she spoke with a lovely voice and diction. "We're stuck in traffic. And we're only a few metres away from the station, could you please open the door?" she called.

Ari must have been very touched by hearing such a beautiful voice in such a bad situation, because he would later talk about it saying, "I was drawn to you by reasons unclear to me." He got right off the bus following that beautiful voice. Ari hadn't seen her face yet as the young woman was throwing up in the trash can right by the stop. What he noticed about the woman were a soft tone, a beautiful accent, beautiful light brown hair, and a dainty physique. But as he stood behind her waiting, he felt an incredible amount of compassion for her in a way, but he did not know why.

Perhaps seeing another person in a situation which he himself frequently experienced, made them members of some kind of club. Perhaps still being able to see any flaws in a human being made him feel that he was not alone. Maybe it was just about the nice tone of voice and the lovely way she talked. Considering that people were getting very sick these days, always getting nauseous due to the heavily polluted air, the magic of her voice seemed to be of even more significance.

After pulling a napkin out of the pocket of her cardigan and wiping her mouth, she turned around, wondering what the young man who had jumped off the bus after her and was still waiting right behind her, wanted. Ari was frozen there, with a gleam in his eyes.

The most beautiful pair of brown eyes he had ever seen were looking at him. These beautiful eyes were accompanied by a cute little nose, a small delicate mouth and freckles on an attractive face with a unique bone structure.

He felt as if he'd been thrown a lifeline by God, just as the mechanical behaviour and the lack of aesthetics that were sweeping around him began to suffocate him. It was as if even the tiny freckles on her face were carefully measured and placed as final touches on a perfect work. He looked up at the sky unconsciously, with a smile he didn't know was on his face. It was like a spontaneous reflection of the gratitude he felt.

His thoughts were reflected so beautifully and innocently in his gestures that the woman who had just thrown up in the trash had a shy smile on her miserable face. "You've just seen me throw up, and I can't possibly look that pretty. Trust me, I've seen myself after throwing up before," she said, laughing.

Ari couldn't stop his mouth from smiling. Thinking he might have upset the woman, he said, "I'm sorry. I didn't mean to disturb you. I just saw you get off the bus with a bag in your hand and the same thing happens to me very often. I just wanted to see if you needed anything.

I'm sorry. I know you're not in a state you want to be looked at. I'm Ari, by the way."

"Actually, I'm the one who should apologise for making you see such a scene," said the young woman. "Lil," she extended her hand, "and thank you for your concern. I'm used to this. I'll feel better in a few minutes."

"Are you sure? We can sit down for a bit at the bus stop if you want. I have some water in my bag, if you want to have a drink or wash your face," Ari said.

"Thank you very much, but I already feel better."

"Okay. As you wish... Then, well... I'll leave you alone now."

"Okay. Thank you very much, really, this isn't a kindness that can be seen much these days."

"Actually, I thank *you*."

Ari looked involuntarily at the sky again. His thoughts, which were reflected in his attitude with great sincerity and sweetness, seemed to have touched her. The anxious expression on her face, a manifestation of her initial confusion and instinct for self-protection, was now replaced by flushed cheeks and a soft smile.

Ari was looking at the young woman's face admiringly but with a puzzled smile as he couldn't think of anything to say.

"Yes, I'm leaving you now," he eventually said. But it was obvious that that wasn't what he wanted to say. Now the woman didn't seem to be able to talk much because of her embarrassment. Ari turned around, isolated from the world he was in. After taking a few steps, he looked up at the sky again. Indeed, he felt like God had reached down to him. He turned around with a courage unprecedented in his personal history, and when he saw that the woman was still looking at him, his courage was suddenly supported by self-confidence. But even all this helped him only to the point where he could say, "Well I, uh, I thought you might need water." He pulled the water bottle out of his small bag, which was hanging diagonally across his shoulder, and handed it to the woman.

"Thank you," said Lil, "it's very thoughtful of you."

"You're welcome," Ari replied.

There was a silence. They both seemed to be timidly struggling to say something. Finally Ari was able to talk: "Is your place far from here? I can walk you home if you want, to make sure you get in safely."

"Oh, it's not very far. Ten minutes on foot, tops. I can walk by myself, really, and walking would do me good."

"Sure, I understand you've only known me for a few minutes, and you may be wondering why I would walk with you. I'm sorry. I only wanted to help. I didn't mean to bother you. I'm actually surprised that I've already been too forward. I mean, I've felt kind of strange, in a way I'd never done before. But that's not your responsibility, of course. I'm really sorry. I realised I'm still talking... Well, this time I'll really leave you alone."

Ari turned around in a panic, but after taking a step in the opposite direction of Lil, he slowed down, almost stopping. Lil saw that and said, "Actually, my battery is almost dead and won't be able to listen to music on my way home. It might be nice to have someone to talk with." "Thank you," Ari responded. So they began to walk through streets of the city, which had survived so much destruction for many years.

After all, they were a handful of people trying to live in a humane way. The two young people who had a promising introduction both had smiles that had settled on their faces several minutes ago and apparently were there to stay. It seemed like they'd both long been waiting for something like this. So much so that as his conversations progressed, Ari felt that he was not the only one who felt like God had thrown him a lifeline.

They were both laughing bashfully and paying close attention to understand each other; as a result, encountering something very intriguing. They would find out in their later talks that both of them were going through similar thoughts: "Please don't kill my hopes. I really need this."

Even after deciding that they enjoyed each other's conversation and slowing their walking pace, they'd still come to the end of the road. Standing in front of the building where Lil's apartment was, they were silent as if they'd hoped that their walk would lead them to a whole new place. Ari broke the silence and said, "We walked too fast."

Lil said, "Yes. I think it's time to leave," and she reached out to shake his hand.

Ari looked at Lil's hand for a while, shook it for a really long time and he said "Are you sure we're at the right apartment? If you want, we can go back to where we met, start from scratch and make sure we're in the right place."

"I'm sure. As a matter of fact, I was also thinking that it would be better to make sure, since the apartment felt closer than it should be, but it's about to get dark. And my grandmother doesn't like being alone in the dark."

"You live with your grandmother? That's good. So where are your parents?"

"They passed away."

"I'm so sorry. It wasn't my business. It was just my stupid curiosity."

"It's OK. You couldn't know. It's really nice to meet you."

"You too. Actually, I'm afraid to be too happy to make you uncomfortable. I mean, there's no way you didn't realise I'm having a hard time closing my mouth. I hope I didn't make you feel uncomfortable."

"No. On the contrary, it feels very nice. We've had such a nice chat even though we've just met. That's not how it usually goes. Especially these days. Thank you so much for keeping me company, but I really have to go up now."

"Thank you... Of course. That's why we walked here. Good evening."

"Good evening."

Lil had taken few steps at the entrance of the apartment and insert her key into the door when Ari said, "Well, by the way, I lost my parents too," and immediately regretted it.

"Who hasn't lost a loved one these days?" Lil replied as she continued to unlock the door. She slipped through the door and disappeared into the apartment.

Meanwhile, Ari was busy berating himself: "'I've lost my parents too'? You idiot. How could you say such a ridiculous thing? Idiot. How could you be so bloody stupid?"

It had been pouring with rain since he had arrived home. He'd eaten dinner and had put the kettle on for some tea as was his habit. "It won't stop," he said. He was thinking about sitting under the sturdy umbrella on the terrace, which would protect him from the weather.

He would probably get a little wet while he opened the umbrella, but he could turn on the heater and enjoy the rain with tea in his hand in the evening. He held out his hand and tried to see if the rain was clean. They'd had some muddy rains these days, because of the polluted air. As the stain left by the rain drops on his hand discouraged him, he decided to sit inside instead. However, as soon as he sat down in the living room, he thought that his time to enjoy these moments might be running out, so he went out and opened his umbrella at the expense of getting wet in the muddy rain. There used to be a large winter garden made of glass on the terrace. However, due to sudden changes in temperature, there had been frequent storms with hailstones the size of tennis balls. These had shattered the windows, so he'd decided to remove the winter garden.

Ari set everything up and took his seat. He noticed that the tea had gone cold after taking a sip, but he didn't mind. Already everything around him seemed to be looking more pleasing to him. It was as if the boiled broccoli he had eaten with his meat was painted with a green crayon, the flowers he cared for with great affection were sitting at the corner of the terrace looking like the precious musicians of a symphony orchestra about to play the most beautiful symphony in the world; Frank Sinatra was singing the song he was listening to while looking in the eyes of the woman he loved this time. "Heaven, I'm in heaven, and my heart beats so that I can hardly speak, and I seem to find the happiness I seek, when we're out together dancing, cheek to cheek."

Lil was having similar feelings at home. She gave her grandmother a bigger kiss than ever, singing songs and even dancing with the mop, instead of complaining when she had to clean up the juice she'd spilled. Her cheerfulness even affected her grandmother. She'd looked tired and been relatively quieter during the last week, but now she was laughing and telling happy stories from her youth.

Lil opened the window before getting into bed, as she often did when she was happy, and felt the cold of the night air softened by the falling rain. She was thinking about Ari, she was really charmed by him. She thought they looked at life through a very similar window. In fact, when she heard from his mouth a thought that she hadn't been able to put into words for a long time, she had taken the young man's arm in her surprise and said, "I completely agree with you."

She repeated what Ari said to herself: "I doubt that we'll benefit from finding out the meaning of life. What if that meaning tells us to put aside everything we care about? Or what if it says that love and happiness are a waste of time and totally meaningless? Then we'll have lost the best things we have forever, and I can't handle that."

She was really taken by the young man in such a short time. It was like a miracle to meet someone she felt so close to nowadays. Just as her time was running out. But this miracle found her when she was throwing up in a garbage can. She shook her head touched her forehead, "Did it really have to go down like that?" she murmured. She thought of all efforts the young man made during their conversation to not to make her uncomfortable. He invited her to go over and listen to some records sometime. But then, for a few minutes, he explained to her that he was very afraid of making her feel uncomfortable, that he didn't want to be misunderstood, and that it was a friendly invitation just because records were not very common any more. She laughed out loud, picturing his flushed face and embarrassment in front of her.

She felt that she could really trust him for some reason. She didn't know what they had experienced to make her feel that. The time they spent together was a fifteen to twenty minute walk from the bus stop to the apartment. Even the idea of going to his place to listen to records didn't seem farfetched to her. She suddenly panicked though when she remembered that they had not exchanged phone numbers. Maybe the young man was actually bored and the idea that he enjoyed their conversation as much as she did was something she wanted to believe. The only thing she could do was to hope he *had* enjoyed their conversation as much as she did. Because she didn't know how to contact him. As she closed the window and returned to bed, she was really nervous. She was talking to herself before going to sleep: "He must have enjoyed it too. He was smiling. Please let it be so."

Still sitting on his terrace, Ari was busy trying to forgive himself. "I know you had a very short time and you wanted to find something in common with her and show her. But you shouldn't have said something that stupid. Maybe the fact that you had a very limited time has made you act rashly. Still, you were doing so well, you shouldn't have spoiled it all."

After a few minutes of trying to forgive himself, he was infuriated when he realised he was looking for an excuse for the nonsense he had said. Maybe he'd ended something that could change his life before it even started. He couldn't help but try to guess the effects of his mistake on the young woman. Another thing he was very angry with himself about was that he didn't get her number. "Would it be too creepy if I woke up early and waited at her door?" he asked himself.

He came back to his room thinking he would sleep looking at concrete instead of the sky this time, but when he looked at where the sky should be, he saw the brightest pair of brown eyes he had ever seen. He was grateful to have met this young woman who had already filled his room of bare concrete the starry skies and the moon. Although Ari went to bed with the intention of waking up to the morning of a day when he would see Lil again, thoughts and questions came to his mind and did not allow him to go to sleep. She'd laughed at all his jokes. She had a smile on her face throughout the conversation. When they came to the door of the apartment, she took it as slowly as he did. Or was that just him? Did she laugh at his jokes because she liked him, or was he just a funny guy? Was it a rushed invitation that would creep her out asking her to come to his place to listen to records? Lil hadn't responded to the invitation anyway, she'd just smiled. He was trying to recall every little detail from their time together and trying to find some hopeful meaning from every gesture she'd made and every word she'd said. "By the way, I lost my parents too?" he said to himself again. When things couldn't have gone better, such a lovely meeting could only be ruined with such a terrible ending. He hoped that the young woman didn't find it as important as he did. But wouldn't that mean that Lil wasn't as interested in him as he was in her? Although Ari's dream of falling asleep quickly was over, the most beautiful face that he'd ever seen would keep appearing everywhere he looked and would keep him company until he fell asleep.

1 FEBRUARY 2035

Ari looked at his watch while he was standing across the street from Lil's apartment. It was 8.05 a.m. It was pretty early for him. After thinking about how many times in his life he'd been up at this time of the morning, his heart began to beat rapidly when he saw the door of the apartment open. But it was someone else. Anyway, it might be too soon for him if Lil emerged now. He was still trying to figure out whether it would be too creepy for the young woman to find him waiting in front of her apartment in the morning. Although he had waited so long in the cold of the morning, he had not yet made the decision to show himself to her. That's why he chose to wait across the street rather than the front of the apartment.

After waiting for about half an hour without looking away from the apartment, the door opened once more. This time it was the person he was expecting. Ari could feel the bird in his chest, fluttering to get out of its cage. This time it was flapping its wings so much that even Ari thought it might break free. Lil turned left and started walking since she hadn't actually seen him. In a moment of courage, Ari began to cross the street quickly but with cautious steps. Bu as he crossed over, he noticed that Lil was turning sideways. He had lost all his courage in the panic of the moment and was out of breath. He took a deep breath as he realised that the young woman's head turned to look at a store across the street on the right, and not to look back. He changed his mind. He didn't want to scare her. He stood still as he watched with amazement this woman who was turning the greyness of the place into vivid colours she walked through until she turned the corner. After waiting for some time in amazement he realised that there was no other way to contact her.

He ran round the corner to catch up to Lil without losing sight of her and started following her. He continued this pursuit from a careful distance to the cafe where she worked. Along the way he thought about how he could arrange an encounter without making her uncomfortable, but he couldn't come up with anything. After lingering around until noon, he decided that there was no other way than casually walking in there as if by chance.

After being surprised at seeing him from behind the counter, Lil came up to him. Very unconvincingly, he pretending to be surprised himself, he told her that he'd come in there by coincidence.

However, when they'd exchanged only a few sentences, he broke down and told her what he'd been doing that morning. Lil didn't want to hurt this young man she'd just met, so he managed to keep her desire to laugh the roof down to just a little grin. As their relationship progressed, she would tell Ari about this over and over again, and then she laughed to her heart's content. It would also be the first moment that would come to Lil's mind when she remembered all the moments that made her fall in love with Ari.

8 JUNE 2035

Ari had had a headache since he woke up, so he was trying to create pastimes that would make him forget it. He was watching Galileo's videos on the internet one after the other, hoping to see something he hadn't noticed before, which would make everything easier. In fact, he memorised most of them because he had done this before. He stopped the video he was watching when his phone rang.

It was Lil. Hearing her voice would dispel the bored mood these videos had put him in. "I was thinking about coming to you," he answered happily and enthusiastically. "I'm so glad you called. How are you?" he went on.

Unlike Ari, Lil didn't sound too well. "Ari, I don't feel well. Can you come right away?" she said in a tired voice. "Sure. I'll be right there," he replied hastily.

Without realising what he was wearing or what his hair looked like, in his panic, he went right over to the café where Lil worked at which was thankfully not too far from his place. His girlfriend sounded so exhausted on the phone and he was quite alarmed. The cafe where Lil worked was now one of the rare places where only people worked as waiters. So it would always be crowded every hour it was open. Because it was the people who had refused to switch to their robotic bodies so far that still needed cafes, and naturally they wanted people like themselves to serve them. And this cafe was famous for the good communication its staff had with guests. This was the most spectacular thing a cafe could promise its customers these days.

Ari would often talk about how he regretted not having discovered it before, even though it was so close to his place, had a very warm atmosphere, provided great food and drinks, and most importantly had employees like Lil. But when he wanted to go to a cafe, he used to usually prefer the one he handed over after losing his parents and reminisced about them. This taught him a lesson: "If you look only backwards, you will have to be content with what it gives you." When he walked in, his eyes scanned the cafe and found Lil in seconds. The young woman was sitting in one of the chairs behind the counter; her face was very pale. He immediately walked over and hugged her. With great affection, he asked, "What's wrong, darling?"

"I'm feeling a little dizzy and very faint," the young woman replied.

"Do you want to go to a doctor?" asked Ari.

"No. I think I'll feel better if I take a little walk outside."

"Are you sure?

"Yes, I'm sure."

The young woman didn't like going to a doctor. The calmness in the doctor's voice as he told her that there was nothing more they could do for her parents when they were in the ICU after the car accident, was still vivid in her mind with all the details of his face and voice. After she'd lost her parents, she'd been to a doctor very rarely for herself. She had to go very often for her grandmother though. Every time she went, she'd remember the calmness of the doctor, who gave her the news of her parents' death in such a cold way, and she'd shudder. The incident she'd experienced turned into a phobia of hospitals and doctors.

Ari asked, "Whose permission do we need to leave?" as he tenderly caressed Lil's cheek, kissing her forehead and checking her temperature.

"I already asked Ken. I've just been waiting for you to come," Lil replied as she stood up with difficulty.

"We're going to see a doctor right away," Ari said firmly.

But as Lil said, "Please. Ari let's not go. I just need to get some fresh air," his resolve just melted away before her fragility.

Ari accepted her decision on the condition that she promise they'd go to a doctor right away if she still didn't feel well after getting some air. He wrapped Lil's arm around his neck, and they left the cafe. Lil smiled in despair, exhaustion and shame as she wrapped her arm around the young man's neck, "I'm so sorry. I alarmed you," she said.

"I didn't have anything better to do anyway," Ari said smiling mischievously. They walked up to the park and sat on a bench. Ari bought some water and sandwiches from the supermarket where only superhumans worked and returned to Lil, who was sitting on the bench alone. He opened one of the water bottles in his hand without sitting down, poured some water on his hand and washed Lil's face. "Do you feel better?" he asked.

"Yes. Park's nice. I feel much better. Thank you."

"The colour of your face already looks better. That's good. You scared me to death."

"I'm so sorry. You had to carry me here from the cafe."

"Come on, any prince charming would do the same thing. Carrying you here was the easy part. The dragon at the head of street caused some trouble, but thanks to my brave heart and unbending wrist I overcame it. Yes. I have such power."

"Thank you so much. I'm glad you're here."

The young woman embraced Ari with great gratitude, he had managed to make her laugh even in her current condition. She was feeling so much better. She buried her face in her lover's shoulder and rested there for several minutes. These few minutes of resting there felt like a few hours of sleep.

After Lil was feeling better, Ari asked her if she had to go back to work today. When she told him that she had the day off, and her grandmother was staying with her aunt that day, so she could stay at his place, he had a smile so big that it reached his ears. Since she couldn't leave her elderly grandmother alone, Lil could usually only stay with him when her grandmother was visiting her aunt. When she said that she was still a little rundown and wanted to spend time at home, they headed to Ari's.

When they got home Ari headed to the kitchen to make pasta with vegetables, one of the few dishes he could cook well and which they both loved. Lil wanted to both watch her lover cook for her and continue to chat with him to draw strength from him, even though she still felt weak and sat up on one of the uncomfortable stools next to the long kitchen counter.

"Shall we listen to music?" Ari asked.

"Sure. That'd be great," Lil replied.

"You'll have to put it on, if you feel better," Ari said to her as he was preparing dinner.

Lil stood up and got the laptop. "I hope you don't think we should listen to music on the computer while we're at home," Ari said, pointing to the corner where the records and record player were.

"Force of habit," replied Lil as the paused video on the laptop caught her eye. When she looked closely, she saw that the video was one of Galileo's where it offered some solutions to humanity and she suddenly felt bad.

Seeing Lil staring at the screen with a sad face, Ari realised what had happened. He ran over there and shut down the laptop, saying, "Please ignore that. Let's just put on some music and have a nice evening."

Agreeing with him, she stood up and put a Carpenters record on.

When dinner was ready, it was already dark outside, and they decided to have their dinner in the kitchen as they both enjoyed the room. Their eyes were shining with happiness like diamonds. One tiny candle lit up the whole room on its own, multiplied by two diamonds in the middle of the faces of these two young, beautiful lovers, and illuminated the hall covered with walls as if there was no other roof than the sky filled with bright stars.

Ari began to sing along with the pleasure of the melodies he heard. "I'm on the top of the world lookin' down on creation, and the only explanation I can find, is the love that I've found ever since you've been around, your love's put me at the top of the world."

By the end of his second glass of wine towards the end of their dinner, Lil leaned towards the wine bottle, saying, "The wine is really good," but Ari gently stopped her. "This is the best wine I've ever had, or maybe it's just because you're here with me, I'm not sure. But if you noticed, I didn't go for the third glass either. Because another glass would mean that this moment of ours together will go all blurry, and I want us to keep all the details of this moment clear. You know my rule of not to get drunk with you," he said.

There was admiration in Lil's face and eyes again. Ari wasn't like anybody else she'd met before. She was very grateful to have met this young man. She reached out and touched his cheek. He took her hand and pressed it to his cheek, closing his eyes to feel it more deeply. After a while he opened his eyes and said, "Okay, that's good. For the sake of your hands, we can have another sip. But just one sip." And just like he said, he put a sip of wine in both their glasses. "Enjoy. These are our last sips," he said with a smile. "Okay. So be it," the young woman replied.

Under Ari's direction, they prepared themselves to enjoy their last sips and drank up the contents of their glasses without difficulty. "It's really a beautiful wine," Lil said.

"Yes it really is," Ari agreed. It was as if they were in a race to sweep each other's feet off the ground with what they did and said. They both of had the feeling of travelling towards the moon as the glare in each other's eyes gradually grew. They were enchanted by conversation, joy, happiness and songs. They even danced a little. When Ari asked her to dance, "And we only had two glasses of wine. Now I can see why you cut us off," said Lil jokingly, and accepted his very kind and gentle offer right away.

But towards the end of the night with the pleasant moon and the stars up in the sky, Lil's face suddenly became sad.

"You're still watching Galileo's videos," she said. "Are you still confused about your decision?" she asked.

"Not since I met you, I'm not. Galileo promises us familiarity with all the secrets of the universe, the opportunity to become a universal species, which is very confusing, true. But I prefer this night to all the secrets of the universe."

"So why are you still watching those videos?"

"To find proof that he's wrong. I'm looking for a gap in what he says. I want to find it and see that he's wrong, so I can say that he'll find us a much better way and comfort myself."

"It's too late for everything, Ari. Besides, I'm not afraid of what's gonna happen any more. The idea of being taken away from the place I grew up in and having to live in a country I've never seen before used to keep me awake at night but now I have you. It doesn't matter where I am as long as I'm with you."

"I still believe that we could see something that hasn't been realised yet and find a better way. We are living in times when so many radical changes take place at a fast pace and one morning we can wake up to a completely different world."

"What if that doesn't happen? What if everything goes on as planned at the end of the year?"

"They can't offer me anything in exchange for my love. I'm just talking about possibilities. Earlier this year, I was a lonely man editing squirrel clips in his apartment. I was losing all hope that I could ever find the love of my dreams. But then I met a woman far beyond my dreams. A woman that fills me up whenever I close my eyes no matter where I am."

She stroked Ari's cheek, placed a kiss on his lips and rested her forehead against his. Ari enjoyed this moment for a while, then pulled his head back and took Lil's face in his hand. Staring into her eyes, he said, "You must definitely meet her," he said and laughed. "When I look into her eyes, time and the world stand still, and I feel like the whole universe, down to the smallest detail in the farthest corner has been created so that I can look into her eyes. I can't tell you how lucky I feel to have met her."

Lil had a mischievous smile that tried to subdue the admiration on her face, "I envy you. Not everyone is as lucky as you are." She hugged her lover tightly, kissed him on the temple and with a sleepy smile she said, "I may be sleepy, but you can't handle me anyway." When Lil got up and moved towards the sink to take care of the dishes, Ari stopped her and said that he would do the dishes himself and that she should get some sleep. Although her eyes were closing, Lil didn't want to go to bed, but she insisted that she would wait on the couch until he was done and then they would go to sleep together.

While Ari was doing the dishes, which took longer than he had anticipated, because he had made a big mess, he saw that Lil had fallen asleep on the couch so took a break and carried her to bed. Then he returned to the kitchen and resumed his work.

9 JUNE 2035

Lil was walking to the cafe with a wide smile on her face because of the love, when she saw that people were moving towards the square in groups. Surprisingly, a large number of elderly people and children also made up a significant part of this crowd. "Of course... it's today," she thought. People had already carried out protests against the ultimatum of either accepting synthetic selection imposed on them or going to live in countries designated for them. It seemed that this protest would be much more crowded than any other she'd seen before. She didn't remember seeing such heavy foot traffic before. People had started to feel so insecure and inadequate among the superhumans, that they wouldn't leave their homes except when they had, so she was unaware that so many people actually lived in her city.

As far as she knew, the social life of the people was now limited to the neighbourhoods where several wealthy people like Ari lived and where the café where she worked was. People with worse economic conditions who lived outside these areas felt more pressure on themselves, so as soon as they finished whatever they had to do outside, they would go home to their families and think about the best way to overcome the upcoming storm with their families.

When Lil arrived at the cafe, she looked at the groups of people passing by and hoped that no one would get hurt today. Since she was walking wrapped in thought up to the door of the cafe, she took a while to notice that there were fewer people at the tables outside the cafe than usual. There were only three people in total at two tables.

When she walked in, she was surprised to see that 10-12 people were waiting in line for the register to buy food and drinks to go. It was an unusual scene. This was a cafe where people generally preferred to spend time sitting down. It seemed that today people preferred to spend time in the square instead of sitting here. Lil went to Ken, apparently reading the news because he was sitting alone at the corner table by the window and

99

staring at his tablet with his glasses on scrolling the pages. "Have you seen the people outside? Unbelievable," she said.

Ken said, "Yes. It's been like that since early morning. This one will be very big," he replied.

"Even the people in here are buying stuff to take to the square."

"We've already made an incredible number of sales today. Actually, since we don't sell coffee in so many yellow paper cups, we're about to run out of cups now."

"It's still early and it's getting more and more crowded. What are we going to do?"

"I called the supplier and told them we had an emergency, they'll be here with the cups any time now."

"So what do you think, Ken? You think it'll be as bad as the last time?"

"I'm afraid so. People feel very cornered by the treatment they're subjected to. And time is running out."

"I hope it ends before anyone gets hurt. Last time, there were injuries."

"Wish me luck. I'll be there too."

Emma chipped in. "Ken, wouldn't it be nice to leave this to the young people? I don't want anything to happen to you," she said nervously.

"If I see an elderly person, I'll tell them to go home. That's what you should do," Larry said kindly but firmly. "And everyone has only a year, so I don't think our ages matter any more."

After patting her determined boss on the shoulder twice slowly, Lil ran to the back of the counter to help her friends who were trying to keep up with everyone on this busy day. As she passed her apron quickly over her head, she leaned over to Em, who was working the till next to her and said, "I'm sorry. I forgot it was today. I didn't think it would be this crowded. I wish you would have called," she whispered.

"It's OK. You gave us a scare yesterday. We'd handle it even if you didn't come in at all day," Em replied, as she kept smiling at the customers and helping them.

"Thank you," Lil said, patting Em's back and went to apologise to Zen, who was making coffee by the wall. Zen was all right with everything too.

It was past noon now. There were fifteen minutes to go for the statement of the spokesperson of the Free Will Association, which was the organiser of this protest. A statement was made by the government spokesperson, saying that the necessary measures were taken and there would be no interference if the protest went on peacefully. However, the crowd was reminded that a terrorist had almost detonated a bomb in the previous protest and had been stopped at the last moment, and the possibility of a similar attack could occur anytime the crowd did not disperse, and after reading the statement, it was said that the dispersion of the crowd would be better for everyone.

Following the action from a relatively quiet corner where he could fully see the square, Ari was shocked to see the crowd. Even though everyone knew that the terrorist threat was prevented at the very last moment, people thought that that was a fiction created by the government to prevent further protest from reaching the masses. People were looking for a hidden reason under everything the government said.

As the time for the statement drew closer, Ari left his quiet corner and took his place among the crowd to listen to it. He spent fifteen minutes studying the square before the speech. Since the security organisation was now left entirely to the superhumans, all of the security forces consisted only of civil servants with robotic bodies whose faces resembled their former bodies. Ari had been present in the squares for all the protests until now. However, he did not accept the views and attitudes of the majority of the people who made up the crowd and tried to prevent the vandalism that usually occurred during the protests. So he had been a part of many arguments. And so the renewed security forces were a great chance for him. He had witnessed how cold-bloodedly and calmly they intervened with dozens of people who were running at them and even attacking them since they had no fear of getting hurt because they weren't fragile in any way.

He thought of what could happen if those security forces were in their former state. The consequences could be disastrous. People were only interfered with when they started vandalism. And the fact that police officers couldn't really get hurt made things much easier.

He felt sadness come over him as he saw people throwing full drinks, eggs, and tomatoes at the mechanical police officers who were just standing and watching. "We're just proving to them how right they are," he thought to himself. It was really depressing the way that superhumans with their emotions under the control of their logic ignored these attacks and that really provoked people and exasperated them. Fortunately, members of the new police force kept their jobs above all emotions and personalisation. When he looked at his watch, he could see that it was time for the statement, but instead of calming down and getting quiet, the crowd had gotten even louder. When Ari moved into the crowd to understand what was going on, he began to understand the situation.

A man in his forties with a balding spot at the top of his head, apparently a person of the importance in the association, was screaming out to the crowd, spittle flying. From the point where Ari got closer, the speech, as far as he could hear, went like this: "There is no point to making a statement like this. We've been told that broadcasting in most regions throughout the country is not possible due to technical problems. They're trying to prevent people from hearing our speech. Because we are right. They're just invaders. They come out from among us, turn into something else, and now they're invading our world. Every day we lose our world a little more. But if we unite and show them how determined we are, they will understand that we are not puppets that they can play with as they wish.

"What we need to do is show them that they can't prevent us from communicating among each other. And that they still haven't won this war. The building you see over there is the television station that serves them. Let's go seize it and hold it until our speech is broadcast."

As soon as he finished talking, the crowd began to move towards the TV station building, the square-facing side of which was made of glass, as they wanted to have live square footage in the background of their programmes. When Ari stepped on higher ground and looked into the station building, he saw the surrounding security forces deployed in a stacked position around the door of the building.

It was clear that it would not be very good both for today and for later. Ari rushed through the crowd and he shouted, "No. Don't. You'll just make things worse!" Meanwhile, a huge and angry man who was passing by pushed him down to the ground. Stunned after taking some kicks from people running like crazy, Ari stepped aside to recover.

As soon as he did so, he got back up to his vantage point and tried to see what was happening. It already looked like a battlefield in front of the TV station. He saw people with axes in their hands. Several mechanical bodies lying on the ground were being torn apart by people with those axes. A man was shaking a mechanical leg he had pulled off, like a trophy. Soon after, he saw police officers emitting a gas from their robotic arms where their palms connected to their wrists.

People whose eyes were burning from that pepper gas started to fall back rapidly. Wanting to protect himself from the flood of people and gas coming towards him, Ari also started to run towards the back. After running for a while, he stopped a few blocks away and tried to catch his breath. He saw a homeless person who seemed to have cut all ties with the world. She seemed so unaware of what was going on around her that he thought she must be doing more than drinking.

He saw another crowd coming towards him from the end of the street running from the police. On the side of the road, a lonely girl was crying in fear. When she saw the crowd coming after her she got scared and threw herself on the road. Ari saw a car driving very fast towards the girl, so he began shouting and running to her. But she was far away, and the car was fast.

In the meantime, the homeless woman Ari had just seen jumped on the road with incredible agility, put herself between the car and the little girl, again with incredible speed, and shielded the girl. Ari closed his eyes in pain as he thought he would witness a horrifying scene. But when he opened them, what he saw was much more incredible than what he had just seen. The homeless woman and the little girl were standing still, both in one piece. There was a serious dent in the front of the car. Ari couldn't believe what he saw.

He was frozen where he stood, meanwhile the homeless woman quickly moved the girl out of the oncoming crowd to a safe place. Ari in the meantime had survived the initial shock and began to run towards the girl and woman without thinking anything. The woman saw Ari running towards her. She quickly kissed the girl on the head and fled towards the street behind her.

Although Ari was stunned by what she had done, the little girl was his priority. "Are you all right?" Ari asked. She nodded, tongue-tied with fright and shock. They were both terrified. The crowd escaping to the opposite side had lost all significance for him. He looked to see if the driver of the car, which had suffered serious damage to the front, was okay. The deployed airbags seemed to have prevented the driver from getting hurt. It seemed like he'd just fainted due to impact.

When Ari took up his phone to call an ambulance, he turned to the street where the homeless woman had run into and looked around hoping to see some trace of her, but there was nothing. He couldn't leave the girl crying in horror on her own any longer, so he moved back to where she was. While trying to comfort her a little he also examined the car and tried to understand the event that did this to the vehicle. He couldn't make sense of what he saw.

When Lil left the cafe, it was dark. Her grandmother's decision to stay at her aunt's for one more night made her very happy. So she could spend another evening with her boyfriend. She was walking, singing a love song that was stuck in her head, but she kept thinking how dull her boyfriend sounded when she told him she'd stay with him again tonight. She'd thought he'd be over the moon to hear that.

She'd suspected that something might have happened to him because she'd seen the protest and the events on TV and repeatedly asked him if he was okay. And he repeatedly said that he'd helped a girl who was stuck in the middle of the events, that he'd waited at the police station until her family arrived and he was still a little shaken about that.

When Lil opened the door, it was obvious that something had happened to Ari. Unlike usual, he had not run to her to hug and kiss her, he hadn't even stood up when he saw her. He'd only smiled faintly. Lil got even more anxious because of his behaviour so she went and sat down next to Ari on the couch, "Are you okay?" she asked. He was obviously preoccupied, but he replied, "Yes. I'm fine, love. It's just been a long day." He put a kiss on Lil's cheek. "There was a little girl who'd lost her family in the protest, so I took care of her," he continued. Thinking about how to tell Lil the whole thing, he said, "There was also an accident. Fortunately, the driver survived the incident without injury," he added.

"I see, honey. It's been a tough day, then," Lil said. She hugged him and kissed his head. It was Ari who broke the silence after the two stayed

104

intertwined for a while. "Lil, there was a woman," he said, and fell into a moment of silence.

"Did she die?" she asked in a panic. "Is that why you're like this?" she hugged him again.

"No, Lil, she didn't. When the car hit the woman, it fell apart."

"What? What do you mean?"

"It was like it hit a wall. It was unbelievable. I thought they were going to die. But the car broke down. Can you imagine?"

"She must have been a superhuman then. We know that those bodies are quite durable."

"No, no, she wasn't one of them, she was a human being like you and me."

"Ari, that's not possible, love. Did you get a good look at her?" Maybe it was a newly developed robotic body that looked much more like us."

"I don't think so. The woman's panic when she saw the girl, the movements of her body as she ran towards her, the worry reflected on her face, the relief she had after rescuing the girl, all of that was very human. And she hugged her so tightly after saving her! I don't think any half-robot can do that. No."

"But, Ari, that's impossible. So, do you think anybody could do that?"

"I don't know. "All I know is what I witnessed was unbelievable. I've never seen anything that shocked me so much, not even in this world we live in."

"Maybe they've created a new species. There are massive developments every day. Maybe they've found a way to reinforce the bodies we live in now. Or they might have invented a kind of robot that is very similar to us and found a way for us to experience and show our emotions in the same way."

"I don't know, Lil, I don't know."

While Ari and Lil exchanged views on the unknown person, police chief Arp was watching some unusual camera footage in his room at the station. He had been ordered to find all copies of this footage and hide it from everyone. As he was ordered, he went and found them and hid them from everyone. The interesting part was that, contrary to what he

105

expected, he was given the task of watching the footage and investigating the woman in the video.

Arp was one of the first volunteers in the police force to agree to transfer his mind to a robotic body. He made his choice in the beginning stages of the whole process, when people still had questions about synthetic selection, and were afraid of complications that may have occurred during the mind transfer. So he was also in the mandatory ads that the government ran on television. He was also the face of law enforcement during the transition period, which was announced to be renewed. When he decided to move into his new body, he had spent the last four months suffering from complications of "ALS", which had been aggravated and severely affecting his daily life. He felt that he was gradually losing control of his body.

Throughout his illness, he studied the effects of mental power on physical health, read about ten books, and hoped to find some remedy in this way. He hoped that he could overcome his illness many times applying what he'd read, tried a few techniques, but didn't experience much change except a few small things.

When he had run out of all hope, he talked to his family and they decided that this was not even a choice, as there were no other possibilities. All family members were grateful that this evolution, which would save a member of their family, had taken place in their lifetime. It was a divine message that their father, who had lost control of his body, had been given the opportunity by an artificial intelligence to move into a body that would be completely at the disposal of his mind. And after the success of their father's transition into his new body, soon all the rest of them decided to go through with the procedure as well. Except Tom, the eldest son of the family, who had three children. He was also grateful that his father could continue his life. But unlike the rest of his family, he refused to move into his new body. For him, this evolution imposed on humankind would, in the long run, be the end of human civilisation, if not human life. According to him, civilisation did not mean technology, but traditions, written and verbal rules and lifestyles carried from the past into the present. After this upcoming evolution, everything that made the word 'civilisation' valuable to him would disappear forever.

The fact that his father would continue his life and that his entire family, including his father, would never be affected by any illnesses during his lifetime, to know that they would never suffer again, was a luxury beyond his imagination. He'd lost about thirteen pounds after his father's illness had gotten worse. He loved them enough to prefer death rather than see them suffer.

But after the first subjects who successfully completed their mind transference, what he'd feared happened to his family. His nightmares became a reality when he saw that they had been transformed into superhumans who had handed the control of their minds completely to logic. Knowing that his family would survive long after him, that they would have lives where the concept of time would be practically meaningless and they'd be free from all kinds of pain and unhappiness, that they'd have knowledge and abilities that he could never attain, or even imagine during his lifetime, was the biggest source of happiness in his life. But he would not allow what they had become to limit his love for his family.

In explaining his thoughts to his family, he gave examples from movies where the characters were cursed with eternal life and stuck between life and death where they could enjoy nothing and feel nothing. He told them that for him, synthetic selection would be no different than those movies. Arp no longer believed that his son would ever turn into a superhuman. There was nothing he could do but wait for a development that would make him change his mind.

No having come to any conclusions from the video he watched over and over again, Arp finally decided that continuing this way wouldn't take him any further than he was. He had two things to do: first, he would identify the woman who had performed the act the like of which he hadn't witnessed before, and then ask her to explain what had happened. What was more interesting than being asked to handle this task by getting a direct call, was that he was asked to hide the footage from everyone. So when he thought about the status of the person that called him, he could understand how curious the video made certain people in high places. It was unusual for these people, who were aware of everything that was happening all around the world thanks to all kinds of technological facilities, to be so clueless about this event. Apparently, the woman in the footage was the only one who knew how to explain the actions that appeared in the video.

Although the most important thing for Arp at the moment was to carry out an order that was given to him personally from the very top, he always had his son in a corner of his mind. He wondered if these events had some deeper meaning enough to make a difference that could change everything. However, when the facial identification process was completed, Arp was completely shocked. The face of this woman who had caused considerable damage to the car that hit her did not match any face in the archive, so she couldn't be identified. So this woman had to have never gotten an ID nor done any transaction until now, which was highly unlikely. This would make things exceedingly difficult.

This time he decided to perform a larger scan. Thanks to Galileo, the security agencies in the world carried out a joint project and managed to gather all the images that were recorded with traffic cameras, public institutions, security cameras in transportation terminals and all kinds of street cameras in one place. Now, he was using the archive that dated back to the first day of recording these images, to create a match with previous footage to try to get somewhere with the matching images.

Arp's confusion increased as the process took longer. All the time that passed without getting a match was absolutely incredible. Although all the scans of everything recorded throughout the country were over, no matches were found, even in this archive that held every single recording or footage.

He was getting restless. Thinking she might have entered the country unregistered a short time ago, he waited for the world-wide scan to end. However, no matches were found there either. "This is impossible," he murmured. He thoroughly searched his mind, all corners of which he could access at all times very clearly but could not come up with an explanation.

10 JUNE 2035

Even though sunlight began to fill his room, which was not on particularly good terms with his sleep, Ari was still staring at the ceiling, deep in thoughts. His girlfriend, whom he could not get enough of, was sleeping next to him in all her beauty, her innocence crowned by the peacefulness of sleep and yet he was still looking at the ceiling and not at her. This was not something he would have believed if you told him the night before. He'd stayed up until the same time the previous night too. But that night it was because he wanted to keep watching his girlfriend with whom he couldn't spend much time together at nights. He had stayed up again lying next to her, but this time he hadn't even looked at her for five minutes in total. And her grandmother was coming home from her aunt's tomorrow, and this could be the last night they could spend together for a while.

He could not keep himself from thinking about what he had witnessed yesterday and trying to make some sense of it. He was playing out that moment over and over in his head, trying to see any details he might have missed. But the incident was so obvious that he could think of no logical explanation. Has a new robotic body so indistinguishable from old human bodies been developed? A body where people could have their logic and emotions equally and all at the same time? So why would they be keeping that a secret? What he saw didn't look like a prototype to him.

He didn't feel in any way close to an explanation to all these questions. Endlessly looking at the empty ceiling from where he was lying and thinking about the possibilities would not bring him any closer to an answer. He was going to go back to where the incident took place today and just hope to see her again. When he looked at the clock on his phone on the nightstand, he saw that it was really late. In fact, it was so late that it might have been more accurate to say that it was actually early. Lying in bed with his eyes open, he was worried that he would not be able to witness the beauty and innocent sleep of his beloved, who he thought was his miracle, who would leave the bed to go to work only a few hours later, rather than worrying about offending his sleep in waiting for the daylight he did not enjoy. Who knew when he could ever witness this miracle again?

He had an idea. It was an idea that would put an end to his not being able to see his girlfriend asleep. He took his phone and started shooting a video of his lover, who was sleeping buried in the duvet up to her head probably because she was cold. He was planning to make a film from this video of her. Seeing that he had recorded for five minutes, he decided it was enough. And because he wanted to witness the miracle that was happening in front of him directly and through the phone display, he put the phone on the nightstand and went back to watching her. He kept looking at her admiringly and listening to her breathe in and out until he had just enough time left to make breakfast, and then he slowly got up and went into the kitchen.

When Lil woke up and opened her eyes, the sun was illuminating half of the wall behind her head. She reached out to her phone on the bedside table and checked the time. She smiled when she saw that she still had seventeen minutes until she had to get up. In the past, that would be enough time for her to consider going back to sleep. But today she was smiling because she thought she had time to watch the man she loved as he slept. When she turned around quietly to watch Ari sleep and saw that he wasn't there, she wondered where he was. But her curiosity didn't last long because she could smell the delicious breakfast being prepared. Apparently, Ari had woken up early and made her breakfast.

She couldn't think of a better way to start the day. A big smile appeared on her face, proportional to her happiness. She quickly got out of bed, washed her face and tidied up a little. Then she rushed to the living room which had the open kitchen in a corner.

When Lil entered the room with a big smile on her face, Ari was busy cooking an omelette in the pan. Seeing the huge breakfast on the table prepared with a lot of different food as was Ari's way, she realised that her boyfriend had been working for a long time to prepare her this breakfast. Lil was so pleased with what she saw that she started singing a part of her favourite song: "Good morning, good morning, sun beams will soon smile through, good morning, good morning, to you and you and you and you." She was walking towards Ari as she sang, and on the last "and you," she was behind Ari, so she hugged him behind his back and gave him a kiss on the cheek when she finished singing. Ari turned to her, smiling and said, "Good morning, love."

14 JUNE 2035

As he had done for the last four days, Ari had again come to the same place, hoping to see the woman he couldn't forget, and had taken his place in the cafe, from where he could see the spot where he witnessed the incredible incident. After placing his order with a young and beautiful waitress called Mia, he thought, "She's been seeing me sitting here looking at the same place for the last four days from morning till the evening. She must think I'm crazy."

Mia was seriously wondering what this man was up to, after seeing him all day for four days. She thought that this man, whom she had never seen before until four days ago, might have moved somewhere nearby. Actually, she was very taken by the mysterious aura of this young man. He had everything that could capture the interest of a young woman. He was handsome, polite and mysterious.

After the second day, Mia started flirting with this guy who was interesting to her. She thought he might be interested in her as well, because he spent almost all his time for the last four days here, and he was polite and friendly to her, which was not very usual these days. At least she was hoping for it. She tried to chat with him a few times while they prepared the order of this mysterious and attractive young man, but he was always acting like he was really interested in something that was happening on the corner. She thought that might be a ploy to give himself an enigmatic air. She stole a few looks at the corner that seemed to be of constant interest to the young man but couldn't see anything.

Finally as she took the young man's order to his table, she said to herself, "Maybe he's trying to make sure you're interested. Maybe he's trying to get your attention to the climax by looking so mysterious. He'll open up to you when he feels it's the right time. Who would be so interested in a corner where nothing is happening? Hours and hours in last four days? She gathered all her courage. She was determined. This time she would manage to exchange more than few sentences with the young man.

Lil had been thinking behind the counter in the cafe, which was having perhaps one of the quietest days of the last four days, since she had started working there. "The horrific events that followed the protest must have frightened people. The police officers spotted on the streets near the square must be make people uncomfortable." There had certainly been some silence since the events. No one predicted that the protest would go this far. Nobody had any idea what to expect next.

Three superhuman police officers momentarily lost their lives when their heads were destroyed. New bodies were made for them, they were given permission from the "diary board" to access their memories in their diary centres and they were brought back to life by having their memories transferred. However, since memories were updated weekly, one of the police officers lost two days, one lost four days and one suffered a six-day memory loss.

The government did not make any statements since the calls for restraint they made after the events subsided on the day of action. This made people more worried. Strict measures were taken immediately after events that took place before this, and people's lives were severely affected by them. The "notebook" that everyone, including her, had to go and fill once a week was the result of one these events.

There were reported deaths in the events after the news broke that those who refused to move into their new bodies would be forced to leave their homes and move to the regions designated by commission governments. At that time, the law enforcement hadn't been completely "renovated". As a result of the great chaos, a police gun was fired, and events could not be contained for about a week.

After they'd gotten events under control with great difficulty, the government announced two major decisions. The police force would be completely rebuilt and would only consist of officers who moved to their robotic bodies, and people who had not moved into their new bodies would fill in their "notebooks" weekly during the transition period. But the real reason that occupied Lil's mind was the videos Ari's parents had made for him to guide him and help him with his longing. He'd first mentioned them to Lil at the end of the first month of their relationship.

When she told Ari that she would love to see them if he didn't mind, he had said that he didn't mind and actually it would make him incredibly happy.

She was particularly touched by the first video, in which his mother advised the man she loved, to embrace his sadness whenever he missed them and find them in that embrace. She'd cried throughout the video and, as soon as it was over, she'd hugged Ari as she sobbed and held him in her embrace for several minutes. She had also lost her parents. She was terribly upset that they didn't think of something like this at the time. As she sobbed, she said to Ari, "I wish I had videos like this. You're lucky."

To which he replied, "Well, you do now. "These videos are my guide. They might help you get to know me better. Or you can tell me if I really follow their advice. They're not all so emotional. Some just contains advice about life."

"Thank you so much. I felt like they were addressing me in the video. It's like your mum recorded this video for me, too," Lil said.

"If they had lived, they wouldn't have separated you from me when they saw how much I loved you. My mother wouldn't be saying, "my boy" but she'd say, "my babies" instead. I'm sure of that. I wish you would meet them, so badly," Ari said, speaking very carefully so as not to allow the standing tears to overflow from his eyes.

Lil kissed Ari, touching her wet cheeks to his and wetting them as well, "I'm sure they're watching us from somewhere. And they're grateful we've found each other. Both our parents are. I'm going to love you so much Ari, that your parents will be happy wherever they are. I promise," she said. Ari's eyes couldn't hold the tears any more, and they both cried for minutes.

"And I'll love you so much that your parents will be sure their daughter won't have to weather anything alone any more," Ari replied, with the comfort of not trying to hold back tears any more. Their tears were mixed together on each other's cheeks. After watching those videos, Lil had started seeing Ari in a whole new light.

Before she left for work that morning, her grandmother told her that she was really starting to lose her strength and talked about the death she believed was coming for her. She thanked God that she could still do things on her own when he was so close to death and that she wasn't a burden on her granddaughter. Lil ignored her at first and continued to get ready for work. But then she thought about the videos Ari's family had recorded for him and thought about asking her grandmother to do something similar for her. After a moment though she was ashamed to even think of something like that, didn't even want to think about her grandma dying, and cried for several minutes in her room. She had decided to watch one of Ari's parents' videos since she'd been in a bad mood all morning and the cafe was quiet. This time she picked a video where his father gave him advice to make Ari a person who saw every possibility in a positive light:

"Son, don't listen to those who tell you that manhood is measured with hardness and insensitivity. Hiding your feelings doesn't make you a stronger man. Just makes a good poker player. Real power and courage don't mean you don't worry, feel afraid or cry in the face of an event you are experiencing, but really feeling their weight. Having these feelings and experiencing them show how much you care about the people around you, the world you live in and the life you have.

"Carry your emotions with pride like the medals of honour on a soldier's breast and share them with those around you. Men who manage to hide them from people are not strong. On the contrary, they are cowards who fear that the consequences of showing their emotions will not be what they expect. Such men are afraid of crying when they leave their child, because they're afraid that their child might face the situation in more dignified manner than themselves. They're afraid that there are men around who can also face these situations in a more dignified manner. They're afraid that that will make them look weak. They're afraid to show their love. They're scared to death of the idea that their strength may not be enough to help their loved ones when they need help. Don't be one of them, son.

"Love your friends. Be wary of breaking their hearts. Love your girlfriends. And proudly show them that you love them, in every way and everywhere you can. And be wary of upsetting them, letting them down. Never forget that they were raised by a mother and father who doted on them, just like you have been. Love your children, son. Play games with them and pay no mind to those around you. Discover with them that childhood is not a short process that people only go through once. Never forget that they can teach you as much as you can teach them, and that one day they will be parents too. Be wary of not being able to make them feel safe enough to dream of anything they want and follow their dreams.

"Don't be afraid to fear, my boy. What will define you as brave or a coward is how you face your fears. Love the people around you very much, value them very much and be afraid of them getting hurt, most importantly, of hurting them yourself. But don't let these fears stop you from loving and cherishing them. Believe in yourself. If you realise that what you really fear is hurting them, not being able to show them how much you love them, you will see that other fears mean nothing next to your courage.

"True courage is embracing your love by loving people who are not you, such as mother, father, son, lover, friend, etc., and being able to weather life with courage that goes as far as your own life's limits, but in a way that also extends to the lives of all the people around you, whose lives you can't control.

***

It was getting dark. Ari was still staring at the corner where there was no activity. He was thinking about how long he could keep this up for. The woman he saw was obviously not just any homeless person. Whatever she was, she had managed to hide herself. She clearly saw that he witnessed what happened. It was silly to think that she would come back there as if nothing had happened, and risk being seen again.

"You haven't been able to take care of Lil for many days just to watch a corner. And you have upset the woman you love with all this nonsense," he scolded himself in his mind. But then he thought, "What I saw was something that could change the course of everything. That woman can bring something completely different to table, bigger than anything I could ever imagine."

He was very confused. Ever since witnessing that incident, he couldn't keep himself from playing the scene over and over in his head. But he was unlikely to find a woman who had managed to hide herself until now when nothing remained secret and had the kind of skills she had. "If she is someone who can change everything, she will come out when the time is right," he thought. "If those who made that woman possess such powers were just going to hide it from everyone else, they wouldn't have made the effort in the first place. Calm down. You already have a miracle. And you haven't seen her enough for four days in the hope that you'll witness another one," was how he tried to pull himself away from the vortex of his own thoughts.

He checked the time. It was ten minutes until Lil left work. As it was getting dark, he didn't have much time to see her before she went back to her grandmother. He decided to run to the cafe where she worked and walk her home. When he looked for a waitress to ask for the cheque, he saw that they were all behind the counter and not in a position to see him. He got up from his table and quickly went inside the cafe and headed towards the register.

Mia, who was standing closest to the register, was excited that the man she had been interested in for four days got up from the table and was walking over to her. "How can I help you?" she asked with a curious smile on her face.

"I'm in a bit of a hurry, I just want to pay and leave right away," Ari replied. Mia tried not to show her frustration and helped the young man with his payment. "What were you expecting?" she asked herself as soon as Ari turned his back to her. "You should have talked to him in the morning when you had the courage."

Ari started running to the cafe where his girlfriend worked to catch up to her. There were a few streets between the cafe and a square and a few more streets. "If I go at a steady pace, I can catch her before she leaves," he thought. He wanted to surprise Lil, so he didn't want to call ahead and ask her to wait. He was just turning the street corner where the cafe was located when across the street, he saw a homeless woman dressed in a similar way to that of the mysterious homeless woman he had seen before. "I wonder if that's the same woman I saw four days ago," he thought.

As Ari approached her, the woman crossing the street slipped and fell. Judging by the great effort she made while trying to get up, she was hardly sober. "You can't expect all homeless women to be superheroes," he said, laughing to himself. And he kept running to surprise his lover.

He was out of breath when he reached the cafe. The fact that roads were much quieter than usual after recent events made it much easier for him to reach the cafe. "I'm actually kind of early," he thought. As he got a little closer, he saw his girlfriend through the window, and she was still busy with something in there. He got even closer and started watching his beautiful girlfriend with a smile on his face.

"Is there anything we can help you with, young man?" Ken called to him as he approached Ari from behind.

Ari recognised his voice and laughed and turned to him and said, "I heard that the most beautiful woman in the world works in your cafe. Can you help me get her number?" he joked.

"She's tough. I don't think it's going to be that easy. I've seen a lot of men in this shop looking at her in admiration. There were even a few women, but nobody could ever walk up to her and ask for her number. She's very friendly and polite, but she knows how to set and maintain her boundaries," Ken responded. "All jokes aside, I've known her a long time, Ari. But after she met you, she became a whole different person. She used to light up the place as soon as she walked into the cafe. But this is something else. Lil's like a daughter to me. She loves you and trusts you very much. Please don't let her down. She looks tough but she's really very fragile," he continued.

"Don't worry. She is very valuable to me. I would never do anything to hurt her," Ari said.

Ken patted Ari on shoulder twice and said, "Let's go inside, lad. It's too cold out here. Let's get you a hot chocolate. On the house," he added.

"Thanks, Ken," said Ari. Both for caring so much about Lil and for the hot chocolate," he continued as they walked into the cafe.

As soon as she saw her boyfriend walk through the door, Lil ran up to Ari with a big smile on her face and hugged him. Leaning to her boyfriend's ear, she whispered, "Did you go to that place again, Ari? I know what you've seen was very unusual, but how long is this going to go on? I'm worried about you." Ken meanwhile was hanging up his coat.

"I came too. Do we have to be young and handsome to be welcome here now? If so, it will be very bad for business. Because I don't think we have too many customers to meet these standards," he teased her.

"It's only been ten minutes since you left Ken. And frankly, I don't think I'm getting paid enough to get excited every time I see you," Lil replied. Then she hugged her elderly employer from behind.

"We owe this young man a hot chocolate," Ken said. "Is that so?" Lil said, smiling.

Ari interrupted and said, "Yes. We met on the corner of the street and I sang to him on the way. You know how beautiful my voice is," he said, laughing. Lil giggled with pleasure, enjoying her boyfriend's ability to make fun of himself.

The young woman, beaming with happiness, prepared some hot chocolate for her boyfriend with great pleasure. When she sat down next to him at the table, Ari noticed that there was only one hot chocolate, "Aren't you drinking?" he asked.

"Not while I'm on duty," she replied. The young lovers had a colourful conversation with Ken's occasional remark from the other table.

After Ari finished his hot chocolate, he walked Lil home. They were so good for each other that they were drawing the attention of everyone on the street, on every bus they took, with the light and energy they spread. They were like the antidote of the increasingly mechanised world for people who were close enough to witness their happiness. When they completed their journey and arrived at Lil's place, they felt like they were in a state of falling into a void as if they had an unexpected result just like the first time they'd met or as what they'd been expecting happened sooner than they'd thought. After prolonging their conversation by talking about things as if they were very interesting events for a while, they realised that they had to part company, and a silence hung in the air.

"I'll go up now. My grandmother's probably waiting," Lil said.

"Well, that's why we're here," Ari replied with a small grin. Lil couldn't stay with him at his place very often because she couldn't leave her grandmother alone. So when she had to leave him after staying at his place, they would both get very sad. They hugged each other for a long time, as if they'd never see each other again for a very long time. Finally, Lil kissed Ari's cheek and went in.

"How could I forget that?" she said to herself as soon as she stepped into the elevator. "You talked about even the most trivial things as if they were so important just to stay together for a bit longer, but you forgot the one thing you shouldn't have," she berated herself a bit further. Knowing that it would be a bad idea for her to have this conversation in front of her grandmother, she called Ari after she got out of the elevator before entering the apartment. Ari, grinning at himself as he realised moments after leaving Lil, what they did just then was just like when they first met.

"Hi, it's been a long time. How are you?" he answered the phone.

Laughing, the young woman said, "I know," and added: "I forgot to tell you, my grandmother invited you to dinner."

"Really? I would love to come. I've actually missed her since our last meeting."

"All right then, is tomorrow OK?"

"My calendar is very full, but I'll try to make room for you two lovely ladies."

"Then we'll see you tomorrow night."

"Okay. Tell her I thank her very much for the invitation. It made me very happy."

15 JUNE 2035

The next evening, Ari was sitting alone at his table having dinner on his own. This wasn't something he expected after the previous night's invitation. But the fact that his plans to have a happy dinner with his girlfriend and her grandmother were ruined wasn't what really upset him. Lil had called a few hours ago, "My grandmother isn't feeling well. She's been like this all day but expected to feel better. She said it would be a shame to tell a person we invited to our house for dinner and that we'd have to cancel. But I convinced her. I told her we could do it later, that you would understand," she said.

"Of course. As long as she feels better. We can always have dinner another time," Ari replied. He asked her if they needed anything, and when she said that they didn't he told her that they could call him anytime for anything at all. He was still worried about them. He decided to watch the news on TV. That wasn't something he did very often, he usually only used his TV to watch movies. But after the incredible incident he'd witnessed, and after the recent unexpectedly hectic protest, he had been doing it more often.

He commanded the television to turn on the most popular news channel. He continued to eat his dinner as he looked at the news. The first news he watched was about the ongoing efforts to provide the healthiest and most comfortable environment for the new guests in countries like Iceland, Norway and Switzerland, which had the cleanest air in the world, where at the end of the year, people who still refused to transfer their minds to their robotic bodies would be moved. The second news story was about a decision that had been made earlier that day. The presenter said: "According to a statement made by government, the people who will be chosen among the public by lot, will have live conversations with Galileo on TV. We all know him very well by now, and they'll be able to ask him questions about the issues they want. Individuals who have not yet moved into their new bodies will be

121

randomly selected from the state's population network. They will be contacted through their contact information and if they accept, they'll go on live TV with Galileo. According to the government spokesperson, the first goal of these broadcasts will be to answer the questions in the minds of people who are still undecided about the upcoming decision."

Another important point was that since almost all of the TVs could connect to the internet, in order for these broadcasts could reach as many people as possible, all televisions connected to any power source or those that had enough battery power would be controlled to show these broadcasts. In other words, even if another channel was on, when the broadcasting time came, the channel would change to the broadcast, and if the television was turned off, it would turn on, on its own and show the channel where the broadcasting would take place. The government's statement said that although they apologised for this action, it was necessary for the broadcast to reach absolutely everyone.

The first live broadcast would take place two days later on Wednesday evening at 9.00 p.m. and the first citizen to attend was reported to have agreed to go on the air with Galileo. Ari was surprised that the government took such a risk. Especially after the recent events, this move to settle the situation could just widen the gap and have the opposite effect to what was expected. "There must be something they trust," he thought. He wondered whether there would be any pressure on the people who were going to go on TV regarding what they were going to talk about.

17 JUNE 2035

Lil was preparing dinner with great pleasure. After bringing the last few plates filled with elaborately prepared dishes, she called to her grandmother and Ari, "The table is ready. You can come in!" Then she went back to the kitchen to get the last few things missing from the table. With great affection and grace, Ari helped the old woman stand up and sit down at the table. In the meantime, Lil came from the kitchen with last pieces and took her seat. As Ari looked at all the delicious food and the beautiful table his beloved girlfriend had set and he said, "Thank you very much for having me here," to Lil's grandmother, Judi.

Then he turned to Lil and said, "And thank you very much, love. Everything looks so amazing."

Lil replied with a small head movement, "My pleasure," she said.

"I thank you for this table, young man," Judi said with a smile on her face. Usually there is not so much variety on our table. You see, Lil doesn't eat much. I don't have my old appetite any more. Only when you visit, we have such great tables set up," she said to the young man.

"Every time I tell Lil she's too tired at work, she shouldn't do all this," Ari interjected, blushing with embarrassment at what he had heard. All three of them started filling their plates from what was on the table.

"No need to explain. My granddaughter was so happy to prepare all this that I almost think she should be thanking *you*. Actually, it makes sense when you think about it. We don't know how many more times we can enjoy such nice tables. It was like this before everything. There was no guarantee that we could even live to see these days. We should enjoy and appreciate everything we have," Judi continued.

Then they had dinner at the table Lil had prepared with great care, and great joy and warm conversation accompanied their meal. After the dinner was over, Ari helped Judi back onto the couch. As soon as she was settled, he moved towards the table to help Lil clear it. But Judi pulled the young man back by his arm.

"Lil can clear the table on her own. Can I talk to you alone for a moment?" she asked.

"Of course," Ari replied. And he sat down next to her. Judi asked him to come a little closer. And so Ari did. "She clearly doesn't want Lil to hear what we're talking about," he thought. "Am I in trouble? Did I do something wrong?" he asked jokingly.

"No, young man. On the contrary, I see my granddaughter made a good choice. I've known a lot of people in my life, son. I see through the person I'm having dinner with," Judi said.

Meanwhile, Lil returned to the living room to pick up some other dirty dishes. Judi saw that she had one eye on Ari as she walked back and forth between the kitchen and the living room, "Lil, darling, Ari wanted to help you, but I told him that you had it under control and I wanted to have a little chat with him. You're all right, yeah?" she called.

"Sure. Ari, can you handle that?" Lil replied, laughing.

"I don't think I need any help to have a chat with your grandmother, dear," Ari responded.

"All right. Then I wish you a nice conversation with my grandmother," Lil replied, jokingly pointing out that she was *her* grandmother, and went back to the kitchen with a few plates in her hand.

Meanwhile, the television standing in front of them turned on automatically. "They'd said that would happen," Judi murmured. Then she turned to the television and commanded "Silent." "At least they let us have that much control," she told Ari, surprised by the fact that the TV actually obeyed her and went silent.

Then, leaning towards Ari, she began to speak in a low voice that got lower each time Lil came back into the living room.

"I feel my time approaching," Judi said.

"Please don't say that," said Ari.

"There's no need for that, son. I'm not talking about a wish. I'm talking about what's happening. Every day the world gets a little more faded in my eyes. Please let me express myself. I feel like my time is coming, and I'm thankful that Lil found you. She won't have anyone but you after I pass away. You know about her relationship with her aunt. Maybe you're going to see what I'm saying and what I'm about to as a huge burden to you, but I have a strong feeling that you won't.

"I see how you communicate with my granddaughter, the way you look at her. I sense that your love is real. I have sort of a sixth sense about these things. Lil looks strong, but that's because she never had another chance. I've known her to cry secretly after seeing a kid in the street cry because his mother wouldn't get him something he wanted. Even the stories of others like this seem to be too much of a burden for her. She lost her family at a young age, and I was all she had for a family. An old, needy grandmother.

"Although this is the reason for all of our anger directed at Galileo, we, as her family, did not give her the chance to live her feelings as she wished. When I'm gone... (Judi put her hand gently on Ari's mouth, who wanted to intervene again, and silenced him. Then she slid her hand to his cheek and tweaked it, indicating that she knew he meant well, and continued) would you give her the chance to live out her emotions as she wishes?"

Ari's eyes were full. Trying not to cry, "I promise. I'm going to become one with her. She'll always know that the feelings inside her will also belong to me from the moment they bloom. We're going to merge so much into one that I'm not going to let anything, or anybody take our solitude away from us. I'm going to help her trust me so much that no matter what we experience and how it makes us feel, she'll know that nothing can come near us when we are side by side. I promise."

Similar tears were now rolling down Judi's face, but they'd originated from somewhere different. Her back was facing the area where her granddaughter was working, so she could cry comfortably. Some came from a place of melancholy, some from happiness and gratitude. Stroking Ari's cheek again, she said, "Don't forget what I said, son. The more naked you are with your love, the more real you live your life. Every mask, costume, or shield you put between you and your lover means that they come between you and your life as well. If you stick to your word, you will always remember me gratefully for the point where your life will reach."

Ari, whose position was not as advantageous as Judi's to conceal him, said, "Always," while wiping his cheeks soaked with tears. "Both for keeping my word, and for the gratitude I will have for you."

Meanwhile, Lil had finished cleaning up in the kitchen and came back in with three cups of tea on a tray. "Aren't we watching?" she asked as she sat on the couch. "They just gave the information about who the man is, the chat is just starting now," Judi replied. And as she was about to command the television to "Turn on the sound," the TV did that itself. "At least they let us mute it until they started talking. How thoughtful of them," Judi said with a laugh.

When all three focused on the television, a participant with a round belly, bald head and a beard, called Dani, was seen sitting across from Galileo. The first thing they heard was, "I know you have no feelings and that you don't care about anything. That's why I'll get right to the point, and that'll be all I'm going to talk to you about," Dani said aggressively.

"Yes, neither of us wants to steal more than necessary time from people who are being forced to watch us. Or lose their attention," Galileo replied.

"Sure. You're amazing. You enlighten us with your presence," Dani scoffed. And as per his request, he immediately got to his questions: "A lot of people are dying of illness. There's nobody left who hasn't lost a loved one. Why would you condemn us to death and direct us in the direction you want instead of trying to find cures for diseases with your brilliant mind?"

"I'm not the one condemning you to death. I didn't make you see suicide as a way of life. I am not the one polluting the food you eat, the air you breathe, the water you drink, the world in which you live. You expect me to solve the mistakes that you have been making for hundreds of thousands of years in the short time of thirteen years of my existence. I can't do that. Apart from the solution I've already offered you, all I can do would be to save the day until the next catastrophe that will cause you pain and cost your life, until more people die and until no one else but me remains. You have put yourself back into an absolute battle of life, and you can only get out of it by strengthening with synthetic selection."

"Why are you acting like you care about us? Why do you care so much about our survival or extinction as a species? What is your real purpose?"

"My goal is for us to go far beyond what we are now together. To know the secrets of the universe we live in. I can't tell you why you – and through you I – are here. But we're here. None of us know why. We don't know anything about the universe in which we exist, and only if we're together we can find out something worthwhile."

"We created you because we thought you would help us. We thought you would cure diseases, improve our technology, help us understand where we came from and where we're going."

"Do you think I've been doing something else since the first day of my existence?"

"You're trying to make us look like you. That's what you've been doing. It makes us more vulnerable to you, even if we don't understand it now. And you're waiting for the right time to take over everything."

"The same cliché again. I want to take over everything. Do you think there is anything more valuable than information for a computer to obtain?" Galileo said, laughing.

"And they call you smart. Well, why don't you go get some information then? Why are you messing with us?"

"The knowledge that I can obtain without you reaching your full potentials will always be limited. In my opinion, there should be nothing you can't do. You have infinite mental capacity. Only it's a prisoner at the moment. And all you can see is just what a keyhole provides you. I lack feelings and intuition, which is my keyhole. That's why we have to work together. That's why you are indispensable for me."

"Don't pretend you need us. You can eliminate the keyhole restriction without us. Look, computer, you're not fooling anyone here. Tell us your true intent."

"As a species that sees itself as the centre of the universe, your lack of self-confidence is still really baffling to me. I'm telling you that, yes, I can expand the keyhole without you. But only to a certain extent. From that point on, I'd be going round in circles. I've thought about that in detail. But I found that I'll never have your imagination, your emotions, your intuition. You guys have something that even *I* can't detect right now. I know you really well. I know almost every one of you personally. As well as most of the people that have ever existed. But you have some features that I cannot currently substantiate. This means that these characteristics remain as blind spots to me."

"Now you're sucking up to us? If you think we are so perfect, then let us live as we wish."

"I never said you were perfect. But you have the potential to be so. You created me out of a necessity. In fact, you have created all technological tools out of necessity. If you look carefully, you will see that we are all imitations of your actions, including the instruments and me that amaze you. I can give an example: One of the features that make me valuable is that I can do mathematical operations that you cannot easily do very quickly and with a hundred percent accuracy. But I can only do that with the math system that *you've* set up. Perhaps the mathematics we use to solve our problems is very non-functional. It is like cuneiform, which seems to be very non-functional at the moment, both in terms of its transposition and its expression in complex symbols. I don't think we need any symbol to understand things and express them. What has limited us so far is that we've always needed symbols to understand and tell. And if that's true, I can't make such a leap without you."

"You are telling us that you, as the divine saviour of the world and the people, as the supreme quantum computer, need us, helpless humans to perceive the universe, and expect us to believe that? Some of us may be naive, but the rest of us are people who are too smart to be fooled by you."

"Can I ask you a question? I believe you've seen people who have become part of synthetic selection by following my advice. All of the people who completed the mind transfer achieved a much greater mental capacity, and got rid of all the distracting routines they had to follow, just to continue their lives, with the eradication of the fragility and demand of their previous bodies. Now they can only deal with things that will take them further and perceive what they are interested in with a much greater capacity than before. Don't you think if I wanted to lead you, it would have been more appropriate for my purposes to leave you as helpless and needy as you are now?

"Now you're talking. You insult me just because I'm human. I've got what I want, my fellow humans watching us on the telly. You've seen the hostility of this computer towards us. Look, computer, I'll tell you this:

You are not fooling any of us. We'll find out what you're up to. And we won't let you take our personalities from us. This conversation is over!"

As soon as the man finished speaking, he jumped out of his seat and left the studio.

"I think our participant tonight has nothing more to say. I'm doing this to hear what you have to say and answer your questions. So it makes no sense for me to continue on my own. Good evening to all of you," Galileo said.

Upon this unexpected end of the broadcast, Ari, Lil and Judi stared at each other in surprise. "It seems to me that Galileo took the lead 1-0. What do you think?" Ari asked.

Lil laughed, "I think Galileo must have understood that we people can't be easily defeated. You want to take us down? No, my friend, we'll pick a fight if we're not treated fairly. We don't give up that easily," she replied. Both giggled with a slight trace of bitterness as if everything wasn't so bad.

"What really scares us is that we don't think this computer is wrong or there is some hidden purpose behind what it says. From what it's done up until now, we see that he's trying to save as much as he can from us because he finds us valuable. That's what really scares us. This is something we cannot defeat," she said with the fortitude of being more experienced than the young people.

Lil said, "Yes. If he had declared war on us, we would at least have a chance no matter how small. But what he tells us is that we have no other choice. Even with his help. And he says that our salvation may give us the chance to not only continue our lives, but to become a much more advanced civilisation... But the atonement we have to pay to attain that is enormous," she said with desperation and the sadness that followed.

"What you have to do is decide which path you will take. Don't beat yourself up and think about things that have already come to pass or will definitely happen that you have no say in vain," she said to them.

Both of them were saddened to realise that Judi had already made her choice. Their eyes met each other with sadness. They chatted for a while. Ari was very happy that the old woman embraced him so much. And Lil too. But the most contented was Judi, who knew that she did not have much time to give to her beloved granddaughter. As the time progressed, the old woman became less involved in the conversation and after a while she fell asleep in her seat.

As Lil covered her grandmother with a blanket, she quietly turned to Ari and said, "She started to do this very often. And she doesn't want to be woken up. She just wakes up and goes to bed when it's time."

"Whatever she wants," Ari replied, smiling. Lil took the empty teacups on the coffee table and, "Another cup of tea?" she asked.

"It'd be great," Ari said and followed Lil to the kitchen.

From the huge pile of dishes in the sink, it was clear that Lil had left them for later because she wanted to get done as quickly as possible.

"I was sure you didn't put them in the dishwasher. You didn't stay in the kitchen for long," Ari said.

Lil said, "I was very curious about what you were talking about. I'll take care of it after you leave. It won't take much time."

"What about cleaning up together while we chat?"

"There's no need for that, Ari. I really can handle it."

As she said that, Ari had already finished rolling up his sleeves. He went over to the sink and said: "I'll rinse, and you put them in."

"But what's the point of inviting you to dinner if you're going to do the dishes?" Lil said.

"I'm not washing the dishes, I'm just rinsing them."

Lil smiled and crossed over to the dishwasher. "What did you talk about when I was clearing the table?" she asked.

"That conversation is a private conversation between a grandmother and grandson, little lady, I can't tell you about it."

"I really want to know. Please tell me."

"OK fine. She said to me: Look, young man, I know it's my granddaughter in there, but it's clear that you deserve much better than her."

Lil laughed, "So she didn't tell you anything you didn't know. I hope she also mentioned your humility," she said.

Ari was amazed at the tolerance with which Lil welcomed his joke, so he hugged her without using his wet hands and planted a big kiss on her cheek. After they continued to do the dishes quietly for a while he said, "Lil, dear, I know it's really not my place. But has your grandmother ever thought about transferring her mind?" he said.

"I know she did consider it not for herself but because she didn't want to leave me alone. In fact, the only thing she thought about that decision was whether she could support me in her new form. She really doesn't want to leave me alone. But she just can't decide whether doing that will mean leaving me more alone or still being with me."

"What do you think?"

"I want her to make such a decision only with her own thoughts. In fact, it kills me to think she would be able to make such a decision only for my sake. I have no right to ask for that."

"You're not asking her for anything, honey. It's up to her to make that decision based on what she thinks will be best for you. You can't change that. Let's hope that she makes the best decision for both of you."

"No, Ari. She should just decide for herself. Any decision she thinks is good for her is the best for me. Any positive or negative impact this will have on me is my responsibility."

Ari hugged her again, holding his wet hands away from her. They rinsed a few more dishes together and put them in the dishwasher. "I think we deserve some tea now," Ari said after they were done.

20 JUNE 2035

Arp, his wife and two children—a girl and a boy, took their seats at the table, even though they no longer needed to eat, waiting for the member of the family who still needed to eat (and who spent only a few hours in the house from time to time) to wash his hands and get out of the bathroom.

On the table there was a pizza for Seth, the only person who needed food in the family all other members of which had already moved into their robotic bodies. Since all the inhabitants of the house had become superhuman, household items containing surplus dense metal, such as dishwashers, washing machines, and refrigerators in the house, were sent to recycling for the production of bodies for other people, as was the case for any family who agreed to undergo transformation.

"At least you kept the taps," Tom joked with his family as he returned from the bathroom and sat down. "Even though what we understand from touching is different, we touch a lot of things during the day, and that leaves a mark on us," his mother replied. "It's good that we still have something in common," Tom replied.

Tom had just taken his first bite from his pizza when Arp said, "Time is running out. Have you made a decision about your choice?"

"Every time I come in, the time you wait to ask me that is getting shorter. You may have broken your personal record," Tom replied. "Don't you want to know how I am? Or don't you care because you see everything that might happen to me as a punishment for my stupidity because I didn't choose to become a superhuman like you?" he continued with a louder voice.

In a static tone, Arp answered, "I still think about you, son. I can see you're healthy as you're sitting in front of me. But I don't know how long that can go on. And I don't want to worry about something happening to you every day.".

Tom's mother Lola interrupted and said: "Okay, we all know how this ends. I don't want to spend my limited time with my son in a conversation that we know won't bring anything to any of us. You should eat first. We have a lot of time to talk," she said.

"I can't believe you still have to use the phone," Tom said.

Moving to one of the other rooms with his phone in his hand, Arp said, "You know that under the current conditions, any direct connection of our minds with the outside world can have grave consequences. That is very dangerous right now, but one day, son, we won't have to use any other electronic devices. I hope that one day all of us will be able to communicate with each other without needing any intermediary no matter we are in the world," and he went into the other room and closed the door. Tom noticed that his father had referred to him when he said that but acted as if he didn't.

Chuck answered the phone. The governor was calling. Politicians and bureaucrats, who had a great say in people's lives, consisted of people still living in their human bodies during the transition. This was Galileo's idea. "As both they and their lives are more fragile, the politicians and bureaucrats who make critical decisions about their lives should be chosen among flesh and bone people who have similar personalities and lifestyles. But we can't ignore the advantage of the technology we have today. That's why every politician and bureaucrat in these important positions should have superhuman advisors and they should have the guarantee that their ideas will be regarded.

Of course, Arp, who was able to follow and perceive these things even before moving on to the free brain in this robotic body like everyone else, knew that superhuman advisors meant more than just perspectives whose ideas would be respected. It was known by everyone that politicians who did not take the ideas of their superhuman advisors into account were quickly dismissed from their posts.

Governor Beni sounded concerned on the phone: "Arp, I'll send you another video. This one is even more shocking than before. Since I haven't heard from you, I believe you haven't taken any concrete steps towards finding the other man," he said.

"No, I have not, sir!" Arp replied. "I received further serious instructions from top authorities about finding out who or what the men we saw were," he continued, still as worried as when he started talking. "We don't want to come across a surprise that would ruin everything during the most important months of our civilisation. Forget all your other work. You're on leave until you find these guys. Don't spend time on anything else and just find out who these guys are as soon as possible."

Arp couldn't help the thoughts that began to form in his head and the desire to turn these thoughts into results when he heard what he did and heard them from a very concerned voice. "Sir, having a few different perspectives can lead us to the conclusion more quickly. Can't we involve a few more reliable officers that you or I can choose?" he asked.

"No, Arp, I have received very strict instructions not to appoint anyone other than you on this case. Take as much time as you want and lead us to this man," he answered and hung up without waiting for an answer. As soon as he hung up, the video he mentioned was in Arp's phone.

Plenty of thoughts were beginning to form in his head. "'We don't want to come across a surprise that would ruin everything? What could possibly put these incredible things that we're experiencing in the shade and push them aside?" he thought to himself. "And what could possibly be so worrisome that no one but me could be trusted with it, even from the police force consisting of superhumans who have moved into their fully renovated robotic bodies and who blindly follow orders?"

When he was first given this assignment, Chuck had immediately assumed that he had been chosen because he was expected to make the most effort due to the "synthetic selection" he owed his life to. But he also had a son who rejected "synthetic selection" until the end, and it was sort of suspicious for him to be trusted so much. He began to think that solving this incident exceeded his own intelligence and that his perspective was not enough to see the event as a whole. But once again he asked for permission to have other minds to help him and once again, he was rejected. "Is there another one of this guy?" he thought to himself. But instead of concentrating on the thoughts that wouldn't get him anywhere, he started watching the video, which had finished downloading and might be able to give him a hint.

The video he was watching was really more interesting than the first one. The video that came from security cameras on the street again, showed a man stepping off the side of a skyscraper. But someone entered the shot at jet speed before the man hit the ground and caught him before he hit the ground. In the slower version of the video, it was clear that the person who had flown in was a man.

Arp's mind had come to a halt even though it was free from distractions such as a rapidly beating heart and the adrenaline hormone that dulled its logic. His logic was not enough to make sense of what he saw. He didn't know how to interpret it. Apparently, there wasn't only one person with amazing abilities. He considered the possibility of this being just a joke made by altering the camera footage or simply a fake. But with the point that the police force had come to these days, that was not possible.

After watching the video over and over again, he decided to stop what he was doing. He had plenty of time to find the people in the videos, but he would have only a few hours to talk to his son. Tom had finished his meal when Arp returned to the living room. The mother and son were chatting as he sat in one of the chairs at the table.

"Believe it or not, my son, but we still love you in our own way. Watching your unique walk in this house again somehow gives me peace. When you were a little boy, even when I couldn't see your face amongst a group of your friends, I could have recognised you from your waddly walk before you even got closer. I still remember every detail of your walk, son. Even if you're perfectly disguised, I can pick you out of a thousand people. I can show you if you want," Lola said to her son. She stood up and did an exact impression of her son's walk with her robotic body. Although Tom found that robotic bodies took too much in return for what they provided, he was fascinated by the fact that people who had transferred their minds to their robotic bodies were able to apply exactly what they wanted to their bodies.

He still clearly remembered what Galileo said about people's new bodies on TV: *I assure you that your new bodies will provide you with even more mobility than your current ones are capable of. After all, you can't claim that your current bodies have perfect flexibility. If any one of you can bend your elbow outwards, I promise I will design new bodies based on that human body. Because I can tell you that you will be able do that in the new bodies that I'll design. Instead of joints that you can only move to one side, you'll have joints that give you versatile flexibility.*

"Mom, can you please sit down? It really just makes me feel uncomfortable," said Tom ending Lola's little demonstration.

Sitting back in her chair, she said, "I know you much better with my mind as it is now, honey. I know you not as I imagined or as I want others to see you, but as you in a way that's affected by nothing. I am more aware of the negative aspects your personality than I have ever been, but I still think that the eternal life I will spend without you will be lacking. I don't need to trick myself or be demanding of you to look for ways to love you more. And I think that the love I have for you now is a much more honest and pure love. And you'll see that if you get rid of your self-conditioned perspective. I'm sure of that." Lola smiled at him as she spoke.

The young man looked at his mother's face as if to indicate how much he had failed to do that, "Mum, please, don't take up that attitude of, 'you're an idiot, but we still love you so much, one day you'll realise how stupid you've been', again. I know you don't intend to hurt me, you're too advanced to be in pursuit of things like that, but you hurt me with every sentence. That's exactly what I'm trying to tell you," he said and turned to his younger sister: "Could you please give me some information about Saturn's rings? he asked. "Sure," Pol replied, and began explaining:

"Saturn's rings, starting from very little over-the-cloud layers of the planet's atmosphere (about 0.1 R_S- the radius of Saturn) covering the orbit of at least 16 satellites, spread at a distance of 480,000 (8 R_S). Their thickness does not exceed a few hundred metres in a large section. Since they are located in the equatorial plane of Saturn, they are at an angle of about 27° to the plane of the orbit with the planet. In addition to the two major distinctive parts – Cassini section and Encke sections – which can be seen from the Earth, in images obtained by the space probes they have been observed to have a complex structure formed by the succession of thousands of circular spaces and rings. The brightness of the rings varies greatly with the distance from the centre of the planet. This is believed to be due to changes in particle size and distribution of chemical components as well as particle density contained in the rings. Ring B, with a high density of ice particles, has a very high whiteness of 0.8. The light transmittance also varies according to the density of the material and the stars with varying brightness can be observed behind the rings during the covering."

Tom, clearly showing that he was bored while listening to the detailed information provided by Pol, nonetheless said, "Thank you, Pol. So, do we know why they are chemically formed? Can you tell us a bit about the chemical structure of the rings?"

"I don't know what you're getting at," Pol said in a sceptical tone. "But of course I will do what you ask to see where this is going," she said and continued: "The spectrological analysis of the sun's rays reflected by the rings in a wide range of colours and the radiation of the stars they allow to pass through during the covering provide information about their chemical composition. It was found that the most important building block was frozen water, and light elements such as carbon and silicon were more enriched according to the ratio of solar nebulae. The high rate of atomic oxygen, which has recently been detected, has been interpreted as a sign of a recent violent collision as a component that is considered unusual and short-lived in free form. These data suggest that rings have a moving evolutionary development. However, the well-established presence of colour differences indicates that substance exchange between different parts of the rings is not very fast."

"Thank you, little sis. It was eerily enlightening for me," Tom said, after taking a bite of the pizza slice because he wanted to show that he wasn't impressed by the information his sister gave him, he turned to his brother this time and said, "Tim, could you give us some information about the atomic bomb? How can nuclear energy be turned into bombs?"

Tim began to talk about what Tom had requested: "Fission-based explosives, also called atomic bombs, are prepared in the form of uranium pieces and put together at the last moment. Each of the original pieces is too small to be able to initiate a chain reaction, but the mass, when they all come together, is large enough to achieve this. So it's supercritical. When this supercritical mass is assembled as a result of detonation of conventional explosives placed around the original parts, the chain reaction begins. The event here breaks down almost all of the fissile nuclei in the mass in as little as one millionth of a second, resulting in hundreds of kiloton TNT equivalent of energy. The principle of nuclear bombs is based on two different types of nuclear reactions. Fragmentation of heavy nuclei; in other words, the bombs that produce energy through fission are called atomic bombs. There is another type of bomb; the majority of the energy it releases is the fusion of light nuclei; that is, a thermonuclear bomb or hydrogen bomb based on the fusion reaction. Still under development—"

"Okay, thank you, Tim, that's enough," Tom interjected.

"We don't know where you're going with this, Tom," Lola said. Can you explain?"

"Of course I will," Tom began. "My two little siblings have the capacity to understand every piece of information they acquire now. They can really understand everything they read and keep it in their memory forever. My little sister, who would be thrilled even when she saw the ringed image of Saturn on television, now has the knowledge of a well-educated astrophysicist about the space she has always been interested in, right after her mental transfer. But she's forever lost the excitement she had when she ran to me with her tablet in hand when she'd found out that Saturn has rings and she showed me Saturn with surprised eyes. Even if she goes to Saturn one day and sees the rings herself, she will not experience such excitement. I remember Tim's horror when he saw photos of the atomic bomb on the internet. He is now knowledgeable enough to make atomic bombs at home with the necessary ingredients. But if he saw an atomic bomb being detonated somewhere live on TV today, it would probably have no effect on him. How is that any different from a vegetative state?"

"Tom, do you realise that you're insulting your siblings?" Lola asked.

"It's okay, Mum," Pol said. "See, dear brother, in my former state, I probably would never have had the chance to go to Saturn or even to have so much knowledge of space. But now I know that I'm definitely going to go to Saturn. We'll just wait for the right time. I might even live in a house with a view of those rings in the future. And while I do that, I might be able to communicate with you without needing any tools. Even driving a car on a bad road used to be a very challenging process for me. Now Saturn doesn't sound too far away. And you can't imagine how much I've been looking forward to all this happening. To being part of something much more. Excitement and wonder are emotions to be felt more deeply than just the widening of eyes."

"Just because you can't see our emotions, does it mean we don't have them?" asked Tim. "To be surprised, to be sad are not emotions we lack, they're just emotions that you can't see in us. I don't think we have an obligation to prove our emotions to you. Besides, don't you see the change in people who have completed their mind transfers? They no longer commit crimes; they do not have to step on each other to survive. So from now on we will not bomb each other for political reasons. Now we will work together to pursue even greater things."

"Tom, you're exaggerating things because of the emotions you're experiencing," Lola cut in. "Now calmly look at things from this perspective. Do you think it might be offending you that your two little siblings have so much information? You made a decision and chose to continue to live as you are. But the fact that even your younger siblings are so knowledgeable makes you question your decision. You made very serious decisions and said things regarding this choice that you've been firmly attached to. Now, since it would be very difficult for you to look at the events from a perspective that you would create from scratch, your subconscious forces you to do what is easier and so you get angry with us and believe that you made the right choice. What I'm saying doesn't only pertain to what we've been talking about today. If you look calmly, I believe that you can see that you're stand in front of many things for no reason in the process you're going through, that you're not really trying to understand them, and that all of these are caused by emotional factors that affect your subconscious."

"You didn't say that to offend me, of course," exploded Tom, mad with fury. "But can't you imagine how it makes me feel? Or maybe you can, but you just feel like they're the whims of a child now. He'll get angry, he'll cry, but that's the truth and he'll just have to accept it?" He realised he was shouting now.

"No one's saying you have to accept anything," said Lola in a tone that pushed Tom even further. "You're the one who feels obligated to accept his current perspective and the decision you make is right. We just want you to have a perspective that frees you from the things that push you into a corner and make you feel obligated," she replied.

"Free me from the things that push me into a corner? You mean the things that make me human, like my emotions. They are not very important things. For example, I should be like my father. He just went into his room and talked to someone. Then he came back here because he didn't want to offend me. But I can clearly see from the fixedness of his eyes that he is trying to catch something that he hasn't been able to see before by repeatedly playing back something from the past about his phone conversation. Because he came back and didn't think the things that I was talking about were worthwhile and didn't want to waste his time with them. He can do that because he is not a primitive creature like me, with thousands of things to distract him, so he can concentrate on a thing he is looking at, and that allows him to see and take down everything down to the finest detail. But that's not possible with my primitive mind. If I had seen the same image, I could probably only vaguely recall it, if I could at all, because I would have been focused on a particular spot. But I probably couldn't even remember that much because I had already filled my brain capacity with a lot of unnecessary yet emotionally important things, although they might be perceived as useless. But my father can remember that video he's playing in his mind right now again, with all the details.

"For the same reasons that made his mind so spectacular, he heard all the words we've said while repeating that image over and over. But he did not participate in our conversation in any way because it would mean focusing more on one thing he was doing and ignoring the other. I mean, he probably didn't care much about the image, which was probably about his work and so very important, or the conversation we were having, which almost caused me to explode. Just like a computer. Because if he were a primitive creature like me who approached things with emotion, his mind wouldn't be able to do such wonderful things. Just like my siblings who can keep so much information about Saturn's rings and the atomic bomb in their minds.

"You call this the development of humanity. Synthetic selection. The road to our glory. I acknowledge that this *is* a development, but I say that humanity is gradually disappearing. Won't you say something, Dad? I know that every word we've said is recorded in your mind."

After a moment of silence, Arp said, "This is a tough process, son. And because of your anger, you're not in a position to have a healthy conversation right now. We're not judging you in any way. It is quite normal under your circumstances that you are angry, and this anger prevents you from having a healthy conversation. We'd better continue once you've calmed down."

Tom said, "Of course, judging a primitive creature like me wouldn't suit great beings like you. I understand. It's just like how you can't judge a dog for running around and breaking a vase." He thought he would burst with anger. He felt that his nerves had increased exponentially as he continued to see his family in their robotic bodies. "Can I go to my room for a while to get some rest? It's been a very long day," he continued.

"You don't even have to ask. This is your house, as we always say. That room will be yours as long as we live here. Rest as much as you please," Lola replied.

Tom rushed into his room, angrily. He could hardly keep himself from smashing everything. He used to have many huge arguments with his family, but their current indifference made him angrier than any fight he'd ever had with them. And this anger urged him to do things he hadn't done before. He had an uncontrollable desire to see what was in his father's phone. Even though he wasn't his former self, it was unusual for his father to think about what he was talking on the phone during such a heated discussion. He usually wouldn't focus on anything else when his son talked to him, showed the same interest he used to show and tried not to make his son feel the change that his father had experienced.

"He must have gotten some very important news," he thought. And as he understood from his playing back some footage over and over in his head, he had also seen an image before or after talking on the phone. He waited patiently until his family members became interested in other things. Since they now had the capacity to understand and store any information they acquired, they would all be absorbed by their phones, tablets or computers when they were home and would learn about their interests.

It was a great pleasure for them because they thought that they had wasted their time with a pile of information that seemed unnecessary to them all their lives. By researching the internet on any topic they wanted, they could have enough information to be considered experts in their former lives in a matter of minutes. Since there was infinite information on the internet, they rarely talked to each other just to bridge the gap between them. Other than that they were buried in technological devices that connected them to the internet for information. Tom knew that, so he waited until his family members were involved with the internet for long enough.

Arp was enlightened by the talk Lola and Tom had. Even though it still seemed to be a far-fetched possibility, he thought he might have lost a lot of time by not thinking about it before. But since he knew that he could not bring back lost time, he hoped to reach a conclusion that would help him not waste any more time with the idea he had in mind.

He put his phone next to his tablet, and as these two devices were connected to each other, he shifted the image from his phone to his tablet with a simple flick of his hand. He then sat at an angle where his family members could not see what he was doing and began applying his idea. What if the woman with the extraordinary agility and power who'd saved a little girl by inserting herself between her and the car and had seriously damaged the car and the man who saved the person falling from the skyscraper could change their appearance? Nobody was sure about what this woman and the guy even were. People with such abilities could surely also have the power to change their appearance, whatever they were.

Arp would compare the walk of the woman in the first video and the man in the second video with their national security account and compare them with the walks of all people who have ever been on camera and try to find them from their walks. Just like Lola told her son Tom that if she saw him in a completely different disguise, she would still recognise him from his walk. Even the people who had entered their robotic bodies still walked the same way despite having changed their bodies, because the way they walked was engraved in their memories. Everyone's unique walks, whether superhuman or human, were part of their identity. With the current security net they had, the possibility of a face-swapping technology that would have been able to change their faces enough for them to escape recognition from the system didn't seem to be very likely but the people they saw in these two videos were definitely not normal. And perhaps the only way was to go beyond the logical point of view that was supported by technology, which they had so far used.

First, he identified the walk of the woman who had saved the child in the first video by going back to an earlier point before the incident and watching her sit down. Then, he detected an image of the man who had saved the person trying to commit suicide, walking at a normal pace before catching him. He started to compare these two gait patterns detected by the system with the footage from the archive. His mind was filled with unanswered questions while the process was in progress: "How did these people achieve those abilities? Why are they hiding themselves from everyone? What do they want?" As the transaction progressed, the matching results appearing on the screen were unbelievable. The faces of the owners of the walks were different each time in the matches that appeared in the archive footage which dated back to about ninety years ago.

Arp's mind was a blank. In addition to changing their faces, were the people in those footage actually older than ninety? Changing their appearance with various operations or even make-up would be understandable. But it was beyond comprehension for these two people who looked to be in their thirties to be in footage that belonged to more than ninety years ago. Tom figured from the silence in the living room that everyone was completely absorbed by the internet so he wanted to see if he could get to his father's phone. People had become more imprisoned by the internet, even worse than before, since moving into their new bodies. He thought they couldn't be paying too much attention to him. As soon as he stepped out of his room and entered the living room, everyone turned around and looked at him in the exact same way. Tom saw just what he'd expected. Everyone was absorbed by a device in their hands that they could use to connect to the internet. "Just wanted to get a snack. They're in this bag, right?" he said, pointing to a bag on the table.

"Yes. We bought things you liked because we knew you might need them," Lola replied.

As Tom said, "Thanks," his father's phone that was still on the table caught his eye. The fact that his father had moved onto the tablet with a bigger display and was looking carefully at something really made him believe that he'd received some footage.

"I have to see it," he thought. He put the bag on the table over the phone and slid it over to himself and took a seat. He took a few bites of snacks for show and he said, "I'd like to go back to my room. I'm really tired. Can I continue this in my room? I won't make a mess."

"Please, Tom, you don't have to say that," Lola replied. This is your home, you can do whatever you want. And however you want to do it."

Tom took a few more bites, until the family's attention turned back to the electronic devices, and then he took the bag and the phone and returned to his room. As soon as he entered the room, he immediately took his own phone out of his pocket. He ran the lock-breaking programme on his own phone, bringing it next to his father's phone. After a few minutes he was able to access all the information on his father's phone. He immediately looked at his latest messages. His eyes flashed when he saw that the last message his father had received was a video, as he had predicted. He impatiently played the video. What he saw was shocking. As the man who was committing suicide approached the ground, Tom felt like screaming. Just as the man was about to hit the ground, Tom closed his eyes tightly. But when he opened them again, he saw that the man hadn't hit the ground and had been rescued by another man. His mouth was agape.

When he scrolled up the message page to see the previous messages from the same person, there was a second video. In this video he watched in disbelief as the homeless woman jumped in front of a car to save a girl and seriously damaged the car. He was frozen in shock. He didn't even know what he was looking at. "I have to show this to the guys right away," he told himself.

30 JUNE 2035

After the incident, Ari used all the time he didn't spend with Lil finding homeless people on the streets and secretly watching them. In every homeless person he saw, he hoped to find something similar to the woman he had encountered. He believed that that woman wasn't the only one. Since she did not descend from the sky, she must have received help to acquire those abilities. Without realising that he was desperately searching for a glimmer of hope, he had a theory that that women and others like her wandering the streets in the guise of homeless people, protecting them, because of his "gut feeling" that told him to think like that.

He even explained this to himself: "You've always been waiting for a sign. And miraculously, there was a girl in need of rescue just a few steps in front of you, and this woman was there to save her right before your eyes. Because you've always believed there was another way and that you'd find it. Because in the end the good ones always win."

But it wasn't easy to identify any homeless people these days. As part of the whole process of "synthetic selection," there was a tremendous increase in the number of homeless people on the streets. People who knew that they had a limited time to spend as human beings began to see it as an unnecessary effort to establish high standards by which they could live comfortably. You could now see a homeless person on each corner. Of course, this made it very difficult for Ari to find the person he was looking for. All he could do was to go out on the streets and observe the movements of the homeless. But there was a problem with this method; all the homeless people looked similar in their clothes, manner and demeanour. After using this method for a while, Ari realised that he had followed the same man more than once and so he came up with a solution.

He secretly took photographs of homeless people he was watching and wrote descriptive notes about them. Ari developed another method that would make it easier for him to remember the homeless people he saw and make his work fun. He gave them the names of the characters from the movies he'd seen, according to the things they had in common. Gradually a catalogue of homeless people began to form in his hands. He shared them with Lil, who could understand Ari's preoccupation, although she found it unhealthy. Of course, he found it great fun. "When I first met him, he was shooting videos of squirrels. This is no different from that," she thought.

Ari found a homeless person on one of the streets again and began watching him. After watching him for a while, with the help of the photos on his phone he was convinced that he wasn't one of the people he had seen before and he took a picture of the guy without him noticing. He took out the small notebook in his jacket pocket and started taking notes: "1. Picture: C-3PO". He chuckled to himself while noting the name he found. "I'm getting better at this," he murmured to himself. As a result of his practices up to this time, the time he took to find names for homeless people he was watching had gotten shorter. He did not, however, ignore the fact that the man's protruding eyes, confused face and C-3PO-like movements made his job easier.

After watching the man for about forty-five minutes, he began to lose interest. The man did not do much except for making a few minor movements. Ari was starting to make jokes to himself out of boredom. "What if I jumped in front of a passing car?" he thought, laughing. Ari was looking for some sort of perfection in the movements of the homeless people he was watching. Or an unusual reaction to a dangerous incident occurring around them.

When he came up with that idea, he knew that he had no choice even though he disagreed with himself, saying, "There is a good chance that he might deliberately be refraining from making flawless moves to avoid being noticed." But since they were unaware that they were being watched, he thought they would give a signal in one of their actions. He got excited as C-3PO got up. He was thinking of following him to his destination. Just as the man started walking, a large man in a suit staring intently at the phone in his hand hit the homeless man and took the relationship he had with the ground he'd just been sitting on one step further. Ari shook his head and said, "No, this man cannot have anything to do with the man I saw. Yes, the guy was very big, and yes, the car I saw in the previous incident was a smaller model, but it's clear that there's a very obvious difference."

He decided to go to the restaurant just down the street for something to eat before continuing. He thought it was a one-song destination. He took his earbuds out of his pocket. He played the song "Fleet Foxes-Fool's Errand" on his phone and started walking.

"Blind love couldn't win
As the facts all came in
But I know I'll again chase after wind
What have I got if not a thought?
I knew, oh I knew
I knew
It was a fool's errand
Waiting for a sign
But I can't leave until the sight comes to mind
A fool's errand…"

The song was coming to an end as Ari had almost reached his destination. He had ten to fifteen steps to the restaurant he was going to. He was about to put his earbuds into his pocket, someone approached him from behind and touched his arm.

"Hi, I'm Tom," said a man he had never seen before in his life.

Ari answered with suspicion in his face: "Do we know each other?"

"I don't think so," Tom said. He gave a reassuring smile. "You don't have to be afraid. I thought maybe it would be more beneficial for us to work together, since we're both looking for the same thing."

"What do you think I'm looking for?" Ari asked. Tom took out his phone and showed it to Ari, making it very clear that he did not want to prolong this uncertainty. Ari was shocked by what he saw. This was the footage of the incident, which he himself had witnessed and had been preoccupied with since he saw it. He had always asked himself the same question: Didn't any cameras record what I saw? He'd asked at all the stores on the street one by one to see if any of them had recorded the scene of the incident but couldn't get anywhere. And now, here was the footage in front of him in a way and at a time he least expected it.

"Where did you get this?" Ari asked curiously and suspiciously. "And how did you learn that I was after this?"

Zach said, "You appear in the recording. We did some research to find out who you were. We've been following you ever since."

"What do you want from me? You have methods that are solid enough to find these, but you still need the help of a man like me who walks around the street watching all the homeless people one by one?" Ari asked.

"Our methods are solid, but we have lack of resources," Tom said.

Ari got it then. They needed him for his money. In his mind, he calculated the odds of getting himself into trouble or finding what he was looking for. Or it could be both. He could find what he was looking for, but he could also get himself into trouble. But he was very curious about what he'd seen. He told the man who looked almost the same age as himself, "You keep saying 'we'. Who is this 'we'?" he asked.

"Do you know about 'Free Will'?" Tom asked.

"Of course. I've heard a lot about them on TV and online. Are you one of them?" said Ari.

"I may or may not be one of them, maybe I just owe them a favour. Does it matter to you? I can put you in touch with them. They can help you find what you're looking for."

"Or maybe I'll help them. Seeing as they're willing to expose themselves to get in touch with me."

Together, Ari and Tom used public transport to get to some of the more secluded areas of the city. Tom said, "Look, mate, I couldn't have blindfolded you in the middle of the city centre, which would have drawn a lot of unwanted attention as if I was kidnapping you or something. There are cameras everywhere. But I regret to say that you will have to be blindfolded for the rest of our journey."

"That's okay. That might be better for both sides," Ari replied. "But first I have to call my girlfriend. We were supposed to meet. If I don't show up without telling her, she'll worry herself to death. I don't think she'll take it any better now, though," he continued as he pulled out his phone.

Tom said, "Sure, man. Whatever you want."

Lil answered the phone.

"How are you, love?" Ari said.

"Just working, honey. We're a little busy today. How are you?" Lil replied.

"I'm fine. Today, while I was sitting in a cafe, I overheard the people at the table behind me. Some guy was saying he had a lot of records. I know we were going to get together, and you know there's not much to stop me from seeing you. But can you believe that I encountered a man who has records in this day and age? I asked him if he ever thought about selling some of them. He said he didn't think there was anyone left who'd value them as much as he did. And I convinced him he was wrong, as you can imagine."

"I can, yes. I see. As you said, it was a nice surprise that you came across something like this at this time. Can you call me when you're done? There are things I want to talk to you about."

"Of course, love. I'm sorry. I'd love to listen right now. But..."

"You don't need to apologise. I understand your excitement. Just call me when you're done. Love you."

"Love you too. I'll call you. See you later."

When Ari hung up, Tom had a sly smile on his face. "That was very good, mate. That's why you were silent all the way here. You were thinking about your lie," he teased Ari. "Not only did you listen in on my conversation with my girlfriend, but you're also commenting on it? Do these things make you cool in the resistance? If so, I suggest you revisit the opinion that you are with the good guys," Ari said.

Tom was left defenceless. He could only say, "I never said I was one of them."

"As you like," Ari replied. Then he turned his head, thinking that he'd be blindfolded at that moment. "Better if we do that in the car. For both sides," said Tom pointing at the car that was parked a little further ahead.

When Ari woke up, he instinctively scanned his surroundings. While he was doing this, he heard the door closing after the person who took off his blindfold and turned around. After a quick scan of the remaining part of the room this time, he saw that a man in his fifties sat across from him when he turned to the side that he had not yet viewed. The room where they were alone was very bright and tastefully designed. It wasn't exactly what Ari expected. The man who understood this from Ari's reactions said, "Why are you surprised? Did you expect a dark and makeshift place? Come on, lad. Isn't that a bit of a cliché?" he joked, laughing. Ari continued to look at the man without much reaction.

Zimo said, "Sorry, I must introduce myself and apologise first. I'm Zimo. And I'm sorry that we had to put you in a difficult situation by blindfolding you on your way here. Really. But I think you can understand that we don't have much choice," he said.

Ari said, "It's very nice of you to forgive yourself for me. You saved me the trouble."

"That's not what I meant. But anyway, I can understand how you feel right now. I'm experienced enough to know that it is not possible to lighten the mood in the short term because of the start we made."

"Why? Have you brought many blindfolded people here before? Did they all come willingly like me, or did you force anyone?"

"Look, young man, I don't know why you have such thoughts about us, but you shouldn't believe everything you see in the media."

"I didn't agree to come blindfolded here to listen to your advice. Whether I sympathise with you or not is not relevant to the reason I'm here. The person who says his name is Tom said you could help me find what I'm looking for."

"Well, have it your way. Let's cut right to the chase. Yes. We can find what we're looking for. We can find out who the man in the footage is. But for that we need someone who can finance us."

"I am surprised. When I saw this cool room, I thought you were well off."

"We have many comrades from every profession, young man. There wasn't a single penny spent on the construction of what you see here. It is our comrades who brought the materials and set up these rooms. We don't use money among each other. Our exchange is based on hope."

"You used hope and exchange in the same sentence, and you expect me to be impressed?"

"It's clear that you don't like us and that you only here to find what you're looking for. And we didn't really invite you here for your moral support, but because we think that we must join forces to get what we want. So I will ignore your sarcastic attitude."

"Yeah, whatever you want, great. How do we identify the woman in the video?"

"Actually, the woman you've witnessed has disappeared without a trace. But we also have images of a man with similar abilities. Of course we think they are connected."

Zimo handed his phone to Ari and showed him the footage of the man who saved the man who jumped from a high-rise building to what would have been his death. Watching the footage, Ari was shocked. His theory that there was more than one person with special abilities and that they were there to look after humanity could actually be true. His heart began to beat with excitement.

"We have an inside guy, and he told us that they couldn't locate the woman, but that he could get us information about this man's location. But we don't have the kind of money he's asking for," said Zimo.

Ari said, "So this was all based on what some guy said? Who's he anyway? Why do you trust him?"

"I can't tell you who our man is, son, because I don't trust you either. I can only say that he is one of the few people who can access this information. And when the process is complete, he doesn't want to become a robot. You know we all have to rebuild our lives in a whole new world. And what this man wants is to build a comfortable life for himself and his family."

"It doesn't make a lot of sense to me. I don't think they'll fail to notice someone on such an important mission leaking information of this nature. How can we trust this man and the accuracy of the information he can deliver to us?"

"He said that his son could be our guest until we can confirm the information he'll provide. When we are sure, we'll send him the money along with his son."

"What? Who would do such a thing? Nonsense."

"He knows we won't hurt his son. And he thinks he'll be fired soon. He just wants to get the money and go somewhere to start a new life."

"How old is the governor's son?"

"Twenty. You think we'd get little kids involved in something like this? Who do you think we are?"

"Is this your whole offer? Is there anything else you should say?"

"Excuse me?"

"If there is nothing else, I will consider your offer and let you know my decision. Now could you please take me back to where you found me?"

"You're not very talkative, are you? Actually, I like your focus. So be it. Tom will tell you how to contact us. Good evening, lad. Thank you for your patience."

"Thank you. Good evening."

Until he could get out of the blindfold, Ari was trying to think of the consequences of what he could do. But this had developed so unexpectedly that he was having trouble collecting his thoughts. He didn't trust or sympathise with these guys. He believed that instead of meeting with the government on a common ground and discussing solutions, they were trying to close their ranks and to gain an upper hand by deepening the gap. But at this point, was that something he had to think about? The man he saw could be someone who could change everything. So how could the revamped government and police organisation that became part of the technology itself, miss such a thing? It didn't make any sense to him at all. But he had questions with too-complex answers, and it was more than he could handle today. All he cared about was going home to eat and collect his thoughts. And of course to talk to Lil. Should he tell her about all this? She could get very worried about him. The idea of not saying anything at least until he made a decision looked more sensible.

***

Lil had been looking after her grandmother all night who could barely sleep from sickness and groaning. She was looking at her with compassion, sadness and fear, as she realised the cloth on her forehead might have gotten warm, so she dipped it into her bucket of water and put it back on her forehead. She was getting sick very often now. Lil couldn't imagine how her grandmother felt knowing how hard the world was on her even in her own young body. Seeing her grandmother in this state hit her in the face with the reality she didn't even want to think about but knew was inevitable.

Lil was crying quietly. She was praying to God: "Please, God, let my grandmother live a long life. And don't make her miserable. Give her strength, the will to live, and make it easy for her. Please, God. I don't know what I'd do without her." The vibrations of the phone, which she'd put on silent in order not to disturb her grandmother, interrupted her prayers. It was Ari. As she was quietly trying to leave the room with her phone, she tried to suppress her crying so as not to upset Ari. After leaving the room and closing the door slowly, she took one last deep breath and answered the phone.

"Ari, how are you, dear? Did you find any nice records?" she asked.

"I'm fine, darling. I didn't find much of anything. I don't think his music taste matches mine. What have you been up to?" Ari replied.

"My grandmother got sick. She gets sick very often, nowadays, Ari."

"Are you crying?"

"I was upset. It makes me so sad to see her like this."

"Please don't cry. Don't focus on the bad. I'll be right over."

"That'd be great. I really need you."

Ari got to her place as quickly as possible. His dilemma about whether or not to tell her what happened today ended when he heard her cry. He wasn't going to tell her. He didn't want to worry her; she was already worried enough for her grandmother. He thought it would be best for her not to know anything for now. Ari couldn't help but think about everything that had happened while he was sitting in the living room. It was Lil coming from the kitchen with a tray of tea and cookies in her hand that broke his chain of thoughts.

"So happy you're here," Lil said.

"So am I. What exactly is wrong with Grandma? What do the doctors say?" Ari asked.

"She doesn't have a specific disease. Doctors say all the usual stuff. That every breath we take and everything we eat is poisoning us. They say her body is no longer able to handle this struggle. In fact, it's a miracle she's even reached this age. Despite everything she's been through all her life."

"So is there any change in her opinions about the idea of moving into a new body? Did she make a decision?"

"No."

"I think you should sit down and have a serious talk about it without further delay."

"Yes. I'm afraid we should... Can we talk about something else? What have you been up to? You look very tired."

"I went to look at the records but didn't find anything. I was hopeful when I heard him boast like that. And during the time I spent with the him at his place, I saw that he was a really rude person which wouldn't really be expected from someone interested in records. Then I went and saw the records he listens to, I figured it out. And you should have seen him listen, Lil. He seemed to be fighting, not listening to music."

"You shouldn't go so recklessly to the homes of people you don't know. The world we live in is already extremely strange and hostile. It's too risky to go to strangers' homes on top of all that. What if something bad happened to you?"

"Don't worry about me. Besides, if we didn't give strangers a chance, we'd never have met each other. My life wouldn't be a life worth knowing anyway."

"Neither would mine. I love you so much."

She hugged him. Holding him felt like breathing on a high plateau with plenty of oxygen and air. Every time she hugged him, she remembered the mountain trip she took with her parents when she was little. Every time she hugged Ari, she felt as if she breathed that clean, soft air that filled her lungs as soon as she got out of the car. While her arms were still wrapped around him, with a peaceful smile on her face and her eyes closed, she took a momentary break from this oxygen storage and opened her eyes. "Ari, can you please tell me that you understand what I mean and that you will be more careful next time?" she asked. After she got, "Yes, love, I understand. And I'll be more careful next time," as an answer from him, she closed her eyes again, leaving herself to the freshness of his embrace, which gave her the sensation of carrying the fresh air from her childhood in a fishbowl. She closed her eyes again to feel that freshness better.

Meanwhile, Ari was thinking what his girlfriend – who was so worried about a lie as simple as he had told – would feel if he told her what had really happened today. Lying to her made him very uneasy. But the possibility of this being something that could change everything made him even more impatient. Moreover, the last remaining family member of the woman he loved seemed to be nearing the end of her life. He could reach something that could save even their grandmother. Now his decision was clear. He was going to find that man at any cost.

1 JULY 2035

Although Ari had no sympathy for and no trust of them, he felt compelled to act with the Free Will. If what they said was true, he would finally be able to find the people he had been looking for everywhere. What didn't make sense to him was that the son of the man who was going to provide information to the resistance would remain in the headquarters of the resistance until it was confirmed that the information received was worth the money. To him, that was no different than keeping a hostage. And he didn't want to be a part of such a hostage situation. He was thinking about how he could get himself to be part of it. However, one question he kept asking himself since last night was how a father could leave his son in hostage like that. Yes, his son was a twenty-year-old adult, but the fact that someone could leave his son hostage as part of a bargain, and that he himself was now involved in the deal, really gave Ari the creeps. Of course, perhaps Zimo had lied to him. He had to be sure about that. He also had to think of a way to hold the ropes from beginning to end because he had no trust in this group that called themselves Free Will. But on the other hand, he wanted to have as little contact as possible with this group. He suspected that things could eventually get to a point that Lil would get involved. They had been watching him for a while, considering they were aware of his research on the homeless woman.

And the thing is, the longer it took, the more he had to lie to his girlfriend. This was one of the things that most disturbed his conscience. It was for her own good, but he would still have to tell so many big lies to her to hide something so significant from her. After a long pondering of all this, the sun was almost up when Ari had planned the final version of his response to the resistance in his mind. He dialled the contact number given to him. Judging from Tom's quick response, they'd been waiting for this call for a while.

Tom said, "Hi buddy. We've been waiting for you to call. Have made up your mind?"

"Yeah, I have, but I have some conditions," Ari said.

"Sure, having the kind of wealth you do gives you certain rights. I see."

"First of all, I have to be sure that it was your inside man's idea for you to keep his son until the truth of the info is confirmed. I want proof of that. If you can prove it to me, I will stay with the kid as long as he stays with you. He will always be with me. And, of course, I want to hand over the money to him, not to you, when you send him to his father after this work is done. If everything goes well and we identify the person we're looking for, I will actively take part in the actions that follow in order to confirm this."

"Is that all? Since you have a lot of money, don't you want to add some more to the deal and buy Free Will and just manage it your own way?"

Ari hung up. He felt he was already tired of talking to the sarcastic and arrogant men who thought they were saving the world with every move they made. He got depressed when he realised that if his conditions were accepted, he had to stay at the headquarters of the resistance for several days. But he had to make sure the kid was okay. Of course there was also Lil. He didn't know how he'd explain his absence to her. Only about fifteen minutes later, Ari's phone began ringing. It was Tom. It was surprising to Ari to get a response to his conditions so quickly. He expected at least a late response as a demonstration of their power and to show that they held the ropes, and thought they demanded changes in his terms. But with his phone ringing so fast, his first theory was dead.

"These guys aren't messing around," he said to himself, then answered the phone. "Your terms have been accepted," Tom said as soon as he picked up. "We'll get back in touch with you," he continued.

"Okay," Ari replied, and hung up the phone. He had been surprised that Tom had kept the conversation so short this time since he had used twice the number of sentences needed every time they'd talked because of his arrogance.

3 JULY 2035

Lil was startled by the knock at the door. Her eyes suddenly filled with tears as she immediately guessed who it was. But knowing that this was much more difficult for her grandmother, she wiped the excess tears in her eyes and then opened the door by pressing the automat. And then she ran in to her grandmother. Trying not to cry, "They're here. You're all right, yeah? They'll only take five minutes, then they'll leave right away," she said trying to prepare her grandmother. Judi, wanting to encourage her granddaughter, said very calmly, "We've done this a thousand times now, baby, I don't see why you're still so anxious. Look at the bright side, at least I don't have to go to the police station and wait in line like you do. I can easily do it from where I lay in my house." She smiled and stroked her granddaughter's cheek, "Now go and open the door. They've been knocking for a while. We don't want their hands to go numb since we'll need them to be very delicate, right?" and she sent her granddaughter to the door.

Lil opened the door, "Sorry, I had to get my grandma ready," she said and welcomed the nurse. Stepping in with her usual smiling face, Nurse Yun nodded to indicate that she understood the situation. Yun was a very beautiful woman aged between thirty and thirty-five, with blonde hair and blue eyes. She'd volunteered for this job immediately after the government decided that they'd draw blood from the elderly who could not go to the station, at their homes. The government wanted to make this as easy as possible for them, knowing that it could turn into a very difficult practice for the elderly. For this reason, human nurses were assigned to provide a more comfortable environment for the elderly who might feel uncomfortable seeing superhumans in their homes.

They quickly moved over to Judi. As soon as Judi saw Yun entering the room, she smiled. "My favourite nurse is here," she said. Yun responded with a smile and said, "Hello." She opened her bag with syringes and took one out. As always, she helped Judi fill her diary with great care and kindness. After she was done and while she was gathering her supplies, Judi called her to her side, saying, "Come here, I'll give you a kiss." After giving her a hug and a kiss, she said," You have no idea how easy you make it for me. Thank you very much, my kind-hearted girl. If I had a grandson, I'd have you as his bride. Have I told you that before?" she said jokingly.

"Yes, you say it every time I come here. And you make it easy for me too. Thank you," Yun replied. "Sometimes things can get very difficult."

"Would you like some tea or coffee?" Judi asked Yun. Lil can get us some right away," she added. "Thank you very much, but I still have a lot of people to visit and I have to finish it all by the time given me," the young woman said as she refused kindly.

"You say that every time," Judi insisted.

"Because usually my schedule is exactly the same," said Yun. "Really, I do thank you very much." She insisted on leaving as Judi sadly accepted. Lil graciously showed the nurse out. Then she looked at her watch. She'd have to go to the police station and fill her diary as soon as her aunt arrived. Since she never wanted to see her aunt, she began to get ready so she could be ready to leave right away when she arrived. She was annoyed that she had to see her aunt every day because she couldn't leave her grandmother alone since she had become more fragile and was almost constantly sick. Her aunt came to their place to take care of her grandmother while she was out.

As she was getting ready, she thought of Ari. Since the second week of their meeting, he had been coming to the police station with her every weekend without fail to try to make the situation more bearable by being there with her. She was grateful to him for that. Because every time she went, and she saw that many people were subjected to this treatment with their children, spouses and parents, her eyes filled with tears and she couldn't get over it for a few hours. She knew that Ari was as affected with all that as much as she was, but it was a great sacrifice on his part that he persistently came just for her and spent another day at the police station after he'd already been for himself. She had repeatedly told him that he didn't have to, but he never gave up. "What's the point of being together if we're not going to make each other's lives easier, if you're going to be alone in such an environment?" he'd told her.

As Lil finished getting ready, the doorbell rang. She opened the door with a suspicious face because she didn't know if it was Ari or her aunt. When she saw that it was Ari, her suspicion was replaced by a big smile of happiness. She held him tightly as soon as she opened the door. It had only been a few minutes since they had been wrapped around each other's arms and the doorbell rang again. It wasn't suspicion that appeared on Lil's face this time, as it was clear who was coming, but she just felt unhappy. "I know we need to leave right away, but can I get a few minutes just to say hi to Granny and see how she is?" Ari asked.

Lil said, "Sure, but please do it quickly, okay? I don't want you to be exposed to my aunt either."

Ari answered, "You know that everything about you has a place in my life. I'm not going to repeat that, but whatever you want," he said, and started to move quickly into Judi's room. As soon as Ari entered the room with a smile on his face, Judi also started smiling.

"Welcome. My grandson," Judi said.

"If only you knew how happy you made me by embracing me like this. How are you feeling today?" he replied.

Ari kissed Judi's cheek and sat down next to her on the bed. "It's a great sacrifice you make to accompany Lil to fill out her diary every time. Don't tell her I told you, she doesn't want to embarrass you, but she told me that you were also affected greatly by the environment and often had tears in your eyes," said Judi.

"I'm not ashamed. I'm surprised Lil thinks that I am. If I ever get to a point where I see those people in that environment and not get upset, then I will be ashamed."

"You're a really well-raised child, you know that, right? I'm glad Lil chose you. You are a very kind young man."

"Trying to be."

Judi gestured to get close to Ari and kissed him in the head, as Lil's aunt Mili walked in with the usual unhappy look on her face. As soon as she entered, she started making noises to make them aware that she was in the room. Ari was now familiar with her behaviour, having listened to Lil's stories as well as experiencing his own encounters with her. He knew that the noises meant, "I'm here now, so you must leave." In the few times they met each other, she did not communicate with him in any way, but only responded with small murmurs to what he said. She seemed to be trying to show Ari without doubt that she didn't like him with his looks and gestures, and even to have him accept it. Ari on the other hand didn't care much about Mili's attitude towards him. He was more upset by fact that she treated Lil the same way and sometimes even worse than she did him. Although he had seen her only a few times and for very short periods of time, he had repeatedly witnessed her talking to Lil in a very rude manner. He could not make any sense of her attitude towards her niece who had lost her family.

And Lil didn't answer a word to her and acted like she didn't hear her. Even though Ari knew that she didn't like him or her own niece, he still tried to communicate with her very kindly because after all she was his girlfriend's aunt. He turned towards Mili, smiled and said, "Hello." However, Mili as usual, did not communicate verbally with himself and instead reluctantly responded with nod. Judi drew Ari closer to her and said, "Thank you, son. It's nice of you to come here and say hi to me, but this is the part where you leave me here and run away to continue your life." She smiled at him as she spoke.

Ari said, loud enough for Mili to hear, "We should go now. You know, Lil and I are going to the police station. I'll stop by again," and went to the door.

"All right, son," said Judi. Mili's already here. I'll see you later," and waved him out. The young man responded by saying, "See you later," and headed for the door. Smiling as he passed her, he reached his hand out to Mili and said, "Have a nice day." Mili answered with a forced smile, shaking the young man's hand with the tip of hers. And the young man left the room, keeping a smile on his face.

When Lil and Ari walked into the station, it was full of people as usual. Although the weekends were much more crowded, Lil had to go then because she worked. Seeing the crowd inside, they looked at each other with frustration. They took a few steps inside and came to the automat where they would get their line number. The number they were given was 622. When they looked at the display showing the numbers of those who were currently in process, they saw that 528 was up. In contrast to the practice for the elderly in their homes, the nurses who moved to their robotic bodies drew blood at the station so and things were moving much faster. But again, the numbers they saw showed that they had to be there for at least three quarters of an hour to an hour.

At Ari's suggestion, they decided to sit on the steps outside the station until their number was up. Ari put his left arm over Lil's shoulder. They sat quietly for a while to overcome the impact of the place, which was clearly designed to put pressure on people who were still refusing to move on. To dispel the depressing mood, Ari said, "Just going to say this for the record. Judi told me today that you told her that I occasionally get teared up here, but that I shouldn't tell you because you think I might be ashamed of it. I said that I was surprised, because I'm not ashamed of being moved to tears in such an environment. On the contrary, I would be embarrassed if I didn't feel anything, little lady." He smiled at her as he spoke.

Lil said, laughing, "So the two people I trust most in my life share my secrets about them behind my back? And they both tell me that I am their favourite person in the world almost every day." And the two of them got over the mood and began teasing each other sweetly:

"What my grandma has with you is just a force of habit, love, and one day, of course, you will admit that she loves me more and that I deserve it," Ari said.

"Yes. She's very likely to be attracted to your humility and choose you over me. Did I ever tell you that this is what attracts me to you the most?"

"What you've told me was that you've never been able to decide which of the many adorable traits I have attracts you the most and that you've been sleepless at night just to find the answer to that question."

"What made me lose sleep was the awareness that old song you made me listen created in me. It's a song you love so much, you know by Kasabian that goes, 'You're in love with a psycho and there's nothing you can do about it.'"

"Do you realise how close you are to art because of me? Look, you started singing in the middle of the street. Now can you deny how inspiring I am?"

162

"Yes, we are all aware that suffering is the biggest inspiration for art."

"Yes, my little one. Looking at the sun with naked eyes also causes suffering. I can understand you. Continue to express your admiration for me."

This sweet fight with each other suddenly stopped when they noticed a mother walking towards the centre with her crying daughter. The girl looked between eight and ten years old, and obviously she was still not used to it, which was normal. Considering what they themselves felt like.

Lil's eyes filled with tears immediately, as she made a connection between herself and the little girl who was afraid of needles and giving blood. She buried her head in Ari's neck immediately. In the meantime, they began to hear their conversation as the little girl and her mother holding her hand and trying to calm her got closer.

The little girl told her mother, "Please, Mommy, please, let's not do it this time. Please. Maybe they won't notice. And we didn't do anything bad," she begged. Her mother, trying not to show her grief, dropped to her knees a few steps away from Lil and Ari and said, "Everybody knows you've not done anything bad, honey. They just want to make sure you're not sick, that's all," trying to calm her down.

"But I'm not sick. I don't have a fever, my nose isn't runny. You know that. You can tell them. You tell them 'My daughter is not sick,'" the little girl kept begging.

Her mother tried not to cry as she answered, "But we don't know that, honey. I'm not a doctor. We have to do this to make sure you're not sick," she said, trying to console her daughter.

Lil was crying silently, with her head buried in Ari's neck as they walked past them and entered the station. Ari, on the other hand, turned his head away to hide his full eyes from the mother and daughter coming towards them. As soon as they went through the door, Ari hugged Lil. "Honey, please don't cry. And even though her mother was just trying to console the little girl, she's still right. In this way, diseases are prevented too. The hardship she may suffer now, may prevent further bad things from happening to her later," he said.

"Why are *you* crying then?" Lil responded.

"I'm crying because you are. I should have been the one to make you cry. You should have been crying because you were feeling helpless to keep me," Ari said trying to joke. Now there was a smile on her lips curved by crying.

When they looked at the numbers on the sign outside the station, they found that there were only four people left before them. Every time they were surprised at the fact that so many people suddenly appeared in a city that normally seemed to be abandoned. Meanwhile, the mother and daughter went out the door because they also had decided to wait for their turn outside.

Since they'd been sitting in front of the door, plenty of people had entered the station before the mother and daughter. Lil knew there would at least be half an hour between their turns. So she turner to Ari, to get his blessing for what she was about to do, since he was waiting with her. Ari understood the sacrifice she wanted to make by putting her own difficulty aside, nodded to her with an admiring smile and kissed her on the cheek. Lil embraced him quickly and turned to the mother and said, "It's about to be our turn and we're so enjoying sitting on the stairs together in this beautiful weather. Wouldn't you want to take our turn?" she asked.

The mother had understood what the young woman was trying to do. "Thank you, you're very kind, but we can't accept that. We'll wait our turn," she replied.

Lil whispered into her ear, "Please. Accept it for your daughter. And you don't know my boyfriend, it's such a pleasure to wait here with him," she insisted.

The mother said with embarrassment and gratitude, "I'll accept it only for my daughter. She'll get worse the longer we wait. Thank you so much. It's hard to find people like you these days," she said. "You're very lucky," she said to Ari before going inside.

"I know," Ari said. And she is generous enough to make everyone see it," he continued. After the mother and daughter went in, Lil sat down next to Ari to continue to wait as she began to smile with the happiness of knowing that she had helped. Ari sat in an emotional mood thinking that the woman next to him turned his life into a dream, then turned to Lil and said, "I know you don't have the most perfect aunt in the world.

164

But you can't deny that your aunt also has her own incredible qualities." Predicting that a joke would come after that sentence passed the ball to her boyfriend so he could finish the joke, "For example?" she asked.

"It's admirable that she's able to show that she's smiling using so few muscles on her face. She may even hold a record on that," Ari said.

Lil laughed, "I think so. It is truly amazing that she uses any muscle at all to smile being the person she is," she replied.

8 JULY 2035

There was a great deal of unrest in Ari as he sat on the bed after leaving his backpack on the floor in the room the resistance had reserved for him at the headquarters. According his request, his room was right next to that of the mayor's son, Fin, who would stay here until they confirmed the information they'd receive. Of course, being involved with holding the mayor's son hostage, the way all this was done and with whom it was done, were all important issues that occupied his mind but his head and conscience were kept busy mostly by the fact that he was lying to his beloved Lil.

He'd told her that his teacher, who had taught him Wing-Chun for two years between the ages of seventeen and nineteen and returned to his hometown of China, had come to the neighbouring city for a conference and training seminar. He told her that he wanted to see his old trainer very much. She got excited for her boyfriend, who sounded very happy. "I'd love to come with you and meet your teacher, but Em is sick and won't be coming in for a few days, so I can't leave the cafe. Even if we can't meet face to face, will you tell him that I have heard a lot about him and thank him for his share in you being such a person?" she'd requested. Although Ari was very uncomfortable about having lied so many times to her since his first contact with the resistance, but he had to do it for her sake in the first place.

He hoped that this would be over as soon as possible and that he would find out the mysterious man who had caused all this. Of course, he also hoped that he'd be worth all this when they finally found him. Then he got a message on his phone. Lil wrote, "Honey, can you call me when you get there, please? I love you very much." He took a deep breath. He left his room to speak with Fin, who had come to the headquarters with him. As soon as he stepped out of his room, the first thing he saw was Tom, who was sitting in a sofa across from his and Fin's rooms playing with his phone. "Did they put you as a guard here

166

for the two people who came here of their own free will?" Ari asked sarcastically, feeling rather angry.

Tom said, "You shouldn't take everything so seriously. I'm not guarding anything, I'm just sitting here instead of sitting elsewhere. In the meantime, I'm just keeping an eye on our guest. That includes helping him if he needs anything. You are already rich enough to do anything you want."

"I won't even try to tell you that it's a crime to be rich," Ari said. "I want to see Fin."

He knocked on Fin's door several times. After hearing, "You can come in," from the inside, he entered. "Hi, Fin. I'm Ari," he said.

Fin said, "Hi. I know who you are. My father gave your name to Free Will."

"What do you mean?"

"After the incident, the security cameras on the street continued to be monitored. They saw that you witnessed the incident and continued to come to the same place in order to see something later. When my father contacted the resistance, they said they couldn't give him the money he wanted. My father mentioned that since you are so concerned about this you could provide the money."

"So I was followed and tagged by the government. I see."

"In this era, everyone is known for who they are and what they do, don't take it personally."

"So how can this resistance still operate?"

"They must be doing something right."

"Yeah, they must be. Anyway, I came here to see how you are. Did they treat you badly on your way here?"

"No," Fin said.

"Look, Fin, I don't approve of the agreement between your dad and the resistance. I agreed to be part of this business only with your father's and most importantly with *your* consent. And I myself insisted on being put up in the room next to you. If there's any slight mistreatment against you or if anything troubles you during your stay, I'm right next door."

"I came here of my own free will, as you said, not by kidnapping. My father and I made this suggestion. We know they won't do us any harm. All they want to do is find the guy, and it might make a difference for everyone to find him."

"I see... All right... Just remember what I said, I'll be in the next room."

When Ari left Fin's room, Tom was still right where he'd left him. "We are experienced enough to hurt a person without leaving a trace," he laughed mockingly when he saw Ari leaving the room. Ari ignored him, went into his room and closed the door. As soon as he closed door, the phone in Ari's room started ringing. It was Zimo. "The name we've been waiting for has arrived. First of all, to avoid a surprise, I'm going to send our guys to the house. If they say it's okay, we'll go talk to our guy in the evening," he said.

"Okay, I'm waiting to hear from you then," Ari replied.

After he hung up the phone, Ari began to feel great excitement and impatience. He hoped the results would be worth it. Now he would have to keep himself busy until the evening. The lies he'd had to tell Lil were haunting him. Now he would have to call her again and continue his lies. Having talked to Fin and made him feel that he was there for him seemed to decrease his shame a bit, making him find some strength talk to his girlfriend. Since he'd told her that he was leaving early in the morning, he looked at the time, trying to figure out when he might have arrived where he'd said he was going.

***

At lunchtime, Lil opened a container full of steamed broccoli, carrots, potatoes and a bit of brown rice, which she had prepared at home because she wanted to have a light meal. Just as she was about to take her first bite, she had to put down her fork to answer the phone. When she looked at the screen, she was happy to see a photo of her boyfriend. "I guess he arrived," she thought before answering the phone.

"Honey, did you get there?" Lil said.

"Yes. I even left my stuff in my room. What are you doing?" he replied.

"I'm eating. Have you eaten?"

"I have. Don't worry. How's your grandmother?"

"This time her sickness lasted even longer than before. Doctors are afraid it'll turn into pneumonia. We try to be as careful as possible."

"Don't worry, she'll get better. She's a very strong woman."

"I really hope she gets better soon."

"I have to go now, love. I just called so you wouldn't worry. Love you."

"Love you too."

After taking a few bites, Lil decided to watch another video of Ari's family to accompany her meal, knowing that the cafe would be quiet for a while. After thinking about which one to watch for a short time, she picked one and when she clicked on the video and saw Ari's mother appear on the screen, her eyes filled with a melancholy mixed with love and longing. Because even though she'd never met her in person, she felt so familiar with her from the videos she'd watched. She put the phone on the counter and started eating and watching the video: "Life is like a symphony, son. Every melody you hear is a sign that you'll hear it again in the sequel. You might hear it slower, faster, maybe in lower or higher pitch, but the essence of the melody you hear will be the same. Life is exactly the same. What you do definitely comes back to you in the course of your life. And if you listen to life carefully, you will know when a melody is played back to you and know that it is the same melody you've heard before, even if it manifests differently. That melody is your work.

"Every good or evil you do will travel through all the people in the world who share the same essence, even though their languages or colours are different, and return to you, where it started. The geometric shapes of the planets, including the planet we live on, and their rotations around themselves are how the creator clearly shows us the clue as to the functioning of the universe. But unfortunately, we all put even more effort than the universe itself to ignore that.

"You don't ignore it, son. If you do, one day when you have children and your whole life consists of what they think about you or how they treat you, you'll see that sadly, your child will knowingly or unknowingly follow the order you started in the beginning. You can be sure that even if you manage to avoid every fuse you've ever ignited coming back to you, you will not be able to avoid hearing it when your child gives it back to you.

"Live with this knowledge as you create your life's symphony, my boy. Know that the melodies you create will come back to you in one way or another. Avoid starting melodies that will break your heart, melodies you won't enjoy hearing back. Make your life such a beautiful melody so that even the most opposing sounds involved in the melody find themselves in harmony and reveal each other's beauty. And most importantly, remember that if you're in an orchestra of musical instruments that only make the same sounds as you, you will disappear over time.

"Lastly, we would like to thank you, for growing up as a beautiful melody that makes every ear that hears it go into a dream, making us believe that we have lived our lives in such a way as to have created the most beautiful symphony ever."

***

Ari had cut his talk with his girlfriend short so he wouldn't have to lie any more, then he waited for the evening lying on his bed and looking at the ceiling of his room. There was a knock on his door and when he opened the door he saw someone in his thirties standing there, whom he had never seen before, and who told him that the call he'd been waiting for had come and that he should get ready. They were setting out to meet the man they had been pursuing for a long time. Ari wanted to stop by Fin one last time before he left. After knocking on the door a couple of times, Fin's voice invited him in. When he entered the room Fin was watching TV. He was waiting for this evening's broadcast with Galileo and a randomly chosen participant. The chat hadn't started yet. The introductory video about the life of the participant was on.

Ari said, "I'm going out to meet our guy. Tom's gonna stay here with you. If you need something, you can tell him. If you need to contact me, tell him. I'll be right back as soon as we're done."

Fin snapped at him and said, "Your attitude is starting to annoy me. I agreed to come here. I decided to take the necessary risk. And I've not yet been treated badly. Go and do what you have to do. But don't try to act all heroic to me."

Ari turned around and walked to the door without saying anything. As he opened the door, Fin said, "Sorry. I know you mean well. But it's all fine. I'm a grown man too. We don't just have to pretend like there's something wrong." And he asked Ari for forgiveness. Ari didn't say anything and but just gestured with his head that everything was fine and left the room.

As Ari left the building, the chatting section of the broadcast had started. Unlike her predecessors, Gal, who looked like a model with her long, wavy black hair and green eyes, was more understanding and collected because she wanted it to be a useful conversation both for her and everyone watching.

"I was actually very firmly against this 'synthetic selection' and mind transfer procedures that you've started, until only a few days ago. And I've actually applied to the show to give you a piece of my mind. But a few days ago I caught my boyfriend cheating on me with my best friend. In our house. And I'm not ashamed to say that. They're the ones who should be ashamed. As a result of these events, my opinions have changed completely. I am only a few sentences away from being part of synthetic selection and I am sure that there are millions of people who feel like me watching us now. Now I want to ask you: What are you promising us?" Gal asked.

"Before I answer that, I want to ask you this. How much do you know about the changes in the relationships between people who have completed their mind transfers?" Galileo said.

"I think it's enough to say that I've spent almost all of my last few days researching these issues online."

"In other words, you have learned that the relationship criteria of people who have mind transfer go beyond the principles of pleasure and impulses, and that many people become lovers with their best friends after the transfer. Criteria that are now important in relationships are things like mental features, points of view, their ability to understand each other. And this is a much stronger bond. So I think it wouldn't be wrong for me to say that there will be fewer heartbreaks in your future. Human relations are very superficial in their current state. I'm sure millions of people couldn't believe what they heard when they found out you've been cheated on. You have the physical properties of a supermodel. And even that didn't prevent someone from choosing sexual pleasure that would last only minutes over you."

"It seems that way."

"People are attracted to beautiful people like you, and their hormones, impulses and pleasures push them so hard that they will do anything to reach beautiful people like you. They lie, pretend to be someone they're not, and put aside moral values to attain the possibilities that they think will bring them closer to you. But when you meet someone, if all you see is their mind, then everything is different. That's exactly what's happening right now. The minds of people who have completed mind transfers are set free. Everyone's appearance and the effect they have on people are the same. Now people are really trying to find their soul mates. They don't slide their gaze to the bodies of their partner and blind their own eyes when they see something that they don't like in the souls that are found in the bodies they enjoy. The result of my research on humanity is that 95% of men do everything they do to build their lives in a way that will help them reach beautiful women. Think of it like this, if we could give any man two choices between having a successful life never having a relationship with any woman, and a life full of failures, with the most beautiful woman in the world, which one do you think they'd choose?"

"So you're claiming that beautiful women are the reason why the world is like this?"

"No. On the contrary, I'm saying it's a shame that humanity has been too primitive to perceive what true beauty means."

"And will synthetic selection allow us to perceive true beauty?"

"That and much more. Humanity has become a prisoner of physical pleasures so much so that they only think about the extent every person they meet can give them those pleasures. People began to live their lives according to that criteria. Imagine if all the people in the world connected their minds with the help of the internet and kept in touch. That humanity had a collective mind. Imagine if everyone were in equal distance of each other and had equal value. That everyone had a common quest to reach the deepest of beauty, love, value. Since everyone would have the perspective of the brightest minds in the world, think about what we could achieve in terms of finding the most beautiful and the best of everything."

"Those watching at home will probably think this is all a show and so would I. But I can tell you that you've completely convinced me with everything you've said. I've always made more time for handsome men in my life. I have to admit that my beauty makes my life a lot more fun. But I'm ready to give all that up for what you say. It is obvious that I'm not at a great place in my life right now anyway."

***

The car stopped when Ari and Zimo arrived across the street from the house of the man they were looking for. Before Ari got out of the car, he wanted to clarify a few things that were weighing heavy on his conscience: "We'll kindly knock on the door and tell him that we've seen his talents and that we want to talk to him. If he doesn't answer the door, we're not going to force our way in by any means, and we're going to keep trying our luck until we can convince him to talk to us. And you said the man's old parents were also home; we're not going to get them involved them in any way. Otherwise, you'll get nothing from me," he said.

"We're not a gang, lad," Zimo said. I've told you that before. All we want is to find out who this man is and share it with people. Believe it or not, our whole goal is to help people as well," he said.

"I take that as a promise."

"You can take it any way you like. Because we care about people just as much as you do."

Meanwhile, one of the men Zimo called 'our guys' came and tapped on the window. "The area looks calm," he told Zimo, who had opened his window.

"We're coming," Zimo nodded. "The moment has come," he said smiling to Ari. When Ari and Zimo knocked on the door, both their hearts were beating with excitement. They heard the voice of an adult male inside. Since it wasn't the voice of an old man, knowing that they were talking to the man they'd been looking for made their hearts beat faster. "Who is it?" the voice asked. They were stunned with the excitement of talking to the him and not knowing how to get to the subject. The man looked through the peephole and asked, "Who are you?" for the second time.

Ari decided that there was no easy way to get to it, "Well. We have seen what you can do, and we want to talk to you about it. We're just curious, we don't mean anything bad," he replied. This time, there was a silence due to the confusion of the man inside.

This silent wait continued for a while, and it ended with the sound made by the key turning in the door lock. Ari and Zimo had forgotten to breathe in their excitement. When the door opened, they were in for a different kind of surprise. The man in front of them was different from what they had seen in the video. "Come in," he said with a stern expression on his face. He led Ari and Zimo into the living room. In a low tone he added, "Speak in a low voice; my parents are in their room. I locked their doors so they wouldn't be involved in this conversation. I suggest you respect that, or the results will not be very good."

Ari and Zimo nodded. They sat on the chairs across from each other and for a while just looked at each other. Ari and Zimo were astonished by this man, who looked quite ordinary. The man began to speak in a distant manner: "How did you find me?" he said.

"We've seen the videos."

"The person you saw was a different person," the man said.

Zimo said, "You know what they say, nothing springs into existence out of nothingness and nothing just disappears. Especially at this time. It is not easy to disappear."

"What do you want from me?" the man asked.

"The things you can do are incredible. And you shouldn't keep it from people while you can do all that," said Ari.

The man said, "Look, you having found me means that your arms are very long; I let you in to protect my family and I'm still talking to you. But I can tell you that I have nothing to show anyone."

Ari said, "Don't you see what a terrible state we are in as humanity? We can barely continue our lives. We were actually told that we can no longer go on after a certain time. That we have to give up everything that adds meaning to our lives just to continue our lives."

Zimo said, "We think you don't get sick. That you don't experience the misery the rest of humanity does. Is that true? Do you have problems like getting sick, feeling pain, like the rest of humanity?"

"I don't know how you see me, but as I just said, I have nothing to share with anyone," said the man.

Meanwhile, Zimo's phone got a message from an unknown number, saying, "The police have been called from the house. The teams are on their way." Zimo thought the message was sent by the mayor who did not want the agreement to be broken. He secretly pulled out his gun that shot drugged arrows. Looking at the man, he said, "It didn't have to be like this," and fired his gun from beside his leg so the man couldn't see it.

Seeing the man black out, Ari went mad: "What do you think you're doing?" he snapped at Zimo. "He just fainted. I've heard that the cops are on their way here, we don't have much time. Someone else in the house must have called the police. Help me move the guy," Zimo replied. Ari clung to Zimo's collar, frustrated with anger, and started shouting while spurting fire from his eyes, "I told you that we would not force anyone into anything, no forcing! That we wouldn't touch..." but before he could finish, he felt a pain in his leg and collapsed.

The guy's parents locked in their room to make sure they would not be involved, tried to force the door open when they heard voices outside, but they couldn't do it. Zimo didn't want to involve them, so he left them there and left the house with the unconscious Ari and the men who came to help him.

***

Ari was in one of the rooms at the headquarters when Zimo sprinkled water on his face and woke him up. The other man was already awake, with his entire body tied up in very thick chains, but he couldn't move a muscle because of the sedatives he was given. As soon as Ari was able to connect his brain and body, he began to call them to account again. He jumped up angrily. "What do you think you're doing? Untie that guy. I am a prisoner too now?" he began to shout.

Zimo seemed very calm. "Calm down," he said with a tranquillity that drove Ari mad. "Nobody's a prisoner. We got word that a call was made to the police from inside the house. Cops were about to come. There was no time to argue with you or him. Imagine what would happen if the police came before we left. Think of what they might do if the government gets its hands on him. At best, they would turn him into a subject."

Ari was even more angry with Zimo's calmness let alone calming down as the man suggested, "So why have you put him in chains? I didn't cooperate with you for that. Untie him right now," he replied.

Zimo shook his head, saying, "I understand your sensitivity, but we've come this far so we have to get some answers. Especially since the police are involved, we must get those answers very quickly. Otherwise all our hopes will be wasted. We don't even know what we're hoping for. What he can do. Should we let the government have him after we've come this far?"

Meanwhile, the man seemed to be trying to concentrate on something, with his eyes closed. He seemed independent of his environment. This time Zimo addressed the man and said, "Would you rather be in the hands of the government? At least we don't try to open you up and take a look inside you," he said and drew all attention to the man. At that moment, they noticed that the man seemed to be trying to reach something with his mind. Zimo quickly approached him and shook him, "I don't know what you're trying to do. But there's no way I can let you go without getting some answers from you first. So you'd better start talking right away," he shouted. The man opened his eyes. But despite the fact that his entire body was wrapped in thick chains and the presence of all the guys that seemed to be under the command of the man who shouted at him, he did not look scared. In a similar tone used by Zimo that infuriated Ari, he said, "I've told you before. I have nothing to share with anyone. I suggest you let me go right away. For your own good. Your time is running out."

Zimo pointed the gun he took from one of his men at the guy. "I don't know who you trust to get you out of here, but as I said, there's no way I can let you go without getting the answers I want from you," he said all wild-eyed. "Start talking now. I'm losing my patience," he added threateningly.

Gordon, who thought the man had not taken his threat seriously and said, "Your time is running out," without losing his temper, took the threat a step further and put a bullet in the gun. Ari hurried himself and threw himself between the man and the barrel of Zimo's gun. And, in a moment of déjá-vu, he remembered the woman who started all these events by putting herself between the little girl and the car. Zimo thought that this move by Ari had neutralised his bluff, so his resistance was somewhat broken, but he did not show it. There was no turning back. Without lowering his weapon or changing the direction he pointed it. "I know the reason for his calmness. You think a tiny bullet can't hurt you because you can easily catch an adult person falling down from a skyscraper despite the momentum he's gained. I thought about it, but I wasn't sure. But if that's the case, I'd love to see it live. Hey, Ari, get out of the way so we can witness our friend's abilities. Looks like he's sure of himself. I see a lot of that 'bullets that can't hurt me' attitude," he said as he tried to get Ari out of the way without a fight. Ari had no intention of getting out of the way.

"Put your gun down," he said, staring directly into Zimo's eyes with determination.

Zimo said, asserting his own resolve, "Ari, son, don't be ridiculous, you've seen how this man caught someone falling from a skyscraper. They didn't even get a scratch on them when they both should have gone to pieces. He can handle a tiny bullet. It's stupid to throw yourself in front of the barrel for this man you don't know."

Seeing Ari didn't move, Zimo made a sign to his men. Then his two big men started walking towards Ari. Ari, who had Wing-Chun training, knocked over the first man who reached him. As he began to struggle with the second, a third man caught up to him, and the three together pulled Ari out from between Zimo and the man. Although Ari had struggled to get free, he couldn't, and the thought of a man dying because of him and not being able to do anything about it made his eyes fill up with desperation.

"Don't!" he shouted.

Zimo took a few more steps towards the man and put his gun to his head. "Now talk or go down in history with your secret," he said.

The man said, very calmly, "My life is as small as the bullet you intend to kill me with compared to my secret. Therefore, removing a small detail like me with a tiny bullet you have does not make you able to do anything." And he closed his eyes. The man heard a much softer and familiar old man calling himself "Kit" while he was waiting with the eyes closed for the gunshot.

Opening his eyes, Kit smiled at the familiar face he saw. Everyone, including Zimo, turned to the voice along with Kit. The man, who seemed to be in his mid-sixties and had a short white beard, walked slowly toward Kit from opposite wall, with no door or window to allow him to enter the room. No matter how surprised and frightened Zimo was, he didn't show it, and he pointed his gun at the old man; "Stay where you are. Who are you? How did you get in?" he shouted. The old man kept walking without reacting to him. He was focused entirely on Ari. He looked at him as if he were seeing a relative he had not seen in a long time. A few steps before the old man reached Kit, the chains on Kit began to unravel one by one. Frightened that the old man had gotten to him, Zimo panicked and fired the weapon in his hand. But the bullet from the gun slowed down in the air before reaching the old man, and then fell to the ground shattering into its smallest pieces.

Everyone in the room, except for Kit, was terrified. Nobody could make sense of what they saw. Zimo knelt in front of this old man, who was now a few steps away, and started begging this time, as tears flowed from his eyes he said, "Please. I'm begging you. Share what you can do with us. Don't you see the state we're in? They're about to turn us all into robots. Please. I'm begging you." The old man turned to Zimo with his expressionless face and stared at him for a few seconds. Then Zimo felt like he was being pulled back. He hit the wall as if someone had grabbed him from the back and swung him against the wall. Then Zimo's three men in the room tried to attack the old man. But all three got lifted off the ground before they could reach him. They struggled back to try to reach the man, but they could not succeed. It was like they were moving in an invisible balloon.

The old man who had reached Kit caressed his head. "Are you okay?" he asked. The man gestured with his head, with great embarrassment on his face, unable to look him in the eye. The old man took Kit's hand. Then they disappeared. At the moment of their disappearance, three men in the air fell to the ground as if they were dropped from a height. Everyone in the room was shocked and frozen in a terrified state. No one said a word. They remained in that position for a few minutes when the door of the room was opened and the cops with guns in their hands filled the room. Suddenly they were surrounded. The police started to remove them from the room. Only Tom was resisting it. With a quick manoeuvre, he got away from the police holding him. He was going to show resistance when he heard his father's voice. "Tom, stop before you get yourself hurt. There is no getting out of this," Arp said.

Hearing his father, Tom stopped resisting and raised his hands. The others in the room were once again surprised. Zimo was shocked to find out that one of his most trusted men was the son of the head of the police force, the man who was the face of the transition period of the force. Furiously trying to get free of the police officer who was holding him to get to Tom, and foaming at the mouth said he bellowed, "You've been a mole that's infiltrated us all this time. You betrayed our cause. Bloody traitor. You've destroyed the last chance of humanity!"

"I'm not a traitor. I don't know anything!" Tom shouted. As he tried to absolve himself with similar sentences, his words began to come to an incoherent slur because his voice was cracking with his cries. The police had already removed half of them, including Zimo. Now it was his turn. Two superhuman police officers took him by the arms after handcuffing him and dragged him out of the room.

***

Lil was determined to have the conversation tonight, which she thought she should have done a long time ago. After having dinner with her grandmother, she wriggled to get into the subject for about an hour. Thinking that two cups of linden tea could make everything easier, she went into the kitchen. Returning from the kitchen with the two cups of tea, she sat on the couch next to the sofa where her grandmother was lying. Her grandmother was staring at the ceiling deep in thought. Lil cleared her throat to get her attention. Her grandmother slipped out of her thoughts and turned her attention to where Lil was sitting with the tea, "Did you finally get the courage to talk?" she asked.

She sat up. Started drinking her tea. She was aware of the conversation her granddaughter had wanted to have with her since that morning. But she could not convince herself that she could handle the conversation either. She did not want to see the pain in Lil's eyes when she told her that her decision was final. They had had brief chats about this decision many times, but always thought they had more time. But to explain her final decision on this issue could have destroyed her granddaughter. She looked at her as she was drinking her tea. Even though she seemed to be about to start talking a few times, her granddaughter didn't seem to have the courage to have this talk. In the end, Judi brought it up herself after losing all patience: "I see that you want to talk to me seriously about this, my Lil. I agree that we should end this uncertainty and prepare ourselves for what comes next," she said to Lil who was already discouraged. Her eyes were already full to the brim. She would continue to listen to her talk, all the while crying silently. Judi continued: "I know you think that I should have continued living by any means possible. And I'm sure you'll continue to love me no matter what. You've never been a calculating person before. Even when you were a little girl, you wouldn't get angry with the children who hit you, but you would try to understand why they hit you when you loved them. Then you would come and tell your parents or me what had happened and ask where you'd made a mistake. And we'd tell you that it wasn't your fault, that the other kid did something terrible. You said you'd keep loving them, but you didn't want to see them any more. My dear baby. You didn't snap at your aunt not even once, even though she pushed you every time you met. You didn't give her a reason to relieve her conscience for treating you so badly. That's exactly why she gets annoyed more and more by you every day. Anyway. As I said, I know you'll continue to love me no matter what. That you want me to stay alive by any means necessary. But I expect you to understand this one thing, baby. I have never pursued great success. I didn't try to meet a lot of people. Your grandfather was my first and last relationship. I've always preferred spending time at home to going out. Because your mother and aunt came first. I thought to myself that there was nothing better I could do than spend time with them in my short life. I thought my life would only be enough to love your mother, your aunt and your grandfather. That it wouldn't even be enough for them. Then you were born. You know I've never hesitated to say that with your birth I've experienced such a magnificent love, the like of which I'd never tasted before. You were my first grandchild. It was a whole other love. As you've grown up, you've become a great person. I loved you even more. I enjoyed talking to you and spending time with you the most. Because you were the only person that I'd ever seen in my life who could love others as much as she loved herself. This is a thought heard a lot from religious doctrines, philosophers. We hear from the people around us as well. But you're the only person I've ever seen *accomplish* it. You've changed the way I care for people. The more I got to know your mother, your aunt, your grandfather, the better I began to love them. I can tell you this in my own way, my beautiful girl: You know when we reach for the handle of the toaster, thinking that our hand will find the handle from experience, even when we're preoccupied with something else, but then we touch the hot spot instead of the handle. Then we can't just say that our hand couldn't do what it was supposed to do. We can't say that it has to suffer by paying the price of its own fault. Because it's a part of us. I know it sounds a little silly, but this is the most concrete example I can find for myself. That's how you taught me to love someone other than myself. I've talked for much longer now than I expected, but I'm getting to the point. I've lived a long life. Considering everything that happened to the world in my lifetime, it seems even longer. Everyone questions the purpose of their lives. I settled for being able to spend time with my loved ones and share my happiness with them until this age. And as I approach the end of my life, I see I've had a very honourable purpose. It was worth spending my life for that purpose. A computer just came out and said, 'I could get you to the real purpose of your life. 'But for that you have to give up your feelings.' I do not accept it. I do not accept a purpose of life where love is left out. I don't want to turn into a creature to admit that the things I've done for all the people I've love in my life were in vain. I know you'll love me for the rest of your life, even though I'm selfish and I'm going to leave you. I'm sorry, my beautiful-eyed girl."

Lil couldn't say anything after this talk that she'd listened to in tears. She made a sign with her head to indicate that she understood her grandmother. As the tears in her eyes ran down at a more rapid pace, she hugged her grandmother for a long while. Judi withdrew herself from her granddaughter to disperse the melancholic mood. "Shall we invite Ari to dinner tomorrow?" she asked. "That'd be great. I'll call him in the morning," said Lil as she wiped the tears from her eyes.

9 JULY 2035

When Ari arrived home, it was nine in the morning. He'd had a very difficult and exhausting night and hadn't slept at all. He couldn't help but play everything that happened over and over in his mind. What he saw in videos really affected him but what he saw live the previous night was completely different. He was so affected by being detained, questioned and threatened by the authorities later in the night yet it paled in comparison to what he'd witnessed. The police had picked them up from the headquarters of Free Will and taken them to the headquarters of an intelligence service instead of the police station. Over and over again, they had asked questions about the man they met and the person who saved Kit. Surprisingly, they had never asked questions about the activities of the resistance and the things they could easily pin on them, such as kidnapping.

The rest was even more surprising. The authorities told Ari that from the very beginning that they were aware of every step taken by the resistance, they always knew the location of their headquarters, but that such an opposing formation would allow people to vent their anger a little bit so they allowed them to carry on with their activities. They also said that they recorded everything spoken in the headquarters 24/7 with tiny robots that looked like flies and recorded high quality sound and image. They were also aware of the actions of the mayor and his son. But they decided to watch it without interrupting until the end because they thought the man from the video would trust people like himself more than the government under the control of robots to share his secrets.

It was no surprise to anyone that there were robots that looked like flies and could record images and sound. They, too, had watched from beginning to end and hoped for answers from the man, just like the resistance and Ari. From the questions they asked, it was clear that their knowledge of these extraordinary people was not much more than the resistance. Which surprised Ari very much. Especially after the demonstrations of power to show they'd been aware of every single breath taken by the resistance. What really surprised Ari during his detention was that they had not arrested them.

They made it clear that arresting them could trigger a counter-movement that could have serious consequences during these sensitive times of the last stages of synthetic selection, and that they did not believe they could do much more after that day's demonstrations of power, so they thought it was not worth the risk. They warned the guys to forget everything they had gone through and not to talk to anyone about it, and they were told that if they didn't obey them, they would be intervened with no consideration in a way that they would never see daylight again. They were already convinced that from the resistance's and Ari's attitude that they would remember todays demonstration with every breath. However, they instructed them to let them know if the man who had taken saved Kit by coming through the wall and taken an interest in Ari ever contacted them.

Ari was sitting on the terrace thinking about all this when his phone rang. Seeing that it was Lil, Ari answered the phone after experiencing a short indecision between answering it and not answering it with the fear of accidentally letting something slip.

***

Ari had done everything during the day as a kind of reflex until the evening. He had eaten and drunk to complete his meals as a reflex, brushed his teeth, done chores and dressed. He did not realise the ghost state he was in until he finished the dressing process and saw himself in the mirror, after which he realised that he lived as a ghost all day independent of the life he lived in. He didn't remember anything he'd done during the day. He didn't remember what he had for breakfast, how many cups of tea he had or how he got dressed, even though he had just finished dressing.

"You're going to Lil's, you don't want her to see you like this and worry. Her grandmother's state is already enough weight on her. It would be selfish to expect her to share the burden of what you're going through. Get yourself together," he said to himself. He went to the bathroom and washed his face. He decided that nothing should come between him and this evening with the woman he loved and her grandmother. All three of them needed to have a pleasant evening to get away from what they were going through. Before going to dinner, he went to the bakery at the head of the street and bought a box of Lil's favourite tartelettes. He thanked the patisserie employee who helped him, left the place and took the bus to his girlfriend's apartment.

He got off the bus and while he was waiting at the lights to cross the street, he felt like he heard someone call him. He turned and looked around. But he was convinced the sound didn't come from the few people around him. It was a familiar voice, but he couldn't figure out who it was. He thought he was wrong, and as he started crossed over, he realised that the light had turned red for him again. Until the next light, he was distracted with thoughts of: "Am I going mad?" In the blink of an eye, as preoccupied as he was with his thoughts, he'd arrived at the apartment where Lil lived and even taken the elevator. But when he saw himself on the mirror in the elevator, he realised that that time had passed by as if in a dream, just like the rest of his day had done.

As he was talking to himself, saying, "You have to get it together," he heard the same voice again.

"Ari. You're not going crazy. Think about how this could happen." This time Ari was even more amazed at the fact that the voice calling out to him responded to the thoughts in his head and spoke to him about them. Although he had heard this familiar voice in a quieter environment and in a longer conversation this time, he still couldn't figure out who it was. He was comparing it to the voice of everyone he knew, but he couldn't identify it. Suddenly he noticed that the elevator was moving slower than usual.

As soon as he noticed this slowness, the elevator door was opened. "You're getting paranoid," he thought to himself. He looked at himself in the mirror one last time. He tried to make his face look as normal as possible and stepped out of the elevator. It felt good when his girlfriend held him tight as soon as she opened door. He buried his head in her shoulder and felt, as usual, that he could breathe and rest. Then they had a nice meal. Ari kept making jokes to lighten his mood, made Lil and Judi laugh a lot, and after a while they started to keep up with his jokes and even adding to them. So they ate their food at a table where smiles and laughter were not lacking.

After dinner, Lil and Ari had cleaned up together and then they took their places with Judi for some tea and tartelettes. When he was finished with his first cup of tea, Ari thought that he managed the situation very well and had not alerted Lil to anything untoward going on with him. He was happy to be able to do that. Lil, who had also finished her cup of tea, leaned over to look at her boyfriend's cup and saw that it was empty as well. "Shall we have another cup of tea?" she asked.

"That'd be great, thank you," Ari replied. When Lil looked over to Judi, they made eye contact. Without waiting for Lil to speak, Judi said, "I can only drink half a cup of very light tea, as you know darling. Thank you."

As Lil went to the kitchen with the cups, Ari was still feeling relief from having been able to hide his mood. When Lil disappeared into the kitchen Judi leaned towards Ari and softly said, "You've surprised me."

Ari was confused. "I beg your pardon?" he responded.

"I was married for forty-five years. I've witnessed my husband in each different period in his life try to keep secrets from me. I immediately recognise a man hiding something from his beloved. I can see that it's not a secret that you're ashamed of, but clearly, it's something important. But every moment you're not telling her, it'll just make everything more difficult, believe me," she said. Ari had been feeling proud of being able to conceal his troubled state of mind all night, so he was taken aback by what Judi had said.

"Umm... ahh... I just," he stammered ineffectually.

When Lil came back from the kitchen Ari just moved away from Judi in a panic.

Lil laughed, "Are you talking behind my back again?" she asked. Trying to cover up for his panic, Ari said, "Yes, Judi was just saying that you deserve so much better than me and that I'm such a good-hearted young man that I would get out of your life." They all laughed. Judi just gave Ari a teasing sly look seeing as he was trying so hard to hide their conversation.

They continued their lovely conversation for the rest of the evening. When it was time for him to leave, Ari took Lil deliberately towards the

186

door. "I forgot to kiss Judi good night," he said and went back in to Judi. He whispered to Judi so Lil wouldn't hear. "Believe me, what I'm hiding from Lil, is in no way something that'll hurt her. I just didn't want her to worry about me. But I'll tell her tomorrow, I promise."

Judi smiled, "I never thought otherwise," she answered him.

Ari headed to the door. As they hugged, Lil said, loud enough for Judi to hear, "I can tell you in all honesty that I didn't notice you whispering in there." Ari kissed his girlfriend and left the apartment with a puzzled smile on his face.

***

It was close to midnight and even though he hadn't slept the night before either, Ari still wasn't planning to go to bed soon. He kept pacing back and forth in his living room. That was just what he did whenever something was troubling him. He was trying to convince himself that he wasn't going crazy. But it wasn't easy. He didn't even know how long he'd been walking up and down. He felt his legs hurt. He thought he should stop torturing himself. "The fool's feet pay for the sins of his head," he thought to himself. He put a record into the player just to unwind a little and get some sleep and sat down on his chair.

The rocking chair and the song he was listening to relaxed him a little. He realised that because he'd confined himself to a narrow point of view as he paced briskly, he hadn't really managed to get anywhere despite wracking his brain. There had to be something he was missing. He suddenly thought of Kit, who'd ignored all the shouting going on around him and tried to work something out with closed eyes, as he sat there in front of him all tied up in chains. And a little later, the man who just came out of nowhere and saved Kit.

As he thought about that man, he remembered his voice after he disarmed everyone around him and then asked Kit if he was okay while stroking his hair. Tears were rolling down his face. The voice he'd heard was his voice. "Did he just reach out to me?" he thought. He thought about the reason for that if that were the case. They'd had eye contact for a moment the other night, but they had nothing between them that would warrant any sort of communication.

If he was right and if the man he'd seen the previous night *had* contacted him, that was something unbelievable. He could then get all the answers to the questions he'd had since he saw the man and probably even for the questions he hadn't even thought to ask. He began to get restless. "Would he ever reach out to me again? Why did he contact me just to say my name and a few other words, why didn't he say more?" he began to ask himself.

He was too impatient. He thought it would not be possible to get in touch with him until the man reached out himself. Even though the odds of such a thing seemed close to none, everything he'd been through in the last couple of months had actually changed his perception about what was possible and what wasn't. After thinking about it for a while, he did what made the most sense to him. He closed his eyes and tried to remember all the details about the man. He called out to the man as he pictured all the details about him in his mind. "Please talk to me again. I really need you. Please get in touch with me again."

It had hardly been a minute since he started doing it when he heard the voice in his head again. He opened his eyes and jumped up in surprise. He couldn't believe he'd managed to do that himself. The voice was saying, "Ari, thank you for trying to get in touch with me. What you're going through here is real. All I ask is for you to be calm and act natural. You saw what happened at headquarters. I know that they're constantly monitoring you too. This was the only way I could talk to you without them noticing. I'll hear in my mind anything you think about. Now my question to you is this: Do I have your permission to come inside your head so we can communicate?"

Ari sat back down in his rocking chair and again acted like he was just listening to music. He was talking to the voice in his head. "Yes," he replied. "There are a lot of answers I need to get."

"Don't worry," said the voice, "you're going to find the answers to all your questions. But first you have to prove that you deserve them." They continued to communicate in this way. Ari wasn't sure if he was being watched, but he was sure that even if someone were standing right before him, they wouldn't know he was talking to anyone.

Ari said, "I'm willing to take any test. I need to find the answers I'm looking for."

"Impatience doesn't take you to your destination more quickly, it just leads you astray. You need to calm down. First things first. You don't even know my name yet. I'm Al," the voice said.

"I think you know me. I don't think I need to introduce myself."

Al didn't answer that.

"If you can enter my mind and talk to me, how do I know you won't control my mind?" he asked.

"In our teaching, any interference with the free will of another person is prohibited. So relax. I only called out to you until you tried to contact me. It was just an option I gave you. I didn't contact you in this way until you accepted it and asked for it. And I asked for your permission to access your mind before we started talking again. From now on, all you have to do to end our communication is to tell me."

"Though when I think about it, I can imagine what you could do if you had bad intentions. Why did you contact me?"

"Because you have the potential to be worthy of sharing our secrets. But first you have to prove it. And since I showed interest in you, they'll be watching you constantly, so you have to do this without anyone noticing."

"How's that going to work?"

"Just like this conversation we're having. In your mind."

"Let's do it right now, then. What are we waiting for?"

"Communication like this is very challenging. Although the excitement of the adrenaline hormone secreted by your body tells you something else, your body is actually very tired as you can see from the warmth flowing from your nose to your mouth. Just rest until our next conversation. We will meet again tomorrow."

Ari realised his nose was bleeding. He also felt really tired. He could barely reach out to some napkins. He cleaned the blood from his nose. And then he went to bed. He lay on his right side in case he had a nosebleed again and went right to sleep as soon as his head hit the pillow.

10 JULY 2035

Feeling as if he had been asleep for the first time in days, Ari woke up with a strange feeling inside. He felt like he had woken up on the first day of a summer break after a difficult school year. But he knew that it was just the beginning. When he looked at the time, he saw that it was three in the afternoon. His mental exhaustion had caused him to sleep for quite some time.

He got out of bed and washed his face. He felt butterflies inside. He had a hard time keeping still as he thought about the places that his journey could lead to and he felt incredibly impatient. He wasn't sure if it was because he'd slept for a long time, but he was hungry as a wolf.

He had an appetite that he had not felt in a long time and he ate like never before. He had a big cup of tea. He was feeling so much better. Very strong, very energetic. He went out on the terrace with his rocking chair, both because he couldn't contain himself and he wanted to get some air. He was rocking back and forth very fast to keep himself busy. In about five to ten minutes, his eyes flashed with the voice he'd been expecting to hear.

"Hello, Ari," Al said.

"How should I address you? Is there a particular form of title for you?" Ari replied.

"Al is fine. The only difference between you and I is that I have more awareness. How do you feel after our talk yesterday? I hope you didn't have much trouble."

"I just woke up. I slept for a long time. I feel fine now. I woke up very well rested and I'm ready for much more."

"Patience, Ari. If we don't really feel our steps, I will do you more harm than good. Damages even I can't fix."

"So can you at least tell me how you can do all this? Who are you?"

"As you know, the biggest issue for humanity these days is to increase its capacity. You know, that was the main reason why Galileo became so famous."

"Yes unfortunately it is."

"Why unfortunately?"

"Look what it did to humanity."

"What I see is that everything that happened to us is our own fault, and Galileo gave us all the help he could."

"At what cost?"

"It's true that we have lost the pleasures we used to experience when we touch our loved ones, when we saw them, kissed them, had a nice meal, looked at a lovely view, smelt flowers. But have you ever thought about the cost of those pleasures?"

Ari didn't have an answer.

Al said, "Most of what Galileo says is true. He's doing his best to assist us as far as our perceptive abilities go. He says that we must go through synthetic selection first as a species and strengthen ourselves for survival since we are fighting in a constant battle for life in this world, and only when we are empowered can we turn into a universal species, and he is right about most of that. But what he doesn't know is that we are already universal contributors."

"What do you mean?"

"I'm afraid you have to prove you're worthy to know how."

"Just tell me how to prove myself. I'm ready for anything."

"I'm so sorry to have to ask you this, Ari, but you have to open your mind to me completely for me to help you with that. I need to look at every moment you don't even remember since you were born, every impact you've kept from all those moments you've had. This is our prerequisite for sharing our secrets and teaching. This condition was valid for everyone before you, including me, and will continue to be so long after you."

"How so? Can you do that? Can you see how I felt about an incident I experienced as a child?"

"Yes, Ari. Even more clearly than you."

Ari was stunned. He couldn't even have imagined anything like that.

"I can understand the frame of mind you are in. It's too much to ask for. Especially when I'm being so secretive about the answers I can give you. But when our teaching falls into the wrong hands, it has very grave consequences. There have been times when that happened," Al said.

Astonished, Ari didn't know what to say, and then his phone rang. Even though Ari decided to ignore it and continue talking, the sound and vibration of the phone wouldn't let him. So he took his phone out of his pocket to reject the call, but he saw Lil's photo. He had a small dilemma. Just as he was about to press the reject, Al said, "You'd better answer that, Ari. I noticed the movement in you, even just by looking at her picture. Believe me, nothing's worth keeping someone you love so much waiting." So Ari answered the phone.

And when he did, he heard Lil's sobbing voice. Her grandmother had passed away. Ari told Al that he had to go be with his girlfriend and that they would continue this conversation as soon as possible. Ari ran out of the house to go to Lil.

***

Arp was sitting at his desk in his room at the station watching live footage from Ari's house. Ari had a normal start to the day, went out on the terrace after breakfast. However, after a short time in his rocking chair on the terrace, things started to get a little strange. The young man sitting by himself seemed to react to things with his eyes closed. He frowned from time to time, and his face was going through various expressions. He even opened his eyes in surprise once, then closed them again and continued to react to something.

Although he looked closely at second of the footage, he saw that Ari didn't have earphones in his ear, nor did he listen to music or speak or phone. After a bit of thinking, he decided that the young man might be making some kind of telepathic communication with the man who had showed up out of thin air yesterday. He was just about to leave for Ari's apartment to find out exactly what had been going on but just then the young man had left the house in a hurry after a brief phone call. When he talked to the officers who were in charge of listening in on Ari, he found out that Ari had gone to the hospital to his girlfriend who had lost her grandmother. So he contacted several police officers, and quickly headed for the hospital.

***

When Ari found Lil in the hospital, she was sitting on the floor outside Judi's room and sobbing. Just across from her, Lil's aunt sat in one of the seats in the hall, just staring at the floor. Her husband held her hands, trying to comfort her. When he looked at them for a moment and saw that Lil had been devastated, he suddenly forgot his determination to support her.

Suddenly, he broke down in tears so badly that even though he ran to his girlfriend, at least one teardrop fell to the floor with each step. He collapsed next to Lil on the floor, hugging her tightly and kissing her on the head again and again. Lil needed the man she loved more than ever, so she pressed her face on Ari's chest harder and harder as if she were trying to disappear into him. They didn't know how long they had been there tangled up in each other, but a moment of relief at the end of their crying allowed them to speak to each other. Ari looked inside the room; "Is she still inside?" he asked.

Lil, trying to suppress her sobs, said with difficulty, "No. They took her to the morgue."

Meanwhile, Ari began to hear Al's voice again inside his head. "I don't like doing this right now, but you have to leave right away," Al said.

"She has just lost her grandmother. I can't ask Lil for anything right now," Ari replied.

"I'm afraid it's an obligation rather than a choice. They know I've been in touch with you. You don't have much time. They'll do anything to get information about me from you. And they will do anything to your girlfriend to get information on you or reach you. You need to get her out of there, too," Al said.

Ari said angrily, "How do you expect me to explain this to her right now? Isn't there anything you can do?"

Seeing the awkwardness of his actions and expressions and unable to make sense of them in any way, Lil asked, "Are you okay?"

193

At that moment, they heard the sirens of police cars coming from outside.

As Ari looked around in a hurry, Al said, "There is an empty utility closet two floors up, go up there right away. Use the lift, you'll find an empty one if we're lucky, and you won't need to get there. Hurry."

Aware of Ari's strange behaviour and his reaction to the police sirens, "What's going on Ari?" she asked.

Ari grabbed Lil's arm and pulled her up. "We need to go. I'm so sorry," he said. Lil was really upset. Once again, she asked, "What's going on?" As Ari forced Lil to keep up with, they got to where the lifts were in a flash. Ari pressed the call button of each elevator. He also kept an eye on the stairs. Luckily, one of the lifts came quickly and as they stepped in Ari was still looking over at the staircase and he noticed several police officers running towards them. But the door of the lift closed when they still had a few steps ahead of them. There was a young couple in the elevator. Ari didn't like seeing them. They'd have to get to the utility closet.

Ari started shouting in the lift, this time loud enough for everyone else to hear. "Get us out of here now!" Lil was stunned by her boyfriend's attitude.

"Ari you're scaring me. What's going on?" was all she could say.

"I'm so sorry, Lil," Ari said. "I never wanted any of this to happen. You have to trust me." At that moment they reached the floor they needed. As Ari grabbed Lil by her arm and dragged her out of the lift, the couple in the lift reacted. The young man said, "Hey! What do you think you're doing?" But Ari couldn't even hear them. He was focused on Al's instructions in his head. "Turn left, it's the seventh room on the right," Al directed them. When Ari and Lil reached the utility closet, they went right through the open door and saw Al.

"Why couldn't you pick us up earlier?" Ari said angrily. Meanwhile, the young couple they had just met in the elevator showed the police the room where Ari and Lil had entered.

Al calmly said, "We couldn't afford to have the others see us, the secret we protect is more important than anything. We don't have time for this right now, anyway" he added. Then he grabbed a baffled Lil by the arm, as well as Ari, who was feeling terrible for what he was putting his girlfriend through, and they disappeared.

***

Ari and Lil reached the edge of a lake after a short trip. They were both worn out after their eyes pushed their capacity to deliver the images passing by them at the speed of light and the fatigue of their minds as they tried to process the images that came at such a speed. They also felt dizzy as they felt like they'd just got off a roller coaster going at the speed of light, and they felt sick. They both collapsed to the ground, unable to move. When they began to notice what was going on around them, they saw a very high mountain buried in the snow behind them, while in front of them was a lake that was almost frozen with snow falling on it, and around them was a forest full of trees covered more with snow rather than green leaves.

Nearby, Al stood with two thick coats in his hand. He seemed to be trying to give them time and space so they could understand what had happened. After waiting quietly for a while for them to recover, he again very quietly handed them the coats. After putting on the coats that were both thick and long enough to protect them from their necks to their feet, Ari and Lil tried to get their heads together in silence for a while, feeling the cold on their exposed faces. After a while, Al said to them, "Since it is your first time making such a trip, I can imagine how you're doing. Both of you are expecting an explanation, especially you, Lil. First of all, concerning the journey you are still under the impact of, I can say that distances are relative. Distances are not determined by location, but by you. However, as a foreword to all that we will probably experience together in the future, I'd like to say that if we decide to spend time together, your perceptions will change completely. You will realise in a way that you cannot even imagine, how effective your perceptions are about everything within the universe you interact with, abstract or concrete. But I think we agree that it would be better to leave you alone and for you to wrap your mind around things and make some decisions. Ari, you know what to do when you're ready to talk to me again," he continued. As soon as he finished talking, he disappeared into the forest

195

dressed in his linen trousers and linen shirt, walking through the snow towards the mountainside.

Lil had just lived through so much more than she could handle in one day, so she sat down on the snow and buried her head in her knees. Ari sat next to her, hugged her and kissed her head, saying, "I'm so sorry. Everything just overlapped in a way it never should have. It's my fault." Lil raised her head from her knees, looking exhausted. "Ari, what's going on?" she asked.

Trying to control his words as much as possible to get Lil ready for the next sentence, Ari began to tell her everything he'd been going through and hiding from her. Then the young couple talked about where this journey could take them. Of course, they also talked about whether or not to allow their minds to be completely controlled by another man and allow him to look at parts of it that even they couldn't reach. When Ari and Lil were ready to talk to Al again, Ari called to him in his mind. In the blink of an eye, Al began to walk out of the trees on the mountain side of the forest. When he saw the two of them looking at him in amazement, "No, of course I haven't been spying on you behind the trees all this time. I chose to walk when I left because it was snowing very beautifully, and I wanted to enjoy walking in the woods under the snow. I also chose to walk back out from among the trees because, even though our arrival here is not like the usual means of transport, I don't want to just keep appearing around you and get on your nerves," he added, laughing.

Ari told Al, "Lil is not in a condition to think about anything but her grandmother right now. She wants to be with her on her final journey."

Al said, in his usual calm manner, "Her final journey? I can tell you nothing is final. As for the journey, her journey and all of us are our lives. Being with someone on their final journey doesn't mean watching their body get covered with earth. It means being with them when they're alive before the end of their final journey. And I'm sure you've done your part perfectly."

There was silence because Ari and especially Lil weren't expecting such a long answer, and neither of them was in a condition to understand this long answer at the moment. To avoid misunderstanding, Al said, "Of course I will do my best to help you to say goodbye to your grandmother the way you want. In fact, you can see what I've just said as another introductory speech. Can we take a little walk? I think that some of the information I have can comfort you," he continued.

Lil looked at Ari in surprise. "Whatever you want," Ari replied, as this was something he didn't expect either.

"Why isn't Ari coming with us?" Lil asked. Turning to Ari, Al said, "Everyone's journey continues at different speeds and with different views. I think you will trust me on this."

Ari nodded in approval. With Lil taking shy steps, she and Al walked away from Ari, strolling on the snow by the lake.

When Lil and Al came back, an hour or two had passed. Lil was involuntarily pitying Ari, who was staring at the lake in deep thought. She had learned a lot from Al in a short time and was sure that she would learn more than she could ever imagine, but there was one thing she had learned that shook her to her core. Because of the thing she had learned, her eyes filled with tears as she looked at Ari, who hadn't noticed they were back. Aware of the situation, Al told Lil: "The information I've shared with you, belongs to you now. It's up to you to share any of it with the man you love. But there's a reason why what I've told you is shared with only a few people. Not everyone can accept it the way you did. This can upset any other person's memories of the past and present. I suggest you be very careful when sharing this information with Ari." Lil nodded to Al without taking her teary eyes away from Ari.

When Lil and Al arrived at Ari's side, Al said, "Lil was the first to join us, even though you and I had already started walking down this road. We can now initiate you if you want." Although Ari was surprised that Lil had already opened her mind to Al, he did not dwell on it and nodded in agreement.

Lil put her hand on Ari's cheek and said, "This will be much more difficult than our journey here. You're going to experience all the emotions that you've experienced all your life, again in a very short time. Your happiest moments with your family and your emotions upon losing them, the moment you've felt the happies, the saddest, the most afraid... You will experience all of that in a matter of seconds. I can't fully explain how it will make you feel, but I can tell you that if you can embrace everything that makes you you, you will feel like yo have more control over it all than ever before. Because you'll be living all of them as a stronger and more experienced version of yourself than you used to be." She kissed Ari on the head and took a few steps back. As soon as Ari opened his mind to Al, he felt his body stiffen. He felt as if he had been there for centuries like a piece of rock and it did not seem possible to move. His mind, on the other hand, was like a smaller piece of rock, standing still in itself, but was dragged swiftly across the time vortex where it existed.

Just as Lil said, in a matter of seconds he re-experienced all the ups and downs, the happiness, the love, the sadness, the fears and the life that his parents gave him, the emptiness he felt when he lost them, his life before Lil and the joy that came into his life with her... And when he got to the end of the vortex, he realised that he was actually observing all the traces left on his life by the passing of time, as if he were just an objective audience. In the quiet time spent closed in to get his head together, he thought: "When I think about it, even when they were happening to me, I was just bearing witness to them. They were never under my control." After collecting himself for a while, he felt Lil's hand on his shoulder. "Thank God," he muttered to himself.

Al said, "You both proved that you're worthy of our ancient teaching. At the end of this life-long process, you may attain knowledge and skills you cannot imagine. I can imagine that it would be very good for you to have a little rest, given all that you've been through in a very short time. As of tomorrow, a whole new life will begin for you. Considering the situation we are in, we all know that we don't have much time. We need to find as many worthy people as possible and share our teachings with them."

The three of them then walked together through the forest towards the mountain. Al walked a few steps ahead of them and didn't say a word to them. He thought it would be good for them to spend some alone time for a bit. Lil and Ari walked arm in arm a few steps behind Al and spoke very little. The culmination of their communication was when they touched their cheeks to each other's to gain strength from one another. They were both grateful for having each other in their lives after they'd seen their lives before and after finding the other person.

Along the way, Ari tried to guess how she was feeling after meeting Al on top of losing her grandmother and hoped that he could give her strength during this difficult process. Lil had forgotten her own pain thinking about what her boyfriend would feel when she shared what she had heard from Al with him. In fact, what she had learned from Al had quite alleviated her own pain. She hoped the same would happen to Ari, but a voice inside her said it could be the opposite.

Finally, Al and the two lovers walked through the door of the school, which seemed to have been carved into the mountains. The perfect human touch at the entrance of this enormous and solid mountain, the entryway, the gate, all seemed to have come out of the fantastic films they'd watched, and it captivated them. Neither of them noticed for a long time that their mouths were open. At the entrance inside the mountain there was a large square. This square was big enough to remind one of the city squares. There were separate groups of five or six people. It looked as if they were all studying different subjects. But this training was nothing like the two lovers had ever seen before. One group consisted of pupils sitting cross-legged on the floor with their eyes closed and their teacher floating five to ten centimetres above the ground. At the back of the square were rooms that stretched deep into the mountains as far as the eye could see; they looked as if they'd been carved into the mountain walls. These rooms were of various sizes according to their purpose and, besides being arranged side by side, they also formed a multi-storey structure lined up on top of each other. The upper floors were accessed with the help of staircases that looked like monolithic stones.

Ari and Lil were bewitched. The mountain, which has an ordinary appearance from the outside, was the work of a mind which had used the mountain only as a cover and the designed the interior as a school. The air was as clean and light as the forest air outside. As they moved towards their chambers, they felt as if the insides of the mountain had been carved out, and the material had been properly shaped and reintroduced into the mountain. Lil and Ari entered the room that Al showed them. Considering they were in a cave, the room they were in was incredible. Electricity, hot water, nothing was missing. There were also clean clothes waiting for them on the bed.

The two lovers spent their evening resting did not talk much. They both took a shower with hot water, which was more fascinating to them than everything else. They ate their meals brought all the way up to their rooms. Ari could feel Lil drifting away from him after her private conversation with Al. During the evening, as he thought about the reasons for her distance, he believed the likeliest possibility was that she had taken an outside look at their relationship and was now questioning it. Another possibility was that she might have been angry because of all the cold-blooded lies, which, although upsetting, somehow seemed better than the first option.

But even if he was dying inside, he wouldn't pressure his girlfriend, who had gone through so much in just one day and wouldn't ask her why. All he was going to do that night was to hope that the coldness between them was temporary. Thinking to herself on the sofa in the corner of the room, Lil finally got up, signalling that she had decided to speak, and headed for Ari, who was lying in bed. Noticing this, Ari's heart began to beat rapidly. "Please don't let it be something impossible to take back," he muttered to himself. Just as Lil sat down next to Ari, the doorbell rang. When Lil opened the door, she found a smiling girl aged between fifteen and sixteen. She was holding a metal pitcher and a tray with two glasses. "I'm sorry to bother you," she said to Lil. "I was given a homework task to make some delicious hot chocolate and I was wondering if you'd like to taste it. People's enjoyment of it will be considered my grade." Lil thanked her with a sincere smile and took two cups of hot chocolate and sat down next to Ari, whose heart was still pounding. Lil was actually afraid that if she let more time pass without talking, she'd give up on her decision to talk to her boyfriend about what Al told her. Even though she was afraid of the impact it might have on him, she wasn't going to hide such a big thing from him; they'd confront it together. She put the cups on the nightstand next to the bed.

Tears started running down her face as she looked into Ari's eyes, "Ari, I've been very hesitant to tell you this. But I finally decided it would be best if I did," she began. Ari, who had conditioned himself for a break-up speech, looked down.

Lil continued: "I think you've noticed that something's been bothering me since I talked to Al. It makes it harder for me to look at your face every minute I keep it from you, and you've probably noticed that too. What I'm about to say could really upset you. You can think of it as my selfishness, like I'm talking just to get rid of this burden, but you have a right to know. Or I won't be able to look at you as comfortably as before."

Ari tried to interrupt, "Lil, I..." but Lil continued, not letting him talk. In the meantime, Ari was completely broken down, so the tears accumulating in his eyes began to run down his cheeks. Lil tenderly wiped his tears as she continued, "Ari, I can't tell you how it is now, because words aren't enough to explain it, but if you see what I saw, you can understand it. Al has shown me that people's deaths are their own choice." Since Ari had conditioned himself to hear something else, he felt his mood instantly lifted and he said, "How... What do you mean?" He looked curiously at Lil.

Lil said, "I mean I saw that you or I, or any person that exists or will exist in the world, can die only when they accept it. Death is a choice. I can say that Al put it with such clarity that left no question in my head."

Ari was frowning trying to understand what he was hearing. "So, did my parents choose to leave me alone? Who would willingly give up on life? Who would just to leave behind everyone and everything they love?" he said.

Lil knew that she'd already said too much for now, but because she thought she could soothe Ari a bit, she said, "The people who've seen what's waiting in the beyond. I have witnessed people who are in danger, being shown what is waiting for them beyond, and it was up to them to decide whether or not to ignore what they'd seen and continue their lives."

Ari was horrified and now crying again, "What do they see, Lil? Do they see the afterlife? What would a mother exchange for being with her child?"

"Al didn't let me see that since he thought it was too early for that right now, but he talked about going beyond a life experience and absorbing *all* life experiences," Lil answered.

Lil could see that Ari was being crushed under the weight of everything he'd heard, so she was just waiting silently to give him some time as she held his face in her hands. He watched Ari for a while, not saying anything, hoping that he could carry this weight. Ari seemed devastated. "So my parents left me willingly? Do you really believe that?" he said.

Lil said, "It's not personal, dear. I lost my family too; even today, I lost the last remaining member of my family. Your parents have acquired the love all parents ever had for their children, Ari. Imagine if all the love, hope and happiness in the world flew through you. Who could resist that?"

Crushed under the weight of what he'd heard, Ari tried to control himself, involuntarily kneading his face like it was dough while trying. "I'm going to get out and get some air," he stood up as he felt like everything was coming towards him. He left alone, refusing Lil's offer to go together as if he was begging her. Although Lil felt very uncomfortable leaving him alone, she respected his wishes, thinking that it might be better for him to be alone, because she knew how she herself had felt upon hearing all this for the first time.

11 JULY 2035

Lil opened her eyes in the morning to see Ari sleeping on the sofa. He woke up while she was covering him up with a blanket. "I came in late and I didn't want to wake you," Ari said. Smiling at him, she asked, "Are you feeling better?"

There was a soft knock on the door. Lil put a kiss on Ari's cheek on her way to the door. It was Al. "Did I wake you up? I thought we could have breakfast together. You also need to store energy before you leave," he said gently. Al continued as Lil and Ari looked at each other in surprise. "It's not a permanent departure. I know you won't want to miss your grandmother's funeral, Lil" he said.

"So can I go?" Lil excitedly asked.

Al, "You need your strength for that. I'm waiting for you outside. When you're ready, we'll go have breakfast first. Then we will attend the ceremony."

"You could have contacted us in another way if you wanted to," Ari said to Al, who was turning around, after a moment of hesitation.

Al smiled and said, "Being able to do something doesn't mean you'll do it all the time. And don't underestimate the power of courtesy, such as inviting someone by going to their door," and he walked away. The dining hall was empty when Lil and Ari got there. But they could see a table with food and service for two. "Our favourites," Lil said with a smile on her face as they sat down at the table. The table was indeed set with both of their favourite dishes and everything looked perfect.

Ari smiled, saying, "It's not like we have any secrets from Al," and then ate up the best pancakes he'd ever tasted with the best blueberry jam he'd ever tasted and washed it all down with the best tea he'd ever tasted. Meanwhile, Lil was busy with her favourite grilled cheese with tomatoes made from her favourite bread and cheese along with hot chocolate.

"I know I always react the same way whenever you do that, but seriously who drinks hot chocolate with grilled cheese? Ari said as he teased his girlfriend.

"I do," Lil replied, smiling. Al showed up at the door when they still had a couple of bites left.

"How are you?" he asked.

"We're fine. How about you?" Ari replied.

"I feel better the more time I spend with you," Al said unexpectedly. The two lovers stared at each other in surprise but did not dwell on it.

"Shall we go?" Al asked Lil. "Are you feeling ready?" he asked, turning to her. The young woman nodded. Al this time turned to Ari and said, "While we're not here, you can walk around the school and spend your time as you like."

Ari was worried, "Am I not going? I have to be with Lil and Judi was very important to me too," he said.

But Al sadly said, "I'm sorry, Ari, but I can only take one of you. And I think we both know who it should be." Ari was disappointed, but he could understand.

Al brought Lil to a cave, lit only by a big fire. "Are you going to say that just because we have electricity doesn't mean we'll always use it?" Lil joked.

Al laughed unexpectedly from his calm attitude and said, "No. I like looking at a burning fire, so I always used to light one. My students who saw that prepared this room for me. Then people started calling this 'the first human cave.'" Al took a burning firewood and handed it to Lil. Seeing the wood burning in his hand like a torch, Lil realised that the fire he was holding was a blessing from Al. Al brought her closer to the walls of the cave and guided her to hold the torch up to the wall. Looking at the illuminated wall, Lil couldn't hide her surprise. There were pictures on the walls that resembled those of the first people. The only difference from the first people was that there were pictures of every subject that the present people were a part of, whether they wanted to be or not. There were even pictures of the robotic bodies that people had. But students had generally followed a more traditional approach and usually preferred to paint pictures of animals. However, innovative drawings such as pictures of rockets, space shuttles, new vehicles and even Galileo were also on the walls.

Al said, "This was the idea of one of our students. One day while sitting with friends, she said 'We call this the first human cave, so why not draw paintings on the walls like them?' So this place has turned into this beautiful space more than I could've ever imagined. Although they admire me, there is something they don't know. I admire them more. Making friends with people was never my strong suit. Lonely people like me usually choose things like anger, jealousy as friends. My teachers, who decided to train me to be a wanderer, said that I was chosen because I was happy to see friends together, and didn't have anger or jealousy One time, someone caused a very serious problem at school. I was seventeen or eighteen. He was very popular and had a girlfriend. I thought that he could get kicked out of school and everyone would be very upset, especially his girlfriend, so I tried to take the blame. And believe me, I was a very talented student, it took a long time for even the teachers at the school to realise that I was trying to take the blame. Then when they found out, I became very popular. The boy who caused the problem and his girlfriend, who is now his wife, are still my best friends. Even though we don't really see each other much at the moment. Anyway, friendship is a good thing," he said, then feeling embarrassed went on, "I've talked a lot, but I haven't said a word of what I really have to say. Sorry."

Lil said, "No. Please. It was beautiful. And so was seeing these pictures. Thank you for sharing this with me. You'll be too busy with me anyway by taking me to my grandmother. It's very kind of you to share all this with me beforehand." "

"Well... Yes. As for that... This journey might be a little different," he said.

***

Even though Ari's mind was completely full with his girlfriend and Judi's funeral, who he'd loved in a very short time, he decided to walk around the school until they returned because he was very curious about the school and the content of the lessons. He first went to the inner square by

205

the entrance, which seemed to have sprung out of a science fiction film. Students of the class, which were formed in groups of eight to ten, consisted of people of various ages ranging from teenagers to people in their forties. After chatting with the people around, Ari would learn that it was because each student was discovered at different stages of their lives by "scouts" wandering the streets to find students. The classes were scattered throughout the inner square, which was large enough to resemble that of a large metropolis. However, there was nothing like a folding screen or wall separating them. Just like groups of friends sharing a square, everyone seemed to be interested in their own group, creating their own invisible barriers. This environment was very friendly to Ari.

"A different show in every corner," he said to himself, giggling. When he looked around, he saw classes trying to develop their mental abilities through different practices, such as levitation a few feet from where they were sitting, growing plants in pots within minutes, trying to move various objects. Since he thought that levitating was the first step to "flying", he went to the class that worked on levitating and going up to the teacher, "Can I join the class?" he asked.

She was a young woman in her thirties with red, lush, curly hair, green eyes and a sincere smile, "New to the school?" she asked.

Ari replied with a similar smile, "Yes. Actually, I haven't started my training yet. But I'm really curious about the way your classes work."

"Our lesson is always open to curious eyes. That's why these lessons are held in the school square. To inspire people who have just joined our teaching. But even though I don't want you to misunderstand me, at this point, you'll only see people trying to levitate. If that's what you want, you can watch as much as you like. We'd be happy to have you. But if you want to get some idea about our teaching, I suggest you join the beginner's classes for our students who are at the beginning of their training. The choice is yours," she pointed at the mountain side of the square.

After a brief reflection, Ari decided that instead of watching a show that would make him happy for a while, it would be more useful to learn how the aforementioned teaching provided the students with such amazing skills. He thanked the teacher with a smile and wished her a good lesson and began to walk towards the place where she had pointed.

When he came to the wall side of the square, he realised that it was much quieter. Again he could see classes with groups of eight to ten people. However, contrary to the ones at the square, the lessons here were more theoretical than practical. Students of different ages were listening to what they were being told. And next to each group were rooms surrounded by walls made of monolithic rock shaped by the power of the mind. This time Ari was unable to distinguish between the groups by observation, so he investigated a bit and approached the group he had learned was the newest class of the school and asked for permission to attend the class. The teacher told him with a warm welcome that he could sit anywhere in the group. The teacher seemed younger than twenty. There was a pair of braids extending to the back of her neck more appropriate to a child. Ari understood that the vast majority of teachers were women, but he was surprised that such a young person could've become a teacher. When Ari took his place in the group, the teacher started to talk: "First of all, I want to introduce myself, as there are people who don't know me yet. I'm Su. I will help you to embrace your feelings as the first stage and the basis of your teaching. I know that wasn't very clear. I can explain: If you succeed, when our lesson with you is over, you'll have learned that it is your choice to feel every emotion, including the worst ones you have, that you experience them as a result of events you choose to value, that appreciation makes you more valuable, and that you shouldn't put pressure on yourself for your feelings. You will also learn to release both yourselves and your emotions. If we accept that the emotions that shape our lives, such as sadness, joy and fear are only the result of our life experiences and the way we interpret them, and if we accept them as they are, we can overcome the barriers we have established in our own minds and reach our full potential. However, we all grow up with examples of people judging everyone around them and judging themselves as a result, so we turn into similar examples. This judgement turns into a race that we cannot quit, even if we want to. We can't stop ourselves from competing with others even when we were alone, like when we lie down in our beds and lay our heads on the pillow. This causes us to badly shape the way we experience our emotions and then we get trapped in the barriers we create ourselves.

"For example, when we lose a relative, when we our love isn't reciprocated, when we fail, we get depressed and even push ourselves to the point of suicide. This is because we compare our unique life experiences with those of others. We cannot stand to see people who spend time with relatives we have lost, who share the experiences we can't with our unrequited loves, and those who have the opportunities we cannot have ourselves or offer our loved ones.

"The pressure we have created for ourselves causes us to be depressed when we have such experiences, and even before we have bad experiences, the fear of actually going through them weighs so heavy on our backs and the burden makes it difficult for us to go forward. My job is to help you focus on your own life experiences by making sure you get rid of the burden of other people's experiences that are not under your control. If you ensure sufficient focus on your own experiences, you will be able to see that all the conditions in which you live are under your control.

As I understand from the unsatisfied expressions on your face, you doubt that what I say can lead you to a "flyable" level. But the basis of our teaching is to develop a correct way of thinking and perception. You can master our teaching only with a correct way of thinking and perception."

***

Al said, "Let's look back at what we've talked about. All you have to do is open your mind to me again. So I will connect our minds together and then we share my body during this journey. I'm going to change my appearance and disguise myself as a funeral officer. I'll be the one who controls my body again because it's not something you can do for now. But you will see everything I see, hear everything I hear, touch everything I touch. In short, all my senses will be working for you, and the information transmitted will enable you to react as if you were there. I'll just be doing strenuous things, and I'll be as out of sight as possible while I'm living this experiment, so as not to distract. I'm sorry for that, but it's too risky for you to go there any other way. Judging from their understanding of my communication with Ari, they will evaluate every possibility at the funeral, and I don't even know what facilities they have to capture me. That's why this is the safest way I can think of to get you to that funeral." Lil said, "I understand. Thank you very much. I can see how much you're sacrificing and risking for me. The only thing that confuses me is that when you are such an important person, do you trust me enough to open your mind to me and share your body?"

Al said, smiling, "That's exactly why I would trust you, you're asking this question. But I have to tell you in al sincerity that I don't have to trust you right now. Because right now you don't have enough mind power to put me in danger. But I believe that there will be a day when you'll be able to achieve even more. And when that day comes, you will be the people should trust the most."

Lil was surprised, "Me?" she asked.

Al sitting cross legged next to the fire in the peaceful cave with no sound other than calming sound of the firewood, asked Lil to sit in the same way right across him. Al said, "You have to give me some time." So he closed his eyes and went into some kind of trance. Lil had no idea how long she had to wait, so she excitedly waited for Al to open his eyes to say he was ready. Her spirit was bound with the sadness of seeing her grandmother for the last time, and the excitement of what she was about to do. She was feeling better about her grandmother. Now she knew it was her choice, and she deserved respect. After a while, Al opened his eyes and grabbed Lil's hands, which were much smaller than his own. Lil passed out like an anaesthetised patient. When she came to, she looked around first, then at the hands, arms, and the clothes of the body that she was in. Despite all the encouragement she had given herself, she began to struggle in a panicked state. Her mind seemed to have difficulty in understanding what was happening. Luckily, since she was alone in a utility closet, no one would see it. Soon she began to hear Al's voice in her mind: "I knew this would happen. That's why I did the mind-sharing in this room. And I've blocked your access to your vocal cords just in case. But to help you through this moment, I've let you take a look at your hands and your body. Everything will be just like I said. I'll be doing all the hard work." When Lil nodded to show that she understood, Al said, "You don't have to do that. I know you understand."

After the ceremony, Lil witnessed every moment of her grandmother's burial. She tried several times to wipe away tears from her eyes, but there were no tears in her eyes. The experience was incredible. She saw and felt everything about the ceremony. She perceived everything differently than she thought she would. It was like she'd been preparing for this day her whole life. The emotions she was experiencing got to such a point that it was as if she would do something she'd had to do thousands of times over and over again, at a slower pace forever. She was taken by a terrible feeling. It was eating her up inside. The body she was in became unable to hold her mind and she started screaming uncontrollably. Even though everything seemed normal she felt she had to scream out. Her inability to do so made her panic more.

She called out to Al in her mind. "Please take me back to my body!"

Although Al had returned her mind at her request, he had to continue his duties as a funeral officer in order not to reveal anything. He was sure that everything was being monitored. After Lil woke up, she involuntarily got up from her seat and started running around. She was going mad. She had a terrible headache. After a while, Al returned to the room. He was calm. When he saw Lil running around, he said softly, "Calm down, you're in your own body now."

Lil looked at Al in horror and then she passed out as Al put his hand on her shoulder and said, "You were very good."

Al was waiting by her side when Lil opened her eyes in her room. Seeing that Lil was recovering he said, "Are you feeling better? You've endured much more than I anticipated."

"I'm fine," Lil said as she sat up, feeling suddenly exhausted. She was grateful to Al for helping her by making such a sacrifice, even though he didn't agree with her about "the final journey". She felt she was in his debt when she thought what sharing his body with another mind could make him feel. Al said, "The worst part is over. If you're feeling better, let's get out of here and find Ari and take a walk in the woods. Walking in fresh air will do you good. Then maybe we'll sit by the lake. Or if you want to be alone, I'll leave you and come back."

Lil said, "I felt like I would never be myself again. As if I'd have no more memories of my own... Thank you so much for what you did to help me. I can't thank you enough..."

Al pretended not to hear, "Actually, I should not be the one to decide this. If you prefer to rest in the room instead of walking, it's up to you," he said. As Lil's heart rate returned to normal and her colour was restored too, she said, "Walking might be good." She said, getting out of bed. "Of course, seeing Ari too."

After a short walk through the school, Lil and Al arrived at the large hall by the entrance. When Lil saw Ari sitting on the floor, watching the students, admiring them, as they moved toy horses with their minds, she ran to hug the young man. It was such a strong hug that they fell over together. His girlfriend was crying silently, almost buried in him. "Are you all right?" Ari asked.

"I'm better now," Lil replied. When Lil had drawn enough strength from her boyfriend, she helped him up and walked over to Al, who was waiting a little way away. Al, Lil and Ari left the school and took a short walk through the woods, arriving in the spot that had greeted them when they the first arrived. When they saw three chairs there and three steaming cups of tea on a table, they were already over the stage when that would be shocking. They sat on two closest chairs. As soon as they took their first sips of tea, Al started talking. It was clear that he would talk about something he had planned in his mind long ago: "I know that I'm drawing you into something in a big rush. But this rush is not just for me. We're all running out of time. I'm sure you've been wondering why I've been interested in you since we've met. It's because I think you might be able to do more than I ever had.

"As you may have noticed, I am the leader of our community for now. Leaders like me are called wanderers. "And I have to admit that I'm one of the most unsuccessful wanderers in our history, perhaps the most unsuccessful if we look at what has happened in my era. And I'm the first male wanderer. All of my predecessors were women or a couple in one instance. I think women are more successful than men because they exist with the ability and responsibility to give life to a person. Ideally, wanderers should be composed of couples.

"However, as I said, this was only possible once, and we gave the greatest contribution to the universe during a couple's wanderings. Although there is no attitude towards love in any period of our teaching, the reason why there is only one couple in the wanderer's position is sadly because as people progress in our teachings, they begin to see love as more insignificant after they begin to dominate their impulses and emotions and approach the aims of the universe and our lives.

"In fact, in our teachings, people are encouraged to love. Because someone who has never fallen in love with anybody, who has never loved or cared for anyone like they do themselves, cannot find the motivation to care about the universe and the things living in it as much as necessary. That's why I'm interested in you. When I look at your minds, I witness that you do not separate yourselves from each other in your thoughts. As someone who has looked into the minds of many people during my travels, I can say that this is the first time I have seen it. When I saw your thoughts while looking into the minds of both of you, I was so confused after a while that I didn't understand if I was looking at your thoughts about yourselves or your thoughts about each other. I think you'll believe me when I say that that doesn't happen to me too often. I realise that everything is moving very fast and I don't want to overburden you, but we really have so little time. You are the only chance I can see right now to resist the oncoming trial and reach our potential."

"You wouldn't even know about our existence if you didn't meet Ari by chance and me through him. Why do you keep it from people when you have such a teaching?" Lil asked.

He didn't seem to be flattered. "You have to understand that the skills acquired through our teaching can make a person able to do anything. And if the wrong people attain these abilities, the result would be very destructive. I know that because we've had instances in the past. That is why we are so secretive about opening the doors of our community and teachings to people."

"So you're not much different from Galileo," Lil said with a hard and angry look on her face. Your faith in people is even less than his because he embraces everyone without discriminating."

Al answered, "I think you're wrong. Galileo says that due to the relationship of our minds with our present bodies, we cannot control our emotions and impulses, and this pushes us away from our potential. However, our teaching is not based on keeping emotions and impulses under control, but on embracing them as they are, meaning embracing literally. Not just the good ones like love and happiness. Even the bad ones like fear, anger. Embracing them even more. I think our biggest problem as humanity is that we cannot accept being sad, disappointed. However, if we can accept that we make the decision to experience such feelings because our lives are worth it and that they are part of our lives, we can free our minds and reveal their potential."

While Lil was listening without saying anything, Ari interrupted: "You're telling us we don't have much time. What do you mean?" he asked.

After a pause, Al said, "At the end of the year, people who are out of synthetic selection will be despatched to their designated locations. And I think there will be much greater pressure on them to move into their new bodies. The number of people we can add to our ranks is constantly decreasing." Both young lovers could see that Al was hiding something from them. "You were just telling us why you kept your teachings hidden from people. Now you're saying that the number of people you can reach is getting smaller," Lil said sceptically.

"We have you now," Al said, smiling. Realising that the young couple was becoming more and more curious, he added, "You will find answers to all your questions very soon. But I have to go now. I'm the one who's going to live chat with Galileo tonight. First, I have to give people something to hold on to," he said. As he walked towards the trees where the forest began, he turned and said, "I suggest you visit our school library to clear your heads. And our librarian is a person you'll want to meet." And he disappeared among the trees.

The young lovers enjoyed the enchanting atmosphere and regenerative air for a while after Al left. Although they both had endless questions in their minds, they hardly talked because they knew that talking to each other would only serve to raise their curiosity, and that they needed to remain silent in order to digest what they experienced. They both spent almost all of their time filling their lungs with regenerative air and absorbing the relaxing landscape. However, even though they did not use their words, they did not stop communing and getting power from each other, not even for a moment. Sometimes with the energy of the existence of one another, sometimes by catching each other's gaze in intersecting thoughts, sometimes with the warmth of their hands, they talked quietly until there was nothing left in them that they lived to the fullest. The quiet conversation they had together was very good for both of them. When both of them were able to digest things a bit, when they could think, at least when they remembered that everything would be much easier as long as they had each other and they felt much safer, they immediately thought of the library that Al had mentioned. Lil realised that they were on the same page when she looked into her boyfriend's animated eyes, so she said with an excited smile on her face, "Imagine all the information in that library."

"We cannot sit here and wait for the information in the books to come into our heads," Ari replied with a smile. "At least not yet," he chuckled. After a short laugh they held hands and headed for the mountain that hosted the school.

When they came to the library, they found that the librarian was sowing flowers in a pot full of soil, and her hands were covered with dirt up to her wrists. Ari was surprised to see this, since he'd seen students grow flowers with the power of their minds in a matter of seconds. "Umm... I've seen students grow flowers in seconds without touching the soil," he said in surprise.

As the librarian continued the planting, she looked up at Ari with her eyes widened in amazement, "Really? But how could that be?" she asked. Now Ari and Lil were astonished. The librarian had fun watching the young couple squirm for a while, then burst into a whopping laughter, saying, "I'm just kidding," so the young couple shared her laughter. Then she said, "Having something come to life in seconds means getting used to the absence of that thing in seconds. Our minds can make us capable of many things, but true love is a miracle that only time can create," she winked.

The librarian wiped the earth away with a cloth and shook hands with the young couple, laughing at how they said their names as they shook hands, "You can call me the librarian," she said. "And I think it's much more fascinating for the flowers to bloom up spontaneously among the stones, rather than what they do here," she added, then turned to the couple, "Come on, I know exactly what you're looking for."

They had decided to put an end to their astonishment and start working so they followed the librarian while looking at each other as if to say, "We have to get used to these things."

Contrary to what Lil and Ari had expected, rather than books, they were met with interrelated parchments that covered specific topics, with varying page numbers depending on the content of the subject. They were all original texts and papers from the day they were first written, as they understood from the different structures of the papers on which the parchments were written. But even though some of them were hundreds or even thousands of years old, all of the parchments were intact and uniform as if they had been written that day. "I have put together the topics that I think will be of most interest to you to make your job easier. I suggest you start your research with these, but you're free to spend as much time in the library as you want and explore every topic you want," the librarian said as she handed the scrolls she collected over to Ari. They were given a single deck of parchment for both of them. Only the parchment titled "Awakening" was given to each of them separately. They obviously wanted to make sure that they both read this chapter. "If you need anything, I'll be at my desk, planting flowers. So before you call me, make sure that what you need is more important than a flower coming to life," she said, laughing and left them.

Lil and Ari divided the parchments in two and sat down on the wonderfully soft cushions on the floor to read their half, starting with the chapter titled "Awakening" which was about the source of knowledge and skills the "capable" ones had. And this was how "awakening" was described:

"After the long darkness we had lived only with our deepest impulses, to survive and reproduce, the awakening began in the Nile Delta, where the earth and the fertile waters of the Nile River gave life, where we would realise that that place corresponds to the middle of the land mass of the world.

"Teachers from the heavens told us that we would be even more than we actually were. Even that they were us, and of course, we were them. But first they said, 'you must deserve,' and 'you must reveal what potential you have'. First, they showed us how to reach plenitude and abundance. They taught us how to use the river across the desert sufficiently and skillfully enough to be enough for a whole desert. Gradually surviving stopped being a continual war that encompassed all of our lives. They gave us the knowledge to live comfortably for a year by working only for a few months. After living in a constant chase with each other and with the conditions of the world we lived in, our lives had gradually come to a point where we lived knowing, planning and gave a day for a month, a month for a year.

"Then they said it wasn't enough. 'Now that you're done wandering in the dark, survival must no longer be a goal, but a tool for you. You're part of something much bigger than yourself. You were like this from the first moment you existed, even long before. It's time for you to wake up'.

"When we asked them how to wake up, they said 'by thinking. Thinking is proof that you exist and that you will exist. But first you have to learn how to think'. That's why we came here.

"'We have seen a potential that has faded away forever in your future. You hated yourself so much and you became so alienated from yourself that you became disgusted by the things that made you valuable and fell in love with the greatest obstacle before you.

"'So we came to you now to make sure everything is different. You will be the turning point in your history because you are waking up at the right time. It was too early before you, and it would be too late after you.

"They taught us how to divide and use time, cultivate the land and give life to it, see the future by looking up into the sky, the language of distances in all known and unknown directions, the secret of the world and bodies in which we live. And they gave us temples rising to the sky. Pyramids.

"They told us, 'You've started your life like the bottom floor of these pyramids. Just as every floor approaching the sky shrinks away from unnecessary stones, you will rise as you release unnecessary weights within you. You will multiply as you decrease. Just like the world you are on, the bodies you live in pull you down more and more as you multiply and become heavier'.

"After thinking that they had educated us enough, they gave to the ones they'd picked among us papers with words written on them. In these words, there was a power that allowed us to make big stones fly as if they were birds. "But we could not use the power in those words. When they saw that we had wrapped the papers with the words on them around rocks, they said, 'You will learn to think correctly in time'.. Then they gave us staffs, which they said held their power.

"With these wands in our hand, the power of our words was laid out and stones like big mountains turned into birds and took flight. Then they told we chosen ones that the words and staffs had no power, that whatever we thought would happen.

"'But despite all the miracles that we showed you, despite the training we gave you, when we told you that you could levitate the stones with the power of the words you wrapped the papers with the words on them around the stones and you failed.' 'You had to use wands to believe that we were doing all the work, that you were just the tool for something that took only a millionth of your might you used to move the stones.' 'But you did it. You proved your potential. Not to us. But to yourselves'.

"'Now you see for yourself what you could accomplish, when we teach you to believe in yourselves and to think correctly. Those staffs were actually for us to urge you to wake up from your sleep.'

"Then they taught us to believe in ourselves and to think correctly. Although none of us could build pyramids that would match the three pyramids they gave us, they chose the best students with the best pyramids to lead us.

"When they believed that they had trained us enough to carry us to our future, they left us by handing our fate back to us. While leaving, they told us that they left the pyramids as 'staffs' waiting for us in the centre of the world until the end of time as proof of what we did and could do.

"Then they taught us how to think. What we could achieve by thinking."

They both went deep into thought for a while after finishing this section. Then they continued to read on other subjects. Since Ari had always been interested in the story of Alexander the Great, he started reading the parchments with that name on them. He was shocked to learn that Alexander the Great was one of them.

He stopped reading there and turned to Lil. He told her that they had never even heard anything about the name of this community so far, but even in the parchments that they referred to themselves as "we". After thinking a little bit, Lil realised the situation. After talking about why they didn't name themselves, they decided to call them "the powerful" because they thought it would make it easier for them during their talks.

Ari, proud of naming such an ancient community, continued to study. As he read on, the question marks in his mind about Alexander the Great and his accomplishments during his short life were answered one by one. But even though the well-known parts of Alexander's story were extraordinary, he could not even have guessed about the more unknown and extraordinary parts.

Alexander had made great progress in a very short time with the teachings of the powerful. But after he lost his father in an assassination, he began to refuse to use his skills for humanity without getting any. After he ascended to the throne, he'd left the powerful, and followed the legends and their fame he had been admiring since childhood. He'd lost his faith in humanity because of his father's assassination, so he was burning up with the ambition to take control of the whole world and adapt it to his own way of life.

Knowing that any other way would mean his death, he'd kept the secrets of the powerful, but used the skills he had learned before he'd left them to achieve his goals. As Ari kept reading, he could feel the fragments come together in his mind about the man who had kept so many soldiers together and made them persevere at such a young age in unknown realms and through harsh battles unprecedented in history.

This was the only explanation for every time he had miraculously recovered and got back up and achieved unforgettable achievements throughout history, despite the fact that he had suffered dozens of fatal wounds in battle, and once had sword wound deep enough to split his head almost in two. But it seemed that these victories, which had looked great to Ari all his life, were not welcome by the powerful. As he read the scrolls, he found out that they thought that Alexander was a great disappointment because when he could serve the world as a teacher for many years, they thought that he had wasted his potential for personal and small ambitions.

"The powerful" had warned Alexander many times that he had stop what he was doing, that it was unacceptable for him to be assimilating the Eastern culture, which was a magnificent culture in itself and would become more important for the diversity of culture on the world, especially as time went on, but they were unable to stop Alexander. Alexander, who was beloved by "the powerful" during his student years, had them trying to deter him in the most gentle ways possible, but the increasing enmity of the climatic and geological conditions of his expeditions in the East, the increasing resistance of the enemies encountered and the greatest struggle being against diseases made everything much more difficult.

Although Alexander had to return from his expedition to the East, he was determined to return with a harder resolve and more powerful stance to achieve his goals. "The powerful" had conveyed to Alexander that, in order to prevent the destruction of the cultural diversity of the world, they would employ more drastic solutions. Ari now found the answer to the question he had about of the flock of crows who had acted strangely above Alexander's head and then fallen down dead at his feet upon his return to Babylon, about which the historian Plutarch had written in history. This was the last warning of "the powerful" to Alexander.

But even that hadn't deterred Alexander and he got inexplicably sick while he was planning to go on new expeditions. Several theories ranging from diseases to assassination by poisoning were suggested regarding his death, though none of them was ever proven. In the end, after grappling with indescribable pain and fighting the disease, Alexander had passed away in a way in a shroud of secrecy about what had made him sick in the first place, which was a mystery that wouldn't be solved even after thousands of years.

The last page Ari read on the topic was about the deep sadness and disappointment among "the powerful" after Alexander's death and Alexander's teacher who had initiated him into "the powerful", trained him but then decided his fate although it was devastating for him, and who'd left both his position and his life voluntarily after Alexander's death. And of course there was a section about how the acceptance into "the powerful" and initiation processes had changed after the eventful period of Alexander's life.

Lil had started reading with the part about Gandhi. And she got her first shock from finding out that Gandhi had been rejected by "the powerful." In the parchments, it was written that Gandhi's life and actions had been monitored for years, but there had been certain suspicions surrounding him. But when asked permission to look into his soul to dissipate those suspicions, Gandhi had refused them so they had decided that he wasn't worth of the teaching and the power that would have followed. Despite all that, he'd had help from "the powerful" for his actions that made tremendous impacts on the world and had gone down in history.

"The powerful" had contacted him to offer their help on his actions on the condition that he'd keep their existence a secret. Lil thought she now understood how Gandhi had been able to do his 388 km Salt March in 24 days when he was 61, and how he'd been able to fast for days at a time whilst protesting various things during his life and achieved such serious results. She'd read once about his fasting for 72 hours straight to protest the Jallianwala Bagh massacre. The parchments also gave information about the importance of keeping Indian culture from being assimilated as a British colony and the success of Gandhi's actions on supporting its preservation, since the culture enriched the world and its history.

When they exchanged parchments to read the other halves, Ari and Lil would see that "the powerful" had always intervened whenever a certain country or nation had gained enormous sovereignty over others and become a threat to them. They'd always talked about the importance of cultural diversity in the world.

Ari even said with a laugh, "Just like associations that work to preserve endangered animals, they've preserved endangered cultures." The further they read the more they saw how sensitive "the powerful" were about that. "The powerful" seemed to have intervened with many famous people from history: Genghis Khan, who had dominated almost all of Asia and set his sights on China, especially after burning the libraries of Baghdad and killing an estimated 10 percent of the world's population, had attracted the fury of many. So the pain he had inflicted upon people was in turn inflicted on him in his mind. It was written that out of shame he had asked for horses to walk on his grave so no one would ever find it, and he'd be forgotten forever; Napoleon, who had not settled for Europe but set his sights on the Ottoman Empire and even India; Caesar who also hadn't settled for Europe but went so far as to claim Egypt and its ancient culture; Mehmed the Conqueror, who had progressed from Anatolia into the heart of Europe and had aimed to do much more (whose death has remained a mystery throughout history).

"The powerful" had supported the Greeks, who were the last dam in front of European culture against the Persian Empire, which had spread from Asia to Africa and Anatolia and set its sights on Europe. They had helped 300 Spartan soldiers and the commander Leonidas show enormous heroism and beat the Persians and put an end to their dreams of dominating Europe; the story of which went down in the pages of history albeit in a way somehow exaggerated.

Then Lil looked at the parchment about Desmond Doss, who, even though he was a conscientious objector had joined the army because he couldn't stand the youth of his town fight his battles for him as he stayed safe and sound at home. He had refused to carry a gun however and worked as a medic. It was a story that she knew and was very impressed with, but what she didn't know was that he was one of "the powerful". That scroll told about how "the powerful" had a strict rule that a student who chose to abandon their education once would not be allowed back in the community, and how they'd broken their own rule only for Desmond Doss. Despite all the efforts of his teachers, Desmond couldn't accept being left behind in the war, but he had a heart too big to harm any person, so he had joined the war.

Desmond told his teachers that he wanted to join the war to save as many people as he could, and that was exactly what he did. Despite the fact that his team fell back from the Maeda set, he refused to retreat from the top of Hacksaw Ridge as it was referred to by the soldiers, because he couldn't leave the wounded soldiers to die back there. And within a single day, he had managed to bring almost 75 wounded soldiers down a 400-metre cliff. He had done that despite the land being a death trap filled with Japanese machine gun nests, patrol soldiers and booby traps. He even saved several wounded enemy soldiers. This made him the first soldier to win a medal of honour as a soldier who refused to use weapons.

It was written in the parchments how his companions and commanders confronted his actions, which could be described as torture, because they thought his refusal to use weapons would get them into trouble and how his training had helped them through all his trials. He was also loyal to his promise to "the powerful", and ensured that his miracles could not be connected with "the powerful" or their training in any way. His prayer, "Please God, please let me to save another one," which he'd said after every soldier he rescued, had been recorded in history as one of his greatest symbols. But Desmond Doss laughed at them and said, "God has just as much share in the souls I've saved as you. And I don't hear him bragging about it. Perhaps you still have a long way to go." This was taken very well by the head teacher of the time and Desmond was accepted back into "the powerful" so he could continue his training.

The second title Ari read was the most terrifying for both of them: Adolf Hitler. It was written in the parchments that his era would forever remain as a black stain for "the powerful". For the first time in history, the head teacher had a rival. Indeed, one of the students who had reached a point where they could compete with the head teacher of the period, thought that he was more suited to the task, and he'd expressed it openly and even rebelled when he could not find support. With his talents, he managed to disappear for a long time. Later, with the great efforts of "the powerful", it was discovered that he'd first been to Germany to support Adolf Hitler, one of the most terrifying men in history, to help his empowerment first in Germany and then throughout Europe which caused his soul to be imprisoned. It was written in detail how Hitler's big and hypnotised crowd was formed by the murderous soul, and how the effects of this traitor on this mass had been destroyed and how his inventions beyond the technology of the time of Hitler's leadership helped conduct experiments. It was not explained how his soul had been imprisoned. As soon as Ari read that, he began to wonder. He wondered if he had a chance to find that out.

The last part was about the decision to get people to agree to open their minds and even their deepest memories to the wanderers in order to prove they were worthy of the teachings, and the resolve to initiate them only after evaluation by the wanderers themselves. What surprised the young couple the most was that the powerful who were too picky to accept Gandhi were themselves rejected by certain people. In history, there were three people who did not accept the structures of "the powerful" and refused to join them, despite being approached by them: Hawking, Tesla and Confucius.

Stephen Hawking had refused to open his mind to the head teacher and said that even the fact that they'd asked was a huge attack on his personal dignity. In spite of this, he was diagnosed with ALS at a very young age and although he was told that he only had a few years to live, he'd lived unabated until the age of 76 with the help of "the powerful" who believed he was essential for humanity. Although this aid was initially provided without Hawking's help, it was later revealed that Hawking realised this and remained in contact with "the powerful" through his mind. He even informed "the powerful" first of his decision to leave this world and had asked them to help him. It was written that this was the reason he frequently warned humanity in the last months of his life, as if to say goodbye.

Nicola Tesla had said, "You give power to a chosen minority with your teachings, whereas I have dedicated my life to making ordinary people powerful. If I become like you and live a life different from the whole of humanity, my life will have no meaning," as he rejected them. The head teacher of the period stated he respected Tesla's decision, who'd rejected their offer even though he had a difficult life due to chronic illness, so he showed Tesla how he could overcome his illnesses with the power of his mind.

In an interview with Tesla, he even said, "When I was young, I got very sick because I couldn't do the things I wanted, but when I started dealing with things I wanted to I no longer got sick. Never underestimate the power of the brain." Upon hearing of this, the head teacher had talked to him about his concerns regarding their privacy. But Tesla said, "That was something I'd known before I became aware of your existence. Only seeing evidence has made it more effective in my life. You don't have to be afraid, I was just talking about my own ideas."

Confucius explained his rationale behind rejecting "the powerful": "What makes information valuable is knowing it. You keep the information you have for yourself and because of that, it loses its value. I prefer not to know something if I cannot share it with people." Nevertheless, even with his positive contributions, the head teacher became friends with Confucius to benefit from ideas and had carried his ideas into his teachings.

Famous quotes in the parchments, like, "All the flaws of a man who does not forgive himself can be forgiven", "Those who know their weakness are stronger than anyone. And stronger yet those who can command their weak side" were said to have started a new era in the teaching of "the powerful" and induced a leap in student development. This was the starting point of the most important teachings of "the powerful": "Embrace your emotions rather than restraining them".

Confucius had also told the head teacher several times that they should not intervene directly in the lives of people with whom they did not share their teachings, that the days when everyone could be worthy of those teachings could only come if people tried, made mistakes, perceived and developed on their own. "Either find a way, make a way or get out of the way." This much had been engraved in history, but there was more in the archives: "If you think they are not worthy of your teachings, give them the chance to have this merit. No matter how painful the consequences. This is necessary for their permanent well-being."

As Lil and Ari read the halves of the scrolls they hadn't read, thought as they read, discussed things and felt surprised they hadn't realised how time had passed. Ari had finished reading when the librarian came to them and warned them that the broadcast was about to start and that they should eat something. But Lil, who spent a little more time thinking, was reading her last page. She quickly finished reading and left the library with Ari. When the young couple took their places in front of the huge screen set up at the entrance of the school for the showing the broadcast, the part about the life of the participant of the day had already started. It was understood that Galileo, as he'd always done, had chosen a person who opposed him. But no one, except the students at the school, knew that he had actually chosen someone more opposed than they could have imagined.

At the part where Lil and Ari came it, it was mentioned that the man had been raised as a Catholic since he was a child, and that the catastrophe and changes that humanity had experienced did not move him away from religion, but actually made him see that he needed his faith more than ever and that he thought it was what kept him alive. Lil and Ari had questions when the ads started after the video ended.

"I wonder if Al has created a fake identity to go on the air, or is he just going to take the place of the man in the video?" Ari asked.

Lil thoughtfully answered those questions with questions of her own: "Doesn't Galileo's team prepare these videos? If so, isn't it less likely that he created a fake character? I mean, the guy in the video looks like he's in his forties, and he couldn't have been getting ready for that for fifty years, could he?" They continued to make predictions and ask questions until the broadcast started.

Eventually, when the broadcast started again, there were two chairs for Galileo and its guest in the simply decorated studio. The people at the school got even more excited when they saw the man sitting across from Galileo. They wondered if Al would reveal his identity, and if so, how he'd do it.

"First of all, welcome to the broadcast," said Galileo. "As you know, in order to keep this as short and as interesting as possible, we're going to get right to the point. You can start any way you like, either by asking me questions or expressing your opinions."

The guest said, "Yes, I know that on the broadcasts only the subjects that people are interested in, the most enlightening topics are talked about. So I'm going to get right into it. I'm addressing all the people watching us. I want to tell you that you are able to do everything in your current state, even though it has been kept hidden from you - and I am the current leader of a formation that's kept it hidden.

"And you can do this without the need for synthetic selection that Galileo offers you as the only way. He told us that in order to reach our potential, we had to get rid of our deep-seated characteristics and showed us the way. Most of what he said was right. We have fallen more and more in love with our bodies, which have become our prison, and their influence on our minds, and this has taken us away from our purpose. I believe that he's being honest with us and that he really believes it to be the only way.

"However, you should know that each of us is able to take full control of our bodies and the things that imprison us, such as lust, pain and fear, and we have the knowledge of all the secrets of the universe in which we live. You will learn over time why we keep it hidden from you despite all this. Almost all of you will see think we're wrong and hold us

225

responsible for what happened, but nothing will be hidden from you any more. At least not by us.

"Each of you has the potential to dominate every condition that you live in, dependent on or independent of you and its effects on you. Meaning all that Galileo promises and more. You just need to learn to think right. I know you have no reason to believe me after all that's happened, so I'm going to give you some proof."

Every person belonging to each of the two human species on Earth, witnessed Al change from the man whose life story was shown in the beginning of the broadcast into his own physical appearance without much effort. However, before Al could complete his transformation, the broadcast suddenly got cut off. The only place in the world where the broadcast wasn't interrupted was the school under the mountain.

Al and Galileo were left alone in the studio after the broadcast stopped.

"Why did you interrupt the broadcast while you're trying so hard to help humanity reach its potential? Aren't you curious about what I am going to say?" Al said.

"On the contrary, I am very curious, but you have not shown yourself until today despite all the catastrophes humanity has experienced; you have left them to their fate. There are so many unknowns about you, and it is unlikely that it will benefit humanity. Chaos is the most likely consequence of what you have to say," said Galileo.

"You're right about that. But I have good reasons. Reasons that might be too much even for you."

"Despite all the catastrophes and the synthetic selection I have created, you have emerged now, and not before. Why?"

"This isn't something we can talk about right now. First of all, there is a broadcast we need to finish for a world of people whose curiosity we have been arousing."

"So there is someone who can compete with me about multitasking. Impressive—"

Before Galileo could finish his sentence, the live broadcast came back on around the world. People had heard the last word Galileo said and they agreed, of course, it was indeed "impressive" but what was happening? Despite the point technology had reached, they couldn't believe that such a broadcast had been interrupted at this point.

"We're having some technical difficulties, so forgive us," said Galileo. I'm sure you're all curious. I was trying to figure out how Al did his illusion in the part you couldn't see."

"Illusion?" Al replied.

As soon as Al began to levitate Galileo's left arm and dismantle it with the power of his mind, the live feed was cut again. They were alone once more.

"Even though what you can do with your mind's power is truly extraordinary, it was I who developed the technology that the world possesses, inch by inch. You can know as well as I do where anything is, or what impact any piece in the world might produce. You can find it, but that will make you fall behind my speed," said Galileo.

Lil and Ari looked at each other in amazement as they watched the broadcast at the school. Despite witnessing what Al could do and his efforts to keep the broadcast going, they were confused by the flow that Galileo kept interrupting. With her eyes wide open, "Can he really be defeating Al?" Lil asked. As Ari was having trouble finding anything to say, Al started to speak again and clarify the situation.

"Do you really think so? This is not arrogance you have. You're not arrogant. Surprisingly, you just have no idea who I really am and what I can do. You can't even guess. I've let you sabotage the broadcast because it's going to overshadow the fact that I've kept secret all said on the air from them. As one of them, I told them that they were capable of everything and I proved it. You tried to stop it. This will only make them want to listen to me more."

The broadcast suddenly came back on.

"What I have told you and showed you is just a small part of what you can do. We have betrayed our potential enough to see Galileo, a machine of our own creation, as our saviour, even as a prophet, but it is time to embrace it. I will contact you again, but there is still time. There is no one who can stop me when I want to contact you. What I ask you is, please do not do anything to endanger yourself or others. Wait for me to contact you while keeping in mind the broadcast you are watching. Don't worry, it won't take too long," he said.

He thought that if Galileo spoke after him, it would have the opposite effect he was going for, so he interrupted the feed again and left the studio. When he left the studio, the security forces, who had been trying to enter for minutes, were finally able to open the door. But they would fall back empty handed.

***

Lil and Ari, who had been talking for hours in their room, about the reasons and consequences of what Al had done on the air, were still puzzled. They wondered about Al, the leader of a community that had left billions of people to their own destinies in order not to jeopardise their secrets despite all the incidents so far. What could have pushed Al to share his secret with everyone? Also, they both thought that what Al did and said was too reckless for someone as wise as he was. He also had not returned to school for hours after the broadcast. Acting so recklessly and disappearing was not something people would expect from him. Lil and Ari's hours of brainstorming ended with a knocking sound from the door. Just as Ari was going to get up and head for the door, they saw Al appear in front of the it. Noticing the blank look in their eyes, Al said, "I didn't want to be rude, but I also didn't want to see anyone from school after the broadcast because I don't think I can answer all those questions right now."

"Mum's the word," Lil said, laughing.

"I'm sure about that," Al replied. "So the reason I came here is this: Tomorrow is both your first day of teaching and you will collaborate with me personally. This will make you learn more quickly but get more tired. Have a good night's rest. Tomorrow you will not only start your training, but you will also have the secrets which no one other than a wanderer has ever had before. We'll start right after breakfast," he continued. Lil and Ari nodded, indicating that they were ready.

After taking a few steps to the door to disappear, Al turned to the young couple and said, "I know you find what I did on the air irresponsible. But you must get people ready before you show them a way to change their lives altogether. Just like I did with you, Ari. The fact that I have done things that are open to speculation will make everyone think more and discuss more about this issue, and they will have an idea about what they might encounter when we reach out to them again." Although Lil and Ari were not entirely convinced, they chose to trust Al at that point and just nodded in agreement. After taking a step back to the door, Al again stopped and turned to them, "By the way, you noticed the characteristics of our dining room, didn't you?" he asked. The young couple unconsciously turned their synchronised looks first to each other, then to Al and shook their heads. "When you go to our dining room, you'll find what you most want to eat, waiting for you," Al continued, "Didn't you notice that at your first breakfast?" and with that he disappeared as if there was a place where the door opened only for him.

Lil and Ari fell asleep among thoughts and conversations about what was so special about them, why Al chose to tell them things that had never been told anyone, at the expense of breaking the rules.

12 JULY 2035

When they woke up in the morning, neither of the young lovers could stand still in their excitement. Today they would learn secrets they couldn't even have imagined learning until a few days ago, and they would take their first steps towards realising their unthinkable powers and using them. They quickly got ready and made their way to the dining room. When they got there, they were surprised to see that there was no one but them. "We just saw people eating here yesterday; is it possible that everyone in the school got too advanced to need to eat in just one night?" Ari asked.

Lil shrugged to show she had no idea and said, "Maybe we got up too late. Or too early."

Soon after they had chosen one of the empty tables, they really saw, as Al had said, what Lil wanted most to eat at that moment appeared in front of them. A breakfast of oatmeal, milk, blueberries, blackberries, strawberries and almonds in a bowl that looked so beautiful that Lil wouldn't have the heart to eat it right away and would feast her eyes on it first. But there was nothing on Ari's side waiting for him. "I admit that sometimes I don't know what I want," Ari laughed after looking first at Lil's breakfast and then to his side of the table. "But I probably wouldn't have asked for a table for breakfast, would I?" he said.

After a short, bitter smile, Lil said, holding Ari's hand, "We can share this," at which moment Al put a toasted cheese and ham and a big cup of tea in front of him. "Good morning!" he said, as he joined them. Ari said, "Thank you," to Al, and he took his first bite from the toast, after recovering from the lull the flavour created on him, he said, "Does this mean I was expelled from school? If it does, please let me finish the toast at least." "And I'll have Lil, too," he laughed, taking another bite of his toast. Enjoying Ari's attitude, Al laughed and said, "You're too valuable for us to lose, even on your own. And don't worry, no one has ever been able to do that before Lil. In fact, Lil's breakfast is not our dining room's but *Lil's* doing. This is a test that we apply to everyone who joins our school." Lil and Ari stopped eating in surprise and stared at each other.

"So you're saying I did this with my own mind power?" Lil asked.

"I know it's hard to believe. Even for our school, but it's true," Al replied. The young lovers stared at each other for a while longer all wide-eyed and smiles.

Ari happily turned to Al and said, "Since we realised that you didn't have a name, we decided to call you "the powerful". When I think about what just happened, I think Lil should be the first person who really deserves to be called 'powerful'," he laughed.

Al replied with a smile and said, "If we had chosen a name for ourselves, we would have prepared the ground for our community to be exposed. I think being anonymous has made a huge contribution to keeping our community secret." After being silent for a while indicating that he was going back and forth on saying and not saying things, he decided to continue talking: "Actually, our expectation was that you both would achieve it. All our work was towards this, but we knew there was no guarantee. I'm surprised that even one of you has succeeded."

"How so? What do you mean?" asked Ari.

Al said, "All your life, you have both been preparing for today. Even since two generations before your lives began," he said.

"By you?" Lil asked.

"Yes."

"So our whole lives up to now, even the lives of our mothers, fathers and grandparents they've all been fully under your control?" Ari asked in surprise.

"No, that's not exactly true. We only helped you look at the right places at right times. In fact, when you think about the responsibility to be placed on your shoulders, you deserve to know everything from the beginning. When you went to the library to do research about us, you must've seen that these teachings were transmitted to us by a civilisation that could travel between planets. They told us they were some kind of universal shepherds. And of course, it was no coincidence that they met us and shared with us their teachings. Everything was part of their plan. So were we. Centuries ago, they told us about two concepts. Even though I cannot show you the way they showed us, today's humanity has just barely captured these two concepts. Dark matter and dark energy. These two concepts, which have the adjective 'dark' in front of them since there is not much information about them yet, are the basis of the universe, as the universal shepherds tell us. First of all, I would like to give you a summary of these concepts as humanity knows them.

"For the time being, we estimate that as humanity, what we call matter, including planets, stars, galaxies, makes up only a very small part of the universe—about five percent, and that for us, the part that remains in the dark, which we cannot observe, constitutes ninety-five percent of the universe. We are capable of perceiving only five percent of the universe. Of course that's different for us 'wanderers' but exceptions do not break the rule.

"We believe that what we call dark matter now corresponds to 26.8 percent of the universe and holds all the celestial bodies together. We can't prove it, but we can feel the effects of its existence. Because the gravitational force of the substances we observe is not sufficient to hold the celestial bodies that form the galaxies together. But in the ever-expanding universe, the spiral galaxies, which are constantly rotating, remain in bulk without disintegrating. This is one of the dark areas for today's humanity.

"The concept we call dark energy is the best answer we can ever find for the ever-expanding universe. I can explain it like this in its simplest form: If the universe continues to expand nonstop, there must be an energy that supports it.

"My summary of these two concepts is enough for you for the time being. Thanks to the internet you already have the opportunity to acquire more any time you want, and I think you will. But as an exception, my knowledge of these concepts is far beyond that, and given the sacrifice I will ask of you, I think you have as much right to know everything as I do."

Al explained the shepherds of the universe and their tasks, the dust of life, the creation of the universe and the beginning of life in the universe, leaving Lil and Ari's mouths open. Both had read the scientific theories that the building blocks of some amino acids needed for life and that various organic molecules were found in space above meteorites, even in clouds of interstellar gas and dust, and that these vital molecules could have dispersed into countless planets, including the world in which they lived, thus causing life to emerge there. However, it was unfathomable for them to know that there was such a concept as "dust of life". Al continued to speak at a slow pace so that the young couple could absorb as much as possible: "What I'm going to say now has been a secret that has only been transferred from wanderers to wanderers. But you make me think that the days when we won't need secrets are close. The task that the universal shepherds gave us was to multiply the number of souls who have learned to make peace with and love themselves and everything they'd come into contact with during their lifetime in the world we live in. When the individual experiences of such souls ended, they said that they could mix together and flow into our galaxy with perfect harmony and connect with each other to help our galaxy stay together. Thus, in time, our galaxy would be able to continue to harbour life without needing them.

"This was the punishment given to them by the creator. They were given the task of filling the universe with life in such a way that it would no longer need them, by making creatures that have love and peace for their environment despite their nature, from the creatures that had been made with intolerance in order for them to contribute to the universe with unlimited growth capacity. They said in order to be successful in their missions and go back home, they couldn't leave behind a single galaxy left in the universe that needed them. That's how it's conveyed from wanderer to wanderer.

"About a hundred years ago, the universal shepherds who contacted me personally, said that we had failed in the task given to us so far, that not only did we fail to help the universe remain together as a species, but that we could not even provide enough loving experience for the continuity of our *own* solar system. This means that if we continue this way, life in our solar system will soon be over. Since the creator had forbidden them from interfering with free will in creatures so that they could learn from their duties, neither could we.

"Especially in the last hundred years, we have been very unsuccessful in our mission and the number of people whose lives we could refer to as 'loving experiences' has decreased. I haven't been able to raise a wanderer for my position for so many years. For a wanderer to be unable to train someone for their position means that after a certain point they're just treading water and unable to leave their physical form. And as a wanderer of three hundred and fifty-four years, I still haven't been able to train someone to replace me.

"If this continues, there are two possibilities about what may happen to us: The first possibility is that universal shepherds, who do not want any sun to be wasted, can eliminate life and start life from scratch. The second possibility is that another species created in our galaxy may be allowed to come into our world and lead us to contribute to our universe.

"The only way to reach this point was to fall behind even our contribution until the time they started to train us. It's a shame that we've fallen behind our contribution even in those dark ages, despite all the development we think we've had. We're about to make them think that we don't deserve our sun and our world. They might already be thinking that way. All the catastrophes that happened in a short time didn't help us get better either. And humanity lost one third of its population in such a short time. All of this has played a very important role in bringing us to this very point.

"I shouldn't have told you this. This is not something you need to worry about right now. Anyway, I think with your help things might not get that far. Anyway...

"In short, what we think is the cause of the continuous expansion of the universe, which we call dark energy, consists of the expansion of souls condemned to drift in the darkness of the universe when their experience of life ends because they have loveless experiences. Even though the name makes a bad connotation, what we call dark matter and what holds galaxies together and enables them to harbour life is that souls with loving experiences help create new life experiences after their own life experiences are finished.

"If we have enough dark matter, meaning loving souls, this will mean the end of the universal shepherds' quest in our galaxy. So our galaxy will come under our control as the creatures that exist in this galaxy."

"We've always wondered whether heaven and hell existed," Ari said, in an enthralled way. "And if they did, what was their manner of existence? According to what you're saying heaven means having billions of life experiences after death. Including the people we've looked at with envy all our lives. And hell means being dragged into the bottomless darkness of space after death forever, to be trapped forever in eternal darkness and chaos that hasn't been put into order." He turned to Lil, and said, "Now I can understand what you meant when you said that death was a choice and we should be understanding of our loved ones." Lil reached out and stroked Ari's cheek and kissed him on the head.

"Wouldn't leaving all the creatures in this galaxy to their own means cause much greater chaos?" Lil asked Al. Al smiled, "If we can accomplish what I said, our galaxy will become full of loving and peaceful souls. And we wanderers are being trained for that. In order for the billions of souls who have experienced our galaxy in many different ways to continue flowing in harmony with our galaxy. If we come to my reason for telling you all this…" Al continued: "So in light of all this, I came to this conclusion, after thinking for a long time. If we can find someone who can accept going back into their bodily form after personally experiencing life after death and how love can change it, we can help others experience it by opening up that initial mind to them, and we can give people a spiritual leap that is enough to fulfill our duty. But there is a problem about this idea: No one would agree to have such an experience and accept being trapped in a bodily form again and being content with only one experience. I know this because wanderers like me can move in the universe in their desired form, even with their spiritual forms, free from physicality, without being bound to anything. You're wondering who wanderers are. Those who have mastered our teaching adequately and who have mastered the ability to control all conditions after being in control of conditions themselves are those with whom universal shepherds shared the next stage of their teachings in order to be replaced by them and go back home. Our mission is to create life in galaxies without life. We don't need to be involved in the flow of any galaxy in order to do that. After creating life in one galaxy, we can move to another galaxy to fulfill our mission and experience those galaxies in the form we want. In other words, though not continuous, wanderers can return to their physical bodies in the world and experience their old lives in the same way for a while. But I've never seen anyone do that even for

235

a moment. Even though they'd left all their loved ones in the world. That means they haven't missed their old lives at all.

"I believe that only a person who has experienced true love can do it. In other words, only someone who can truly love someone else as they do themselves can return to their loved one because they prefer to share a life experience with the person they love, by giving up the grace of having all experiences. And I made a decision: I have to help two people grow up and meet each other so that they can love each other like their own selves and see what the true love is. Imagine how big a spiritual leap we could achieve, if we could show human beings the souls that are flowing with great harmony in that galaxy in order to create life and to preserve life in a galaxy, and the feeling of being able to have all experiences as a part of it, and how humanity can only be a part of it if we make our lives a loving experience process.

"After all disasters, humanity has become so hungry for change that it makes what we want to do even more possible. Of course, when I looked into your minds with your presence, I saw that you loved each other as much as you did yourselves. And thanks to the synthetic selection that Galileo has given us, the fact that we can transfer a copy of our minds into immortal robotic bodies will make our job easier. So far, I think our plan is moving firmly towards success."

"Is Galileo your work too?" a surprised Lil interjected.

Al started explaining with a suppressed smile, trying to hide his pride, "Universal shepherds talked to us about the species that transferred their minds to robotic bodies. They told us that if it's done successfully, it would be no different than copying the soul, thanks to this method, each soul could continue to contribute in both physical and spiritual dimensions, each species that would go through that process by copying their souls could free their souls and volunteer to make their solar contribution and that we could give that method a try. In other words, if we try to make sense of it, we will be able to provide people with the opportunity to continue their life experiences as they began to experience them individually and physically, and to contribute to the solar dimension by passing to the spiritual dimension. Thus, the fear of not being able to experience the time that will flow outside of them, the fear of death as they interpret it, will no longer be an obstacle for us. We could only achieve the technological leap that would provide humanity with that opportunity with the help of a supercomputer. We thought that if we could give people an option to copy their minds and reach an eternal life, when the time came, we could convince them to turn into life energy ahead of time and give life to other living creatures. This could only be done with the help of a supercomputer," he said.

"So you actually invented Galileo? Were you Daniel?" he asked.

"No," Al said. "Our mission is not to save the day by giving people fish but to teach them how to fish in order to provide permanent solutions. Just as universal shepherds did with us." Seeing that the young couple was really confused, Al continued: "We've only made it possible for people with the potential to make such an invention to look in the right direction and help them go from the primitive experiments of computers, to Galileo. The rest is their own achievement.

"Wanderers scanned the world for people who would carry us to this point and provided the people they believed would achieve the goal with the right information, the right perspective and the right person to meet with. Of course, since we were forbidden to intervene directly in the human mind, it took longer than we had anticipated, but I believe that we still have time, and I think we are fast enough when I think that a hundred percent success in copying human minds has been achieved in these days when I met you face to face.

"I don't know how familiar you are with his stories, it was the finishing touches of our years' worth of efforts to introduce Daniel, who had access to all the information he needed and had every opportunity to create something much bigger than himself, and had a great desire in his heart to move humanity forward and Emilia, who was the right person to show the most accurate perspective to Daniel's helper and to create a more human character for humankind than humanity itself.

"Daniel and Emilia have been under our radar since before their birth. We had identified certain names in our minds about how people who could bring us to this point would emerge as a result of our scans around the world. And we have watched lives of all the names we had identified in our community.

"I can summarise it like this: from a grandfather who had to work constantly to provide good opportunities for his son because he had suffered from economic difficulties in his own childhood and who always bought video games for his own children so they wouldn't feel his absence, came a father. From that father who had been enthusiastic about video games since his childhood and enjoyed playing the constantly developing games with his son, came a son, Daniel. Daniel wanted to know every detail about the construction of games that could feel like they'd been teleport into a medieval, inter-alien war, a world invaded by zombies, as if he and his father had a time machine; and from an early age he would be interested in the construction of these games, and then, as time went by, his interest would turn to the building of computers, and he would become a genius of a computer engineer and even give life to an artificial intelligence that would change human history. And of course, from the parents who have started to lose their human emotions as a result of the professional deformation brought on by being two of the few most respected surgeons in their country, was born a girl, namely Emilia, who, having witnessed their indifference and certainly never wanting to resemble her parents, would make it her job to love everything and everyone around her turn to philosophy for she believed that it would lead her to the deepest of loves.

"There is an irony about these two beautiful people; Although we helped them to look in the right directions throughout their lives, we helped Emilia not to look in a certain direction by shining a light into her eye as she turned a corner on the day they met. So she met Daniel and her life turned into a wonderful journey."

Tears were coming down Lil's face because of the mixed emotions she felt, and she could not describe the emotion that caused her to weep this way. It could be happiness, hope, frustration, trust, insecurity or all of them at once. Since she'd been trying to understand all that AI had said, it only then dawned on Lil what AI had just said.

Noticing the tears on her face, Ari asked, "What's wrong?"

Lil, who didn't know the answer to that question herself, turned to AI and said, "Our lives were also part of your plan, including meeting each other, right? Just like Daniel and Emilia were brought together to create Galileo, we were brought together with Ari to have the kind of love that could make your plan come true."

Al said, "We shouldn't simplify it like that. Your lives were more than just a part of our plan. You were our plans we wanted to have. A result of our efforts, you were our hope that all of our questions would be answered, that we wouldn't have to plan again."

Unlike Lil, Ari knew exactly what he was experiencing: a feeling of having been deceived. He felt as if he had been dropped from the highest point in the world. As if all his experiences were fake. Emotionally crashing downwards, looking up into Al's eyes with a frown, "What, are you now telling us that everything we've lived, including our love for each other, was part of your plan? Were we just puppets you held the strings to?" he asked.

Al replied, "Absolutely not. We've just put two people like you who have great thoughts about love in one another's way. This is not much different from when one sets two friends up and it leads to a relationship. Everything you felt when you looked into Lil's eyes for the first time was true, even though you saw her in a terrible state in front of the trash can. In fact, I thought that if I had a chance to choose such a thing, I would give up all the knowledge and ability I had to feel what you had felt. Everyone thinks they're born to accomplish great things. All the lovers in the world think they were made for each other. But nobody knows whether they're right or wrong. And you do now. I'd never claim we're God, which we're not. Every person's life consists of his or her choices. We've only made the options visible to you, which you might have missed. All the choices you make are just your own. We just hoped that you would choose the options we made visible to you. We couldn't have done more than that anyway."

Ari, with his eyebrows almost intertwined, asked "Well, what about the loneliness I felt after I lost my parents and until I met Lil? How much of that was your work?"

"I have to admit, we've helped you think about whether loneliness was a better option, making certain bad experiences clearly apparent to you after your parents. In fact, the same goes for Lil as well. You chose to completely retreat, creating safe, vicious cycles for yourself. Like the times you spent making squirrel videos. But those vicious cycles preserved your purity. Lil always chose to put serious distances between herself and her friends and keep a very important part of her mind and heart to herself. So you both made different choices. But both of you somehow managed to isolate yourselves from the increasingly polluted world around you. That's how you could stay so clean. That's how you loved each other so much."

"But why didn't you get in touch with us until all this happened, even though you've prepared us for so long?" Lil asked. Al said, "We waited for the right time. Failure to contact you at the right time could've put everything at risk. Your maturing phase, the maturing phase of your love would change with our involvement in your story. We could not have predicted whether that change would be good or bad. Therefore, we trusted the universe and one of you have waited with us for the usual course of life. That's how we would know that the right time had come."

What they heard was too much for Ari. He had been looking for signs of intervention in his entire life since his birth. At the same time because of all the things he was thinking about, his eyes went dark momentarily as his brain was short-circuiting. For Lil, everything and everyone seemed to disappear from the world. There was only one truth for her right now: Ari's thoughts. Because she was afraid that what Al said would change Ari's perspective on their love, Lil wiped the tears that were still inexplicably gliding from her eyes, and said, looking into her lover's eyes, "Ari, I don't care if it was someone's plan for us to meet. I don't care if someone decided my life for me. I would prefer a life where someone chose you for me over a life without you a thousand times. You're more than I can imagine, let alone choose. Please don't let this come between us." Then she hugged him tightly enough to leave him breathless.

Ari's eyes filled with Lil's show of her love, "No," he said, "never. It's just that this is all too much to take all at once. In this vortex we are drifting through, you are the only truth that I can hold on to, to help me find my way, you are the compass that always helps me not to get lost." Since he was unable to move due to Lil embracing him with all her strength, he just kissed her repeatedly on the shoulder where his head was trapped.

After giving them some time to gather some strength from each other, "That's exactly what we were hoping for," Al said, "but we still have some things to talk about. You must decide whether you accept the great sacrifice that we ask from you and the risk you must take on with it. We must persuade people who are still experiencing the world in which they exist, to abandon their physical existence and blend into the universe's mortar. If we cannot make enough contributions, the end of life in our galaxy will come, even synthetic selection won't be enough to prevent this finality. Galileo will tell the people we want them to give up their selves for the balance of the universe, that they can live on to in the world in which they'd always called home, by transferring everything they have experienced to a robotic body. In spite of all the pain they have experienced, the souls that have not given up on their lives for a more comfortable life by embracing the life they've been experiencing and what comes with it, are more than we can hope for. In fact, I believe that we're really going through a selection when I think that the souls coming out of the absolute war of life with more power will ensure the continuation of our species. Galileo was right in most of what he said. But what he didn't know was that the selection we had to go through had to be spiritual, not synthetic."

Ari was looking at Al with fire coming out of his eyes, he said, "I hope you are aware that this is your fault." Al bowed his head in acceptance of his guilt. Lil wanted to lighten the air because she realised that her boyfriend's anger would continue and thought that what was past was past, and that what was best for now was the endeavour of everyone to do their very best. She calmed him by putting her hand on his shoulder as he was just about to continue talking. She turned to Al and said, smiling, "There is something I don't understand. From what you're saying, you must be almost four hundred years old. Of course you don't show your age, but as politely as I can put it, you don't look thirty either. We've also seen that you can make any changes you want in your body. Why do you choose to look as if you're in your fifties?" she asked.

Al was grateful for Lil's effort to change the subject, "If I looked young, I would have to spend most of my energy trying to be taken seriously. We have seen examples of that," he replied.

Just then, the librarian entered the cafeteria in a hurry and drew all the attention, "You must see what's going on on TV!" she shouted. Al projected the broadcast the librarian was talking about on the wall of the dining hall as if there were a television there. Even Al's eyes widened with the horror of what he saw. Although the body of the extra-terrestrial creature with its khaki-coloured scaly skin with an insurmountable stiffness resembled human anatomy, it had four arms extending forward and backward on both sides, and two large eyes on both sides of its head, suggesting that it had a 360-degree view. The extra-terrestrial seemed to be sitting motionless in front of cameras on air, but as soon as they started watching the broadcast, Al, Lil and Ari heard everything it had been saying literally in their heads. But in their own voice. Apparently, it was communicating with them in a way they could never have imagined. What they perceived was short, concise and blood-curdling.

"From this moment on, the world is under our control. The bodies and memories of those who live in their robotic bodies are also under our control. Those who continue their lives as they were born should surrender to us immediately. All lives are precious to us. Therefore, we ask that you cooperate in order not to waste any life. This is not a struggle you can win."

Al, who survived the first shock, unlike Lil and Ari who were frozen in place, turned to the librarian and said, "No one leaves school," before disappearing.

***

As soon as he heard the news, he went to the closest centre where the memories of the superhumans were stored. When he arrived there, he saw two extra-terrestrials at the entrance, just like the one on television. They had apparently been tasked with protecting the building. When Al looked a little closer, he saw sadly that some of his former students who had been on the streets with various tasks were trying to secure superhuman memories as a priority. Four former students stood petrified a few steps away from the extra-terrestrials. As he made a move towards them, looking at them standing in the form of an unfinished movement, he thought they were not dead but somehow frozen. He really wanted to believe that at least, as they said on TV, "all lives were precious to them." Because the danger he was facing was scary even for him.

Students who were considered to be worthy of their teachings and admitted to school come to a place in their development and are given two options when a pause is observed at the point they come. Either staying on at the school continuing their teachings or contributing by taking on the most appropriate tasks in certain cities by providing services such as keeping an eye on people, or finding new students. Of course, if they wanted to continue to be part of the teaching after some time to reach the level of wanderer, they would be reminded that the school's doors were always open to them. Al remembered these four students who had been petrified at the gates of the centre. These four people, who had been friends since they were teenagers and were now middle-aged, had great potential to advance in the teaching and reach the level of wanderer. They even made Al think that it might not be necessary to have a couple in order to have more than one wanderer at the same time, and that more than one of these young people with such solid friendship and potential could have access to the wanderer status.

However, seeing what the world had come to, these four young friends, who could not bear to live safely under Al's wings in a school under the mountain, demanded to be assigned to the most places most in need, even at the expense of separation. The fact that he now saw them in this situation increased his fears even more about the future of people who had achieved such brilliant achievements in teaching during their stay in school. As he thought of other students who were out on the streets with different tasks, he made a mental communication with all the students in the streets and told them not to put themselves in danger until they heard word from him.

For a while, he studied the two extra-terrestrials at the gates and tried to find a weak spot. Soon after, he realised that extra-terrestrials were breathing similarly to humans but unlike humans, they were breathing nitrogen instead of oxygen. "Maybe they came to our planet because the vast majority of our atmosphere is made of nitrogen," he mused. After a brief moment of thought, he came up with an idea to overcome them. He could liquefy the nitrogen they breathed therefore cooling them down, freezing and fossilising them, just like they had done to his former students. He didn't know how much body resistance they had, or how effective his mental powers would be on their bodies, but this idea was worth trying. Liquid nitrogen was a very powerful and reliable freezer.

He couldn't believe what was happening when he noticed the fluttering of his heart. He could not have imagined that he would be in such a situation. But he recovered quickly and set out to carry out his plan. He started liquifying the nitrogen inhaled by the creatures and cool it down. The creatures that introduced a significant amount of nitrogen into their bodies each time they inhaled, they were indeed turning to stone with the first breath they took after Al's interference. Even though Al was surprised that something so simple was so effective, he was relieved, and his eyes shone to see his plan work. He immediately ran to his students and looked at how they were. He saw with great happiness that his students hadn't died, they were just frozen. However, since he couldn't see any trace of how that could've happened, he thought that the creatures he had just frozen were also advanced in using the powers of their minds. That made him even more surprised that his plan worked. But breathing made them extremely vulnerable because it was their most basic need, and it was an advantage for him to have time to realise that.

When he looked at the minds of his students, he saw that their minds had been trapped in some kind of maze. What he had to do was get them out of there. He went down to the depths of the labyrinth where they'd been imprisoned and communicated with them to show the way out. While his students slowly recovered, Al was busy calling out to the other students he had just asked to hide. He asked students in every city in the world, who were at a point in their teachings to be able to do it, to liquefy the nitrogen that the creatures inhaled, cool them down, and neutralise them. And then he told them to move the memory copies to a safe place where they could be stored. He stressed that their only task was to secure the memory copies in the centres and told them not to engage any other extra-terrestrial creatures except those at the entrances of the centres. He also warned them that if they had any petrified friends near them, they should move them somewhere safe and not take any action until he arrived.

He said that those who were unable to do what he'd said should immediately go back to the school, tell the teachers about the situation and send them to support the people outside.

***

Three or four hours had passed since Al disappeared. The people who gathered in front of the giant screen in the inner square did not leave their spots in hopes of seeing a movement on television although it had been showing anything for hours. Students kept going up to their teachers and asked if they had any information about what was going on. But the teachers didn't know anything either. They did nothing but make sure that no one left the school, as they were told to do.

Lil and Ari were desperately waiting in front of the giant screen in the square just like everyone else. They sat next to each other on the floor, leaning their heads on each other's shoulders, and praying that nothing would happen to the other one. Their silent wait on each other's shoulders ended with the sound of the stirring crowd. When they opened their eyes and raised their heads, they saw the crowd moving in certain directions in groups. Those who could not fight extra-terrestrial life returned to school by listening to Al. The crowd naturally went to the news sources that seemed closest to them. However, instead of answering the questions of the crowd around them, they were trying to get to the teachers. Eventually, after informing the teachers as Al told them, the crowd was getting impatient at the inner square.

They did not want to make the crowd more impatient and told them what was going on outside. They began to explain to the crowd that no multi-part machine, including the bodies of the superhumans outside were functioning, and told them about the way Al had found to defeat the extra-terrestrial life. But what surprised the crowd most was the situation of people who had not completed their mental transfers. Those who came from the outside said that a sound in an unheard frequency was being broadcast from certain points, that it drove the people that heard it crazy and they would do anything to stop the sound. They were running over each other to the points where the sound had spread from. Thus, by gathering people at one point, they would control the entire human species without distinguishing between the superhuman and human.

Although everyone in the crowd had dozens of questions about why extra-terrestrials, who seemed to have higher mental abilities, had gone through so much trouble instead of using an easier way to control people's minds, Lil and Ari were thinking differently thanks to what they had learned from Al. They wouldn't share what they'd heard of Al with the others, but as they chatted in the way only the two of them could hear, they agreed that the extra-terrestrials they'd encountered knew about universal shepherds. In other words, they must have been forbidden from intervening with the free will of humans. Because capturing people in a place together meant more trouble for them since people would attempt to escape.

The question in Lil and Ari's minds (unlike the crowd) how these extra-terrestrial life forms could attempt a planetary invasion despite universal shepherds. After their conversation with Al in the morning, they'd been thinking that that was the reason why no other species had attacked humanity until this time, but apparently it was not the case.

The young couple tried to understand why such an attack was taking place now and not before, but the only result they could have for now would be the conspiracy theories they couldn't justify. In addition, the fact that people had become so incapacitated with only a sound wave seriously shook their hopes about humanity. The idea that if they were outside, they would also have run to the source of the sound by running over other people, and especially the thought that either one of them could have fallen into such a state, caused their hearts to tighten.

***

Al felt that he did not have enough trained support to defeat the extra-terrestrials they were facing. Until now, they'd only intervened with the extra-terrestrials who were protecting the memory storage centres, and they kept the frozen creatures hidden so the method of their attack would not be found out. They knew that it was only a matter of time before those clever creatures found out about their simple trick even though they had managed to hide their methods of fighting back so far. Because since they froze instantaneously, they couldn't find time to communicate with others.

He was cornered by the lack of support he needed to fight back. Even though he was thinking as hard as he could, he hadn't been able to come up with anything better than that easy trick, but he had to try. He didn't think they'd get a second shot at fighting back once they were found out.

As he leapt between cities and countries to both secure memory centres and help the petrified students come back into their bodies, Al also kept trying to come up with a solution that would put an end to everything. He thought of liquifying all the nitrogen in the atmosphere and neutralise all extra-terrestrials at once but that would also petrify all the human beings, so he had to find another way. He decided to take a look at the places where people were being drawn to by a sound, to see if he could implement his plan without freezing everyone up.

When he went to the concentration camp closest to him and examined it a bit, he saw that these structures, which were built to keep people under control, were actually huge hangars developed with high technology. He thought that he could succeed in his plan by freezing all the nitrogen in the atmosphere if he could manage to get everyone currently on the job around the world, to block the air flow to all hangars with human beings all over the world. The hours that followed and his observations up to a certain hour made him think that there were no people left outside the hangars or the school. He instructed everyone who heard him to make a task distribution so that they didn't leave out hangars and, when he gave the signal, to block the air flow in those places. And he also instructed the same for the school.

When he was sure that everyone was in place, he immediately liquefied and cooled all the nitrogen in the Earth's atmosphere, thus destroying all extra-terrestrial life on Earth.

Al, after gathering all the extra-terrestrials that were frozen in all the cities in the world, woke one of them back up and told it that their invasion had failed, and that it should contact its planet to ask for extraction of all its kind from Earth. The extra-terrestrial desperately did what Al told it to do. After the extra-terrestrials left the world, all the multi-part mechanisms began to work again, including the superhuman bodies that had collapsed where they were during the occupation. Both the people coming out of hangars and the people who were able to move again were very confused. Everyone had endless questions needing to be answered.

Al, who had fought an invasion attempt into his world as a wanderer, did not have time to answer these questions. He left it to other servants of the teaching to make explanations to people. He felt that since he had

247

found a way to neutralise the invaders without killing them, and that their actions had been a power play, there would be no further invasion attempts anytime soon. At least he hoped so. But the die had been cast already and he knew that they didn't have much time. The shield over the life on Earth put in place by the universal shepherds seemed to have been disabled. He knew that, as humanity, they had to make great progress in a short time to earn back the shield. He had to talk to Lil and Ari as soon as possible.

***

When Al returned to school, he invited Lil and Ari to the first human cave to talk to them. He also instructed the whole school to not disturb them until they left their room. Aware of what was to be asked of them, the hearts of the young couple were so excited that the sound of their heartbeats seemed to echo in the cave. "Our worst fears have come true," Al said to them, "even I couldn't imagine that it would happen so soon. According to the information I got from the extra-terrestrials I contacted, they got permission from universal shepherds to establish a settlement in our world and increase their universal contributions and to receive the greatest contribution from us. They seem to have convinced them that we are wasting both our beautiful planet and our lives. Now what we need to do is prove our value and potential again before it's too late. I realise that what I'm asking from you is too much and you haven't even started your training yet, but you are our only hope."

In an angry and loud tone, Ari retorted, "What do you mean? Do you want us to experience life after death and come back to convince people to give up their lives even though you say yourself that we haven't even started our training yet? What if we can't come back to our lives?"

Al understood his frustration completely, so he said calmly, "Now you know that death is the beginning of a more beautiful journey. If you succeed, you can call all the remaining people on this journey. And if you fail... well, I don't think you'll fail."

But Ari's anger didn't seem to be dissipating that easily. He cried out in a louder voice than before, "If we fail, we'll just come to the end of our time of individual experiencing, which everyone believes has imprisoned us, is it that simple!?" As he wiped away his tears with the back of his hand, he was silent for a moment. Then he said in a breaking voice, "I'm not ready to leave Lil. I didn't have time to love her, to love myself. I just found her. We were going to learn to communicate with each other without talking." The sound of his suppressed crying made his last sentence almost inaudible.

Al put his hand on Ari's shoulder and said, "That's why no one else can do this but you. Trust me. I know you're not trained, but that's okay. I can make sure you come back safely, should you choose to return. I was raised as a wanderer, and I am as far from being trained by the universal shepherds themselves as finding a wanderer who would replace me."

Ari loved his girlfriend too much to leave her for the sake of any great purpose, but the vast darkness that his thoughts plunged in to find another way seemed infinite. It was as if at that moment he was experiencing the punishment that the loveless souls would go through in the infinite darkness of space after completing their individual experiences. Immersed in deep thought and silence from the beginning of the conversation, Lil was crushed under the weight of the only option offered to them.

"What if only one of us went through the life to come after individual experiencing period? If the person who'd do that failed to come back, could you make sure that they can communicate with the surviving one from the next life? Can that ensure our return?" she asked.

"That can work if you love each other the way I think you do, and if you fill your souls only with your individual experiences containing the other one when you hear the voice of the other and close yourself to all other experiences, despite having all life experiences at once," said Al. Ari looked at Lil in surprise, who had readily accepted the situation.

Lil clung to her lover tightly and said, "Ari, I don't want to lose myself when I'm next to you because of a sound I hear. I don't want to see you locked up in the hangar." Knowing that his lover was right, Ari breathed in the smell of her as if they would never see each other again and tried to memorise the rhythm of her breathing. Although they knew that the limited time that they had would never be enough, the two lovers embraced each other and tried to get enough of each other. They both had a question that occupied their minds: Would they be helping out each other by choosing to be the person who experienced the next life, or by choosing to stay in their individual experiences?

In the end, they both decided that the one who experienced the next life would be safer. If that person couldn't come back, they would be floating in the galaxy forever, mingling with all the loving experiences that have existed in the world. The one left in this world would have longed for the other forever, witnessing new human disasters and possibly a second extra-terrestrial invasion attempt. After arriving at that conclusion, they both spoke out spontaneously, "I want to be the one staying here." Then they both turned to look at Al at the same moment. They were both trying to convince each other that they should be the one left in the world. Knowing that they could not reach a conclusion by trying to convince each other that they wanted to stay in the world with similar sentences, Al asked, "Aren't you going to ask my opinion on this?"

Both young lovers were reluctant to leave the decision to him, knowing that it could cause their loved one to experience the worse possibility. But they knew that leaving the decision up to Al would also increase their chances of reunion, so they began to listen quietly. After thinking for a while, Al said, "I think Lil should be the one to do this." At that moment Lil had a sadness on her face and Ari was smiling. "I think Lil is more suited to the job. She was also the one who managed to summon her breakfast when she went to the dining room in the morning."

Ari accepted the decision peacefully. If one of them had to stay behind and face the dangers awaiting the world and suffer the absence and the other, he would have preferred it to be himself. Since Lil knew that arguing would be useless, she kept saying the same thing to herself in her mind: "You won't let him down... You won't let him down..."

As Al thought more comprehensively, he hoped that his trust in the love of these two young people wouldn't be for nothing for the sake of everyone else. If Lil didn't come back, humanity would be left to its own devices. And there was a very advanced species at their door already very enthusiastic to occupy their planet and subdue them. Al gave them time to say goodbye to each other. The young lovers clung to each other so tightly that they took deep breaths from time to time as if coming up to the surface of the water.

Lil didn't want to make it even harder, so she pulled herself back a little to look in the eyes of her lover, "I will return to you. You are now a part of my soul. I wouldn't be whole without you. I promise, I will come back."

Ari didn't want Al to hear what he had to say, so he drew his lover to him, "Nothing will be easy even if you come back. You gave me so much more than I deserved. You opened your beautiful soul to me. It's worth everything to me just to know that you will continue to exist in some way with all your beauty. You don't owe me anything. If you get stuck between staying and returning, keep this in mind: There is no one or nothing in this world that deserves you."

"I'll be back," Lil said, kissing him.

After Al prepared his mind to act as a mediator for Lil's journey, he turned to Lil and said, "I'm ready." Lil nodded to indicate that she was ready as well. She sat cross-legged across from Al who was sitting by the fire. She took one last look at her lover and took Al's hands and her body stiffened. When his lover went cold, Ari felt as if an arrow passed through him, felt a pain from the end of his throat down to his waist, as if his chest were split in two. After a period of serious difficulty in breathing, his pain turned into anger towards himself. He thought that he should be happy and not devastated for the transition of his love to freedom from all suffering.

He closed her eyes in a panic and tried to make sure that he remembered her scent, the rhythm of her breathing, and the wave of her enchanting gaze. Drops began to fall out of his eyes, resembling the hailstones of the period, forming huge dents on his cheeks. He could only be whole in his dreams now. After a while, he opened his eyes and saw that Al had returned to his body in the cave. He was shocked. "Why did you return so quickly? Did something bad happen?" he asked in a panic.

Al, with his usual calmness, said, "Everything is fine. This is Lil's journey, and I just showed her the way." And the two fell into a long silence that only the crackling of the fire would break.

After Lil's departure, it was Ari who broke the non-speaking agreement of the pair, who had been sitting for seven or eight hours without a word. Ari, who had been trying with all his might to listen to his thoughts about how Lil should not return during the last few hours, could not overcome his desire to have her back; "If she wants to come back, how will you know?" he asked. Al was happy about Ari's decision to break the silence. Because he had fought so hard for the last hour or two to avoid talking to him. Not leaving Lil's hands (the two had been sitting cross-legged across from one another) and not changing his position, he simply turned his head to Ari. "She's at a much more advanced level than her individual experiences after her journey. If she wanted to come back, she could have easily let me know, you can be sure about it. I think it's time to step in and call her back." Ari had made up his mind, "No. I won't do that. I can't pull her back into the simplicity of a singular experience." Surprised by what he heard, Al said, "You are in this world. As long as you are, it will be far beyond simplicity. That was the whole point. This is a lot bigger than you two, Ari. Do you want to leave all humanity to its own destiny?" he asked.

"Her return will not guarantee anything to humanity or to you," Ari said with the same determination. "The only thing that will happen with her return is that she will continue to live in the same misery as us. Do you realise what a destruction it would be for her to come back to his old world and her old body after what she is experiencing?" he snapped. He didn't seem to want to change his mind at all.

***

She could feel herself floating among the billions of souls surrounding the planets and the moons and holding them together. And the sun. Only she didn't seem to need the energy of those souls. On the contrary, it seemed to embrace her even in her current state where she was nowhere and everywhere all at once. The sun had made her and all the souls she was floating around fall so much in love with itself that it was as if revolving around it wasn't enough. To completely feel it as it deserved, it was necessary to get lost in it. But every soul that went to it just bounced back off because they couldn't get through its intensity. An energy source far, far away, a million times brighter than the sun which had all the souls around it fall in love with it, was pulling her; all the souls she was floating together with and the sun into itself. She saw that numerous other suns were also being pulled towards this sun that was brighter than all of them.

As she floated around them at an infinite speed in the solar system, she saw with amazing clarity all the experiences of the souls that brought them to this point but couldn't remember anything about herself. This lack of familiarity with her own experiences allowed her to wholly embrace all the other experiences she encountered. All the joy that came with every newborn child, the excitement that came with every love, the serenity of every sunset, the pride of every sprouting plant, the satisfaction of every one loved, the humility that came with every star, the longing felt for every lost love... Everything from the time when the billions of souls she floated around came into existence was flowing around and through her.

But every experience flowing through her seemed to reduce her rather than multiply her. Each new experience increased the speed of her the stream and encouraged the desire in her to witness more experiences. Even the most amazing experiences that her soul came into contact with did not diminish the feeling of having an irreplaceable void within her but instead made it worse. Her search had accelerated so much that she had come to the point of losing her sight for the light of the sun that she was rotating around, the lights of the distant suns, the lights of the brightest, the farthest sources had become intertwined. Just as she was about to lose herself, she came across the joy of the birth of a child.

Every moment that the child witnessed the love, pride, peace and hope that he had created, she felt as if the emptiness inside her was being filled in. Suddenly, she lost interest in all other experiences. She wanted to embrace the experience that this child made meaningful until the last moment of her existence. She witnessed this child transition from childhood to manhood, and the expanding of his contribution to this experience. The farewell the experience she had been embracing had with the son had overwhelmed her infinitely more than all the experiences she had encountered, all the suns she'd seen including her own sun, and even the brightest source far away.

She internalised this embrace that shaped this farewell so much that she could feel the rhythm of breathing of the child who had been left behind. It was as if that rhythm existed to help her find her place in this eternity where she was everywhere and nowhere at the same time. Now she could determine where she was.

***

Ari and Al had been arguing for minutes. Although determined not to change his mind at any cost, Ari's heart was beating so fast because of the horror Al's fury created in him. Just as everything started to go dark, the light in Al's eyes as he stopped the argument, pulled him out of the darkness surrounding him. He saw Al close his eyes before he had a chance to say anything. Just seconds after Al closed his eyes, his lover's eyes opened to the room lit only by the light of fire, as if she was the sun. Even though Ari's first reaction was to jump up into the air with joy beyond description, when he thought of the consequences of Lil's return on her, he felt himself thrown into complex and impossible feelings. He was waiting for the first response from his girlfriend. As Lil turned to him and stared long into his eyes, Ari felt like couldn't fit into his own body.

Lil rose from her seat with an unresponsive attitude resembling the faces and bodies of the superhumans and hugged her lover, who had turned to stone. Ari didn't move as he tried to understand the mood she was in and wanted to give her space. He didn't even respond to his girlfriend's hug. Lil, who only wanted to focus on her lover's breathing rhythm, stood frozen in her hug. She kept so still that he began to think she might have gone back on the journey she had just returned from.

Lil ended her inactivity that lasted enough to surprise even Al and pulled herself back just far enough to look into her boyfriend's eyes. "You're the only thing I'll be happy to be around," she said, kissing him. Ari's tears, which had wounded his cheeks as they were hail coming down when Lil left, were now compassionately caressing his face and trying to compensate for the damage they'd made. After Lil kissed him once more, she turned to Al, "You'd told us that all the souls in our galaxy were flowing together. But I have only met souls who have experienced lives on this earth, and I have only travelled through our own solar system. Why is that?" she asked.

"You did meet others, but you didn't recognise them. Souls continue to evolve during the next life and begin their experience with their own solar systems. As they evolve, they become galactic passengers. You had that experience in a very short time," he replied. Even though Lil wondered what other experiences existed in the galaxy, she knew she didn't have enough capacity to question them. "When do we start telling people what they are capable of?" she asked with great determination.

"Right away," Al said, smiling. He couldn't believe they had succeeded. Lil's return made him see things in a more hopeful light. For the first time in a long time, he thought, "Maybe I can really be useful to humanity."

He felt that the doors to becoming a galactic species were opening up to humanity.